Her Sure Thing
Helen Brenna

TORONTO NEW YORK LONDON
AMSTERDAM PARIS SYDNEY HAMBURG
STOCKHOLM ATHENS TOKYO MILAN MADRID
PRAGUE WARSAW BUDAPEST AUCKLAND

Recycling programs
for this product may
not exist in your area.

ISBN-13: 978-0-373-71725-5

HER SURE THING

www.Harlequin.com

Printed in U.S.A.

ABOUT THE AUTHOR

Helen Brenna grew up in central Minnesota, the seventh of eight children. Although she never dreamed of writing books, she's always been a voracious reader. So after taking a break from her accounting career to be an at-home mom, she tried her hand at writing the romances she loves to read. Since she was first published in 2007, her books have won many awards, including a Romance Writers of America's prestigious RITA® Award, an *RT Book Reviews* Reviewer's Choice, a Holt Medallion, a Book Buyers Best, and a National Readers' Choice Award. Helen lives happily ever after with her family in Minnesota. She'd love hearing from you. Email her at helenbrenna@comcast.net or send mail to P.O. Box 24107, Minneapolis, MN 55424.

Visit her website at www.helenbrenna.com or chat with Helen and other authors at Riding With The Top Down.

Books by Helen Brenna

HARLEQUIN SUPERROMANCE

1403—TREASURE
1425—DAD FOR LIFE
1519—FINDING MR. RIGHT
1582—FIRST COME TWINS*
1594—NEXT COMES LOVE*
1606—THEN COMES BABY*
1640—ALONG CAME A HUSBAND*
1672—THE MOON THAT NIGHT
1719—THE PURSUIT OF JESSE*

*An Island to Remember

HARLEQUIN NASCAR
PEAK PERFORMANCE
FROM THE OUTSIDE

For Mark Twomey
Thanks, big bro, for being you and for all you do!

Acknowledgments

Thanks to fellow writer Lois Greiman for letting
me muck out barn stalls and dig fence posts.
With friends like you...
Seriously, thank you, dear, for allowing me to ride
your precious and beautiful Sage,
for advice on this manuscript and for giving
me a glimpse into a life with horses.
If only I had a couple extra acres, a barn and a
pair of those sexy riding boots...

Thanks, also, to my lovely and very talented
niece Angi Twomey for her expert advice and
insight with regard to the Los Angeles
fashion world and for letting me sleep on her
couch while doing research!
What happens in L.A. stays in L.A.
You know that, right?

Love you both,
Helen

CHAPTER ONE

A SIMPLE, UNCOMPLICATED LIFE. Was that too much to ask?
Apparently.

A sense of dread churning in his stomach, Sean Griffin glanced out at the choppy waters of Lake Superior and waited impatiently as the ferry approached Mirabelle Island. How ironic that this should happen to him now. Right now. When he'd finally orchestrated for himself the perfect life.

Well, almost the perfect life.

For the first time ever, he had close, trusted friends. This past winter, he'd bought the business of his dreams while managing to keep his part-time medical practice. He now owned a significant chunk of land and horses, lots of horses. And although the old farmhouse that had come with the Mirabelle Island Stable and Livery operation had needed a lot of work, he'd spent the last several months refurbishing the place, getting every piece of furniture, every wall color and window treatment just right. The only thing he was missing was a woman to share it all with, a wife, and a wife was definitely not coming for him on that ferry.

The afternoon sun, brilliant and blinding, reflected off the wavy surface of the deep blue water, and as he flipped down his sunglasses the truth hit him like a blast of cold air. He wasn't ready, probably never would be. What had he been thinking in agreeing to do this?

That a man couldn't shirk his responsibility and still call himself a man. One way or another he was going to have to deal. *It's only for three months,* he reminded himself. *You can put up with anything for one summer, right?*

"Hey, Sean!"

Sean spun around to find Garrett Taylor, the island's chief of police, walking across the pier with his brother, Jesse. "Hey, guys." The Taylors, Chicago transplants and two of Sean's friends, had come to Mirabelle separately, but had quickly become part of the fabric of the island.

"Want to join us for lunch?" Jesse asked.

"Can't today. Busy." He nodded toward the ferry.

The Taylors both glanced out over the water.

"Today's the day, huh?" Garrett said.

"Yep."

"Good luck, man." Jesse gave him a reassuring smile.

"Next happy hour at Duffy's," Garrett added. "I want to hear how it goes."

"I'm sure everything will be fine," Sean lied.

The brothers went on their way to the Bayside Café. Funny, they'd both found wives here on this little island. Maybe there was still hope for Sean.

He turned around in time to see the ferry dock with a surprisingly light touch against the pier. As the crew lowered the ramps and some of the first of this season's tourists filed onto the island, he glanced at the faces of the people coming ashore. After all these years, would he still remember what she looked like?

The thought had no sooner entered his mind than he saw her face, his ex-fiancée, although their engagement had been so long ago it seemed silly to still think of her that way. On either side of her were two adolescents, a boy and a girl, looking to be around ten to twelve years old. Walking behind the three was a tall, rail-thin teenage boy. Well, maybe walking wasn't the best description of how he was moving. Dragging his feet was more like it.

Sean tried for a clear look at the young man's face, hoping for some spark of recognition, a flicker of familiarity, but the boy's gaze remained firmly focused on the ground. "Denise," Sean called, waving his hand above his head. "Over here."

Pulling a suitcase behind her, she smiled. "Sean!"

Awkwardly, they stood before each other, and then she shook her head and hugged him. "It's good to see you again."

He wished he could say the same.

"This is my son, Jeffrey. My daughter, Erin." Both kids smiled tentatively, and Sean nodded at each one in turn. Then Denise stepped back. "And this is Austin."

The boy raised his head, looking directly into Sean's eyes, and Sean let go the breath he hadn't realized he'd been holding. Denise had obviously jumped through the hoops of DNA testing for nothing. It was almost as if he was looking at his sixteen-year-old self. Sean most definitely had a son.

He cleared his throat. "Hello, Austin."

Through shaggy bangs, the boy silently stared at Sean as if he, too, could see the resemblance and wasn't quite sure what to think, let alone do about it.

"Austin, the least you could do is say hello," Denise said softly.

"Why should I?"

"Because you're going to be here for the entire summer. I want you two to get along."

"Oh. Sure, Mom. In that case, whatever you say." He stared at Sean and bit out sarcastically, "Hi, *Dad*." Then he angrily brushed past Sean and headed toward town.

Nice kid. That attitude was going to make for a great summer.

"Goodbye, Austin," Denise called after him. "I'll call you every week."

The boy's steps never even slowed.

"Austin, wait!" With tears in her eyes, the young girl, Erin, took off after her half brother.

Clearly reluctant, Austin stopped and turned.

Denise touched her other son's arm. "Jeffrey, why don't you say goodbye to Austin, too, and give me a few minutes alone with Sean?"

"Do I have to?"

Apparently, there was no love lost between the two brothers.

"Yes." She gently pushed him forward. "Go." Slowly, the boy took off toward his siblings. The moment he was out of earshot, Denise turned to Sean. "I'm sorry for this."

"Not going to cut it, Denise. Not now. Not ever."

"It's all I've got. All the years we were engaged, you'd made it very clear that you never wanted to be a father. I wanted to start fresh with Glen. Not that it did any good in the end, but at the time, I felt justified." She held his gaze. "Now I know that all the justifications in the world can't make what I did right. I'm trying to fix that."

"So just because you're going through a nasty divorce, you decide to send your…*problem* here? That was the word you used, wasn't it? You call that fixing things?"

"It's the best I can do. Besides, you said you were going to be working 24/7 this summer. Austin can help. He's a chip off the old block. Just go about your business and he'll go about his."

He wasn't entirely sure if that was a cut at him or not, and decided to let it pass. "If he's so self-sufficient, why don't you keep him?"

"I need to focus on Jeffrey and Erin. Their dad leaving is hitting them really hard. Austin's glad to see Glen go. He doesn't care about the divorce. And he's…just…a lot to handle right now. I don't know what to do with the kid anymore. You know?"

"No. I don't."

"What was I supposed to do, Sean? You're his father."

"I *fathered* him. Glen is his father. There's a big difference."

Fathers cared for their kids. They went to school conferences and sporting events. They rocked their babies to sleep, wrestled with their toddlers and disciplined and guided their teenagers. At least that's what Sean had always imagined good fathers were supposed to do. He'd done none of those things with Austin because until Denise's phone call last week he hadn't known the option had even been available. "You never gave me a chance to be his father."

"I said I was sorry, and I know this isn't fair to you. I just need a break. I'll be ready to take him home again before school starts. I promise."

Sean was a lot of things. A man, a friend, a doctor and, most recently, a horse stable and livery owner. One thing he'd never planned on being was a dad, and there was a damned good reason for that. He'd had a piss-poor role model. Maybe that explained why he had no clue what to do next.

He glanced behind him. Austin had hugged both of his half siblings and said a few words to each of them and was now continuing toward town. Should Sean go after the kid? Let him be? Shower him with kindness? Play taskmaster? Maybe, for now, he needed to give the kid a little space.

"Does he know where I live?" Sean asked.

"He has your address." She handed him a file folder. "Here are some things you might need. His cell number, insurance card, allergies, all of my contact information. Oh, and his things." She rolled a suitcase toward him.

"Do I need to worry about him running away?"

"I don't think so." Beside them, people started boarding the ferry for the return trip to the mainland. Denise signaled to her other two kids that it was time to leave. "I think he's curious about you. He'll stay."

"In that case—" Sean picked up the suitcase and started toward his stables "—see you at the end of summer."

"Sean?"

The catch in her voice made him stop and turn. Her two younger kids were already boarding the ferry.

"Glen was...hard on him," she said, her eyes pooling with tears. "But he's a good kid deep down inside. Give him a chance to prove it." Then she turned and ran to follow her other kids.

Three months. Then Sean's life would return to normal. Maybe he'd been worried over this for nothing. He was an intelligent, competent man who'd made life and death decisions for years in the blink of an eye as an E.R. doctor. How hard could playing dad be?

"TAKE MY LUGGAGE TO THE master bedroom." Grace Kahill pointed up the stairs as she walked through the first floor of the spacious colonial she'd rented for the summer, cracking open windows as she went. Since when did Mirabelle Island get this hot and humid this early in June? More to the point, how could she have rented a place without central air?

But then only a few days ago, she reminded herself, she'd been thinking of buying a beach place in Malibu. Given the late notice, she was lucky to have found any rental at all available here for the entire summer.

"Set up the computer and printer in the study at the front of the house," she went on, shrugging out of her jean jacket. "The exercise bike goes right..." She studied the layout of the living room and pointed to a spot near the large picture window. "Here. The treadmill goes next to it. The plasma screen replaces that piece of...junk." She pointed at the old box of a TV in the corner, surprised the contraption didn't come complete with rabbit ears. "And I want cable and wireless capabilities installed by the end of the day. Got that?"

"Um…ah…" The mover glanced at her, then seemed to stare toward her neck.

An instantaneous sense of panic swept through her. *Oh, God.* Quickly, she found her reflection in the mirror hanging in the foyer and scanned her appearance. *It's okay. It's all right.* She hadn't repositioned her layered T-shirts when she'd taken off her jacket. Taking a long, slow breath, she put her jacket back on. Just to be safe. "Did you hear a word of what I just said?"

"Um…yes, ma'am."

"Do I look like a *ma'am* to you?"

"Ah, not really…Mrs. Kahill."

No one *ever* called her Mrs. Kahill, either. "Grace. Just Grace will do fine."

"Okay. Sure."

Two more hulking men lumbered through the front door carrying suitcases, trunks and boxes, everything she owned that wasn't being held in storage. The men stopped and stared at her as if they'd never seen a woman before. No longer worried about her shirt having shifted, she impatiently crossed her arms and transferred her weight to one leg. The novelty of any man's obvious approval of her looks had worn off long before her twenty-fifth cover shot, and these days, more than anything else, it aggravated her. Was it too much to ask to be treated like a regular human being?

"I'm not paying you gentlemen to stand here," she said. "Get this place set up."

"Will do, ma—ah, Grace." The head mover directed the other two men and the three set off in various directions.

She opened a few more windows, hoping to catch a breeze, and glanced around the place. What had ever possessed her to come back to, of all places, Mirabelle Island? Hadn't she left this place, vowing never to return, before even graduating from high school?

If not here, though, where? There was nothing left for her in L.A., she reminded herself. Not anymore. *You're here now. Might as well make the best of it. Besides, Dad needs you.*

She'd already called her father to let him know she'd arrived, but since he was busy all afternoon she'd have the rest of the day to get settled. She'd be comfortable enough in this rental, she supposed, even if the house's blue-and-white seaside decor was a bit dated. At least it was private, located at the end of the road at the top of the hill overlooking Mirabelle's village center, the marina and the daunting expanse of Lake Superior.

Her cell phone rang, and she glanced at the number displayed on the small screen. Excited now, she quickly answered the call. "Are you ready?"

"Yep," the man said.

"You're still at the airport?"

"Yep. If that's what you could call these two short strips of cement. Been busy getting all Louie's things together. He's good to go."

Mirabelle's tiny airport didn't get used very often, but at least the island had one. It had made her move here as simple as could be by having the movers load all of her things on a chartered flight out of L.A. "How's Louie doing?"

"Better," the man said. "Considering he's never been on a plane before, he's doing great."

Their landing had been a bit rough, so while Louie was settling down she'd left with the movers to bring things to the house. "Good." Grace felt herself smile for the first time that day. "You know where you're going to meet me, then?"

"Yep. We'll be there."

She'd no sooner disconnected the call than her cell rang again. The moment she recognized her personal assistant's number, her spirits sank. This call felt like an intrusion, a piece of her old life butting in and dampening her attempt at a fresh start. But she had loose ends to tie up. Might as well face the camera lens. "Hello, Amanda."

"Good morning, Grace. How are you this fine Monday morning?"

"Could be better."

"Sorry to hear that." Amanda sounded sincere enough, but then Grace did cut her generous payroll checks. "Especially since you have such a busy day scheduled. A yoga session at ten and lunch with the fitness video folks at noon. Then a doctor's appointment at three."

"Cancel everything."

"That's not a problem for lunch and yoga, but..." The young woman hesitated. "You're supposed to stick to your doctor's checkup schedule and you missed your last appointment."

"I don't care. Cancel everything." After all the surgeries, physical therapy, and doctor, acupuncture and chiropractor appointments, stacked one on top of the other over the past year, Grace was wholeheartedly sick of every medical care professional on the face of this earth.

"Grace—"

"Leave it, Amanda. You're not my mother."

Grace had no mother. Not anymore.

For the first time since the funeral, she missed her mom. They may not have gotten along once Grace had hit thirteen, but for the first twelve years of Grace's life, Jean Andersen had been Grace's rock. Moms fixed things. They made the world right. Now more than ever, Grace was on her own.

"While you're canceling appointments for me today," Grace went on, "you might as well cancel my entire summer."

"What? As in the next three months? You sure about that?"

As sure as she could be about anything these days. "I'm

falling off the grid for a while, so enjoy the time off with pay, Amanda. I'll be back in the fall."

The moment the words had left Grace's mouth, one of the many knots in her stomach slowly unfurled. The weight that had been bearing down on her shoulders for the past year was slowly but surely being replaced by a curious sense of freedom. She'd gotten out of L.A. Finally. She could stretch out her arms and let her soul breathe.

"Grace, where are you?" Amanda asked.

"Mirabelle Island."

"Wisconsin? But what... Why... When did you..." Amanda sputtered. "I don't get it."

Neither did Grace. At least, not entirely. She chuckled, and another knot unfurled. Her dad could use the company, but it was more than that. Something had drawn her to Mirabelle. Something as powerful and inescapable and deeply rooted in her soul as it was elusive. "There's nothing to get, Amanda. I simply needed some R & R."

"I take it, then, that you're not interested in a house in Carmel. Your real estate agent called and said it hasn't been listed yet, but it's perfect for you. She wants you to get the first shot at it."

"Tell her that for the time being I'm no longer in the market for a house." Who knew at this point what the end of summer would bring? "Is there anything else you needed from me?"

"I don't think so." Amanda hesitated, and then gently, she said, "I hope Mirabelle is just the thing for you."

Grace clicked off her phone and leaned against the nearest wall. Already it had been a long day and it wasn't even dinner-time, but then she still wasn't one hundred percent even a year after the accident. An all too familiar pins-and-needles type tingling sensation zinged up in her left shoulder and spread down her side. Then the itching kicked in. Panic threatened to immobilize her as her left arm became virtually useless and her upper back muscles tensed and cramped.

Holding on to the rail, she climbed the stairs and sat on the edge of the bed. Grabbing the tube of medicated prescription lotion from her purse, she unzipped the top part of the custom compression garment her layered tees hid quite well and slathered the cream over her skin, if you could even call it that. It felt more like animal hide as far as Grace was concerned.

Then she grabbed the bottle of pain meds, shook out two of her quickly dwindling supply and glanced at them. More than likely they'd not only knock out her pain, they'd knock her completely out. Better to save the rest of these for crises. Truth be told, she was sick of her head feeling as if it was stuffed in a wad of cotton.

"Saddle 'em up." A man's voice sounded through the open window.

Grace slid the pills back in the bottle and glanced outside. The Mirabelle Island riding and livery stables were practically in her backyard, and college kids hired to work through the busy summer tourist season were getting ready for a trail ride. With few bushes and trees to demarcate property lines, several large barns, paddocks and, beyond them, acres and acres of pastureland were clearly visible.

This—*this*—was why she'd rented this house. God, how she'd loved spending time with the horses, brushing, riding and feeding them. Arlo Duffy had even hired her to work for him when she'd been only twelve, and from that point on the time she'd spent at Arlo's stables had been the only time she'd enjoyed while on Mirabelle. She'd have lived in the barn if he'd let her.

Time to go find Arlo. Rushing down the stairs, she called out to the movers, "If you need me call my cell." Then she took off out the back door.

A path through the woods brought her out near the paddock closest to her rental. After a short, narrow trail, probably a deer path, through some scrub separating the two properties, she came out in a clearing by Arlo and Lynn Duffy's iconic red farmhouse. As she reached the road, a man leading a very familiar solid black horse passed through the main gate and headed toward her. Louie. Her horse was clearly tired, but the moment he noticed Grace his pace quickened and his step lightened.

"Perfect timing," she whispered, reaching out to stroke Louie's sleek neck.

"You can say that again," the handler said.

"He's tired. Aren't you, boy?" The horse let go a long sigh, as if agreeing, snuffled his muzzle in her hair, and another one of those incessant stomach knots eased. "Thank you for taking care of him." She glanced at the handler. "I've got him from here."

"No problem." He handed over the lead. "I'll make sure your tack and other supplies get delivered here today."

"Thank you." Grace was barely aware of the man disappearing down the road as she closed her eyes and rested her cheek against Louie's warm, muscular neck.

"Well, I'll be damned."

Startled by the deep voice, Grace glanced up. Leading a pretty bay, a man walked across the dry dusty road toward her. Wearing faded jeans, scuffed-up boots and a navy blue T-shirt, he was dressed much like the college kids working out in the pasture, but that was where the comparison ended. The breadth of this man's shoulders and his confident gait clearly separated him from the others. Too rough around the edges to be considered classically handsome, he was still a sight to behold as he led the saddled-up bay by the reins.

Within seconds, Grace could've listed off at least five designers who would've been falling all over themselves to dress this rough-looking cowboy in their latest styles. If he'd been ten to fifteen years younger. As he came closer, the laugh lines around his eyes gave away the fact that he was likely in his mid-thirties.

His gaze, hard and unreadable, flicked over her, and then seemed to take in the horse. "If that isn't a beautiful sight," he murmured. "I don't know what is."

Was he talking about Louie? Or her? The slight smile playing at his mouth caught Grace completely by surprise.

He has the most kissable lips I've ever seen.

The moment the thought crossed her mind, she sucked in a breath. She thought about men as photogenic or stylish, not kissable, and out of her element as she was, her defenses rose. Straightening her shoulders, she glared at the man. "He's a Friesian."

"I can see that." He came to stand on Louie's other side, opposite Grace. "Don't run into this breed of horse every day."

A solid jet-black, Louie's coat gleamed silver in the clear afternoon sun. With typical Friesian characteristics, his mane and tail—which almost touched the ground—were long, thick and wavy, and his fetlocks were silky and untrimmed. His conformation was close to the shape of a light but powerful draft horse, but he'd been bred to be taller and finer-boned than his ancestors. The lines of his neck, long and gracefully arched, showed the quality of his bloodlines.

Laughing about what to give a woman who had everything, Jeremy had given the gelding to Grace for her twenty-fifth birthday, almost as a joke. Her ex-husband hadn't realized it at the time—he'd probably never fully understood—that the spirited but loyal animal had been the dearest gift he'd ever given her.

Grace watched the man slowly run his hands down Louie's neck before patting his back. There was something inherently sensual in the way he moved that she couldn't help but notice his tanned skin, trimmed nails and the light dusting of dark hair on his fingers. *First his lips and then his hands. What next?*

"Nice horse," the man said. He crossed his arms, causing his biceps to flex and bulge. His blue eyes regarded her unemotionally, making him appear as unmovable as a mountain. "What's he doing here?"

CHAPTER TWO

"EXCUSE ME?" THE WOMAN glared at Sean as if he was horse dung stuck to the soles of her obviously expensive gold sandals.

Sean did his best to dismiss her superior attitude, but since she didn't seem to be anything *but* attitude, it was difficult. "Is the horse yours?"

"Yes," she said, stroking the animal's neck.

"We're the only stable here on Mirabelle." It was a damned small island with limited pastureland and even more limited paddock and barn space. Anyone with a lick of sense would know you didn't take a horse anywhere without first arranging his keep. "So what's he doing here on the island?"

"I'm boarding him here for the summer."

Oh, no, she wasn't. Not without asking him first.

She straightened her shoulders, clearly preparing for a fight. "Who are you?"

"Sean Griffin. And you?"

"Grace. Just Grace."

So this was Grace Andersen Kahill? The face that had launched the covers of hundreds of fashion magazines? The body credited—or accused, depending in which camp you fell—for having first made lingerie catalogs and swimsuit editions of popular sports editions look like soft porn? That explained a lot.

Sean had heard she was coming back to Mirabelle and renting the Schumacher's old place, but he wasn't surprised he hadn't recognized her. He'd seen Grace and her husband at Jean Andersen's funeral, but that had been several months ago and he'd never met, let alone spoken, to either one of them. Afterward, talk about her breezing in one day for her mother's wake and out the day immediately following the funeral had fueled the gossip channels for weeks.

Strange, but for a woman known for baring more skin than any other American model, she looked pretty covered up if you asked him. Dressed in a hip-length jean jacket, a couple of crewneck T-shirts and some beady-type necklace, she looked as if she were heading off to some trendy Hollywood hotspot for a two-appletini lunch with friends. Sean had lived in L.A. long enough to know. Too long, in fact.

"Well, Just Grace," he said. "We've got a problem."

"The only problem I'm aware of is that the boarding rate hasn't been settled. That really doesn't make a difference because I'll pay whatever it takes. Problem solved."

As if money solved everything. Typical. "Boy, you really are something, aren't you?" He chuckled. "But I don't board horses."

"*You* don't?"

"That's right. *I* don't. It has nothing to do with money. This is a stable and livery operation." Boss, his horse, pulled on his reins and struck his nose toward her Friesian. "We have over sixty horses here and limited acreage. All the horses here work for their keep. I can't spare a stall, let alone a paddock or pastureland for someone's…pet."

"Well, it's not really your decision, now, is it?" She stalked toward the barn.

"Where are you going?"

"To find Arlo Duffy."

"You won't find him in there."

She spun around. "Then where is he?"

"Home. Eating lunch."

She turned on her heel and headed in the opposite direction toward the ranch house.

"And you won't find him in that house, either."

She spun around. "Who do you think you are?"

"I told you. Sean Griffin. And that happens to be my house now." He cocked his head at her. "I'm the new owner of Mirabelle Stables and Livery." If she hadn't been so high and mighty, he might've cleared that up at the onset.

She looked away and shook her head. "Of course, Arlo would eventually retire." Then she glared at him. "You could've told me you're the new owner of this place."

"You could've been less presumptuous."

"Look. I just talked to Arlo on the phone a couple of days ago. He didn't say anything about not owning the stables and told me it'd be fine to board Louie here."

"Well, you talked to the wrong person."

"So what am I supposed to do?" she huffed, putting a hand on her hip. "Louie flew here from L.A. I can't send him—"

"Well, I'll be." The sound of the man's voice cut through their discussion like a bucket of water on a campfire. Arlo. Back from lunch. "Is that little Gracie Andersen?"

Grace glanced down the drive and a smile immediately spread across her face like the big old morning sun rising over Lake Superior. "Arlo. It's so good to see you." She held out her hand. "How have you been?"

"Gettin' old." He ignored her hand and pulled her into his arms for a quick but tight hug. "Other than that, I can't complain. I see you met Sean."

"I did." Her mouth turned down in a frown—or was it a pout?—but Arlo was already sizing up Louie.

"Nice horse you got here," he said. "So whaddya think, Sean? Where we going to put him?"

Sean had accepted he'd lost this battle the moment Grace had said she'd already talked to Arlo, but he couldn't very well let Arlo think he was still making all the decisions around here. "We're not putting him anywhere, Arlo. *We* don't board horses, remember?"

"I boarded Boss for you." Arlo nodded at the bay next to Sean.

"That's different," Sean said. "I asked you *before* I brought him to the island, and back then *you* were the owner."

"We can make an exception for Grace, don't you think?"

Sean didn't have much of a choice now, did he? He knew all he needed to know about running a trail riding operation from all the summers he'd spent in high school and college working on ranches in Montana and Wyoming. He knew virtually nothing, however, about repairing carriages and training draft horses. For that, he needed Arlo, and Arlo knew it.

"You should've talked to me, Arlo," Sean said. "This isn't your business any longer."

Exasperated, Grace let go a puff of air. "That's just—"

Arlo squeezed her hand, sending her the clear message to let him take the lead.

"But I—"

He tugged a little harder.

Clearly, with extreme effort, she clenched her jaw closed.

"Heck, Sean," Arlo went on. "I didn't think it'd be a problem. Besides, you might be the new owner, but you put me in charge of the livery operations. Doesn't that put me in charge of the livery barns and paddocks?"

Sean shook his head and chuckled. Then he glanced at Grace. "How long did you say you were going to be here on Mirabelle?"

"Just for the summer."

"That's a long time." He glanced at Arlo. "You sure you have enough room for another horse?"

"Ayep. That I do. A Friesian will fit in nicely with the Percheron and Hackneys."

"All right." Sean fixed his gaze on her. "But you're responsible for him. Feeding him. Exercising him. The whole nine yards."

"That was my intention all along." Then she forced out through gritted teeth, "Thank you."

Arlo winked at her. "Grace, you look almost as tired as Louie. Why don't you go on home and rest a bit?" he offered. "I'll just put him in a stall, and you can come back later."

Sean narrowed his gaze at Arlo, but kept his mouth shut. What game was the old man playing?

"Thanks, Arlo, but I can handle it," she said. "Just tell me what stall he'll be using and I'll get him settled."

"Whatever you say." Arlo pointed to the barn farthest away from them. "It's that last barn over there. Put him in the first empty stall on the left. He'll have a nice run out the back, and we'll keep him segregated for a few weeks until he's used to things around here."

"Will do. If you need anything from me—" she pointed to the blue Colonial she was renting "—that's where I'm staying."

"We know," Sean said.

"Of course. I almost forgot this is Mirabelle." She turned and led Louie across the yard.

Sean studied her as she walked away. He might've become the new owner of Mirabelle Stable and Livery, but he was still the island's only doctor, part-time though the position might be. The doctor in him observed and quickly went about diagnosing her stiff gait. She was either in pain or extremely tense, very likely both. Possible back or hip problems. Probably had something to do with the car accident he'd heard about.

The man in him, on the other hand, couldn't help but focus in on those long, slender legs and that perfectly rounded butt encased in skin-tight jeans. Or that long mass of blond hair trailing all the way down her back in natural-looking waves. The woman was perfection incarnate.

"Isn't she something?" Arlo said, the moment she moved out of earshot.

Sean had almost forgotten the old man was standing next to him. "Yeah, something." Gorgeous and aloof topped with an attitude the size of the Chequamegon National Forest, he had two words for Grace Kahill. *High* and *maintenance*. He turned toward Arlo and frowned. "The next time you want to do an old friend a favor, check with me first."

"Ah, heck. What would've been the point?" Arlo laughed. "I knew you wouldn't go for boarding her horse."

"Yet you agreed anyway?"

"Always did have a soft spot for Gracie. She worked for me for years. Hard worker, too. Besides, I wanted to see that Friesian of hers. He's a beaut, isn't he?"

As he watched the horse and its owner disappear into the barn, Sean ran his hands along his own bay's muzzle. Boss had been the first horse Sean had ever owned, and the day he'd arrived on Mirabelle had been one of Sean's happiest. He'd take his no-nonsense Arabian anyday over a high-strung dandy. "Her horse is gorgeous. I'll give him that. But he's a bit like his owner, isn't he?"

"She said he's well trained."

Time would tell.

Arlo patted the bay's neck. "I'd appreciate it, son, if you wouldn't be too hard on her."

When the two of them were alone, Arlo had a tendency to refer to Sean as son. The old man probably wasn't even aware of his use of the endearment, but it meant something to Sean. "Hard on her? In what way?"

"I saw the way you were eyeing her. As if she's like every other woman you knew growing up out in California. Bitchy.

Demanding. What do they call them? Divas?" Arlo brushed the bay's shoulder. "Grace is none of those things."

That wasn't all Sean had been thinking about as he'd been sizing up Grace, but he sure wasn't going to enlighten Arlo anytime soon.

"Growing up the pastor's daughter wasn't the easiest thing here on Mirabelle," Arlo went on. "Especially not for a young one as feisty as Grace."

"Feisty? That what you call it?"

"Keep an open mind. That's all I ask."

"Sure. As long as you remember you don't own this operation anymore. Deal?"

"Deal." Arlo patted Sean's horse and grinned. "Now that I think about it…you and Grace. You never know. You two might hit it off—"

"Oh, no," Sean interrupted before the thought could take root in the old man's stubborn mind. "My life's fine the way it is, thank you very much."

Sean took great pains to make sure no one on Mirabelle had a clue he was looking for a wife. The last thing he needed was any of his well-intentioned friends setting him up with every single available female on the island. He could do his own vetting, not that there was much to vet on a small island like Mirabelle.

Besides, Grace Kahill wasn't even close to what he was looking for in a woman. A pretty package was a good start, but more than anything he wanted a full-fledged partner in life. A woman who didn't mind getting her hands dirty and who loved Mirabelle as much as he did. A woman who would not only be content living in this small community for the rest of her life, she'd be happy to do so. Forever.

Arlo chuckled. "I got news for you, son. You don't know it yet, but your life ain't as great as you think it is. Find yourself a good woman, and *then* you'll know what I'm talking about."

He knew. "Yeah, well, she's married, anyway."

"Separated, is what I hear."

"He came to the funeral."

"Appearances, I guess."

A marriage on the rocks? Only made for more baggage. "Doesn't matter. I have absolutely no interest in a relationship with that woman. My summer's going to be busy enough as it is."

"Speaking of which…how'd things go down at the pier?"

"Fine."

"Then where's your son?"

Sean looked away. "Not exactly sure."

"That doesn't sound to me like everything went fine."

"He left the ferry and took off toward town. Other than making sure he knows where I live, what was I supposed to do? The kid's as communicative as a mule."

"Go after him? Talk to him? Explain your side in this whole thing?"

"Yeah. I thought about all of those options."

"And?"

"What do I know about being a father?"

"What does any man know about being a father until he is one?" Arlo nodded toward the main gate. "That him?"

Sean glanced down the drive and nodded. "Austin, can you come here a minute?"

The boy hesitated before finally skulking toward them.

"This is Arlo Duffy. You ever need anything or have any questions and you can't find me, he's the one you want."

Arlo put out his hand. "Pleasure to meet you, Austin."

Grudgingly, Austin shook his hand and mumbled a hello, then he cocked his head to the side. "That your house?"

Sean nodded. "Your suitcase is on the porch."

"So where the hell am I supposed to sleep?"

Add a mouth to that chip on his shoulder. Sean bit his tongue, but the kid's attitude was already wearing on him. "Take the hallway to the right before you get to the kitchen. Last door on the left. Bathroom's next door."

Austin walked away, and that was that.

"See what I mean?" Sean said the moment the front door to the house slammed shut.

"Can you blame him? He just found out his dad isn't really his dad. He's confused and angry." Arlo sighed. "Give him a chance to settle in. Might end up not being as bad as you think."

Sean grunted.

"Be patient. With him. Yourself. You'll figure it out, son. You're a smart, compassionate man."

"Not according to some folks here on Mirabelle." There was no doubt his bedside manner had been slipping of late.

"A woman just might improve your mood some."

"Let it go, Arlo." Sean headed toward the stables. He had to get back to work. "The last thing I need is more complications in my life this summer."

And Grace Kahill was nothing if not complicated.

CHAPTER THREE

HER FIRST MORNING ON MIRABELLE.

The sun already streaming through the open window, Grace lay in bed staring at the ceiling. The sound of squirrels scrabbling up and down the trees filtered in, along with the chirping of robins and chickadees, cardinals and finches. There were no traffic sounds to interfere with their songs, no smog to ruin the fresh-smelling spring air. She should've felt rested and relaxed. Instead, she was tense and edgy.

Rather than the restful night she'd hoped for, even after taking two pain pills, she'd slept fitfully, if that's what you could call that flip-flopping, sweaty tussle in the sheets she'd suffered through for the last six hours. No point in lying here any longer. That was about all the decadence she could handle for one morning.

Flipping back the covers, she padded into the bathroom, unzipped the compression shirt and stepped into the shower. Once finished, she quickly dried herself off and smoothed some medicated cream over her scars. The tube was nearly empty, but she'd be damned if she'd call her doctor for a refill. No doubt, he'd want her to come in for an exam.

Briskly, she slathered lotion on the rest of her body. Once upon a time, she'd actually enjoyed this part of her daily routine. She would've lingered, taken time covering every inch of skin and luxuriated in the feel of rich, scented cream. Since her accident, though, she hated the feeling of being naked and exposed. The sooner she got clothing on, the better. She couldn't even remember the last time she'd seen herself nude.

Spur of the moment, she spun around and stared at herself in the large mirror over the sink, took in every angle, every inch of skin. *My God, what happened to you?* That skinny, damaged body could not be hers.

Grabbing the bath towel, she strategically placed it over her left side. *There you are. Almost.* With the right clothes on, covering the right spots, no one would be the wiser.

But she knew. She always knew.

The memory of the look on Jeremy's face when he'd seen her scars flashed through her mind. No wonder he'd filed for a divorce the day after her long-term prognosis. *Scarred for life* is what the doctors had said. No amount of plastic surgery would ever completely erase the injuries caused by the fire. Her usefulness to him had gone up in flames, along with the leather seats in her Bugatti. She was now damaged goods.

Quickly, she pulled on a clean custom-fitted compression shirt, zipping it up the front. For a moment, she imagined going about her day without the tight elastic fabric, but the thought had been immediately followed by a sense of panic. She'd gotten used to ever-present pressure around her upper body. There was an odd sense of security, she supposed, in the feeling.

In order to ensure her scars wouldn't spread, she needed to wear the compression garment over most of her torso at least twenty-three hours of every day. That meant she slept and exercised in one and would be wearing one until the day her doctor said her scars had matured.

Matured. How ridiculous was that term? As if a burn scar could ever be anything except ugly.

She was stepping into a pair of white thong underwear, when the front doorbell chimed. Inching out into the hall, she glanced downstairs through the sheers on either side of the front door. A young man, more than likely a college student, stood at the door holding two bags of groceries.

"Newman's delivery," he called out, setting the bags down and knocking. "Hello? Mrs. Kahill?"

She hadn't ordered any groceries.

The boy squinted through the windows on either side of the front door, trying unsuccessfully to see into the house. "Well, okay then. Call the store if you need anything else." Shrugging, he set the bags down on the porch, turned and left.

Her stomach grumbled and she wondered what was in those bags and who had ordered her food. As if in answer, her cell phone rang. That had to be either Suzy or Amanda, but she didn't want to talk to either one of them.

The phone stopped ringing and indicated a voice mail had been left for her. Then, surprisingly, the house landline rang. She hadn't given that number to anyone.

The answering machine speaker sounded through the house. "Dammit, Grace, pick up." Suzy Lang's unique accent, not quite British, but not entirely Indian, echoed strongly through the house. "Okay, fine. Be that way. I ordered you some groceries because I have this sneaking suspicion that you have nothing but celery to eat in that house. Believe it or not, that Newman's store had some decent organic stuff. So eat, okay? Don't make me come there and force-feed you."

At that, Grace smiled as she pulled on a pair of white capris, topped with a T-shirt over her compression garment and finished off with a dark heather-gray hoodie and a light-weight scarf around her neck, effectively hiding the rest of her scars.

"You know I don't have the time. The photo shoot for that new magazine spread has me running around like a runway wannabe." Her long, soft sigh came over the line. "I miss you already."

Grace missed her best friend, too. Apparently, there was one thing left in L.A. that Grace still cared about and that still cared about her. She answered the phone. "Hey, Suze."

"I knew you were there. What the hell?"

"Sorry. Having an awkward time settling in here, I guess."

"Amanda called me," Suzy said softly. "What are you doing back on Mirabelle?"

"I needed some R & R."

"R & R, my ass. You're going to be bored out of your mind in a week."

"I've been working full-time since I left this place. I think I'm due for some time off. Besides, my dad needs the company."

"Okay, okay." Suzy sighed. "Amanda's worried about you."

"Oh, really?" Grace was a paycheck to her assistant. Nothing more, nothing less.

"Grace, don't be that way. You do have people in your life who love you."

Bullshit. Suzy had been the only one who truly cared. The rest had all been using her. Designers wanted her to wear their latest lines. Friends wanted appointments with her agent for their daughters, nieces, nephews, you name it. Editors wanted exclusive photo ops. Photographers wanted in with up-and-coming models. The truth had been revealed when her usefulness to them had ended with her accident.

"I'm serious," Suzy said. "You're not just a boss to Amanda. She really cares."

"If you say so."

"She said you were supposed to have a doctor's appointment the day you left for Mirabelle. I know you're sick of doctors, but you may still need some attention."

"I know." She wasn't entirely out of the woods yet, and she

didn't want to be ninety and still wearing this compression garment.

"So what are you doing about it?"

"Well, believe or not, this tiny island has a wonderful clinic. I promise I'll make an appointment for some time in the next couple of weeks with Doc Welinski." He'd give her a new prescription for any medicated cream she asked for and pain meds, if needed.

"Is he any good?"

"The best."

Grace had never met a sweeter, more compassionate man than old Doc Welinski, except, quite possibly, for her father. Doc had tenderly and with unexpected humor put on her cast when she'd fallen out of the McGregors' apple tree and broken her arm. When she'd gotten violently sick to her stomach after French inhaling an entire pack of cigarettes, he'd given her antacids and kept the secret from her mother. And when other mothers, mothers like Mrs. Miller, had complained about Grace and the trouble she always seemed to be getting into, Grace could still remember Doc Welinski standing up for her in the school lobby. She'd be in good hands here on Mirabelle.

"All right," Suzy said. "I'll tell Amanda she can stop worrying."

"I gotta run. Talk to you again soon."

"Don't wait to answer the phone next time."

"Yeah, yeah." Smiling, Grace disconnected their call. Then she went downstairs and brought in the groceries the Newman's delivery boy had left on her porch. She set the bags on the kitchen counter and put everything away.

The selection of groceries indicated Suzy was well aware that Grace snacked rather than cooked full-fledged meals. Tomato juice, low-fat yogurt and breakfast bars. Pita bread, hummus, sprouts and shaved roasted turkey. Romaine, feta cheese and an olive oil vinaigrette. Shrimp and fish. Blueberries, raspberries, avocadoes and an artichoke, all of them fresh. There were a variety of organic soups. And, lastly, a special treat. Two pints of chocolate fudge brownie ice cream.

Grace grabbed a spoon and dug out a chunk of ice cream before putting the containers in the freezer. As the chocolate melted on her tongue, she groaned. There were benefits to no longer modeling.

Grabbing a hat and sunglasses, in case she encountered any tourists, Grace grabbed a breakfast bar, left the house and set off down Mirabelle's residential streets toward the house she'd grown up in. A strange sense of déjà vu filled her as she walked down the street. She'd spent far too much time here on Mirabelle for these neighborhoods to feel like anything other than home, but the trees were taller and many of the houses had been painted different colors.

In her head, she listed off the names of every family who used to live in every single house, but strangers mowed the lawns and picked up the mail. People had moved, died and retired. Mirabelle had changed. If the Duffys had moved out of their farmhouse, then it was also possible that the Setterbergs had, too. For all she knew the Grotes may have relocated, as well as the Hendersons and the Millers.

But as she approached the cotton candy-pink Victorian next door to her parents' home, it was apparent Shirley Gilbert still owned the bed-and-breakfast. The grand old house was still in tip-top shape as were the gardens already overflowing with pink, white and purple petunias.

The house where she'd grown up couldn't have looked more different from the Gilberts'. Grace turned up the front sidewalk to the modestly sized, but classically designed Victorian and noticed that very little had changed with either the structure or the yard in the years since she'd left home. The house still looked terminally white. What else could you call white shutters and trim on white siding? Virginal?

Her mother had even ensured the landscaping didn't step out of line. Bridal veil spirea bushes. White petunias in the pots on the front porch. A white crab apple tree in full bloom on the front lawn. Other than the grass and leaves, the only color in the entire yard came from the shingles on the rooftop. Green, naturally, so as not to clash with the vegetation.

She glanced up to her old bedroom window in the second-floor turret to find white—of course—sheers hanging in the window. The pale pink polka-dotted curtains she'd had to stare at for most of her teen years were gone. Thank God. She'd always hated those damned frilly things.

A large honeysuckle—white again—climbed up the trestle near the corner. How many times had she climbed down the drainpipe outside her window? If she hadn't been escaping off into the woods to meet some boy vacationing from Chicago, she'd been meeting up with groups of kids to hang around a fire and drink stolen liquor out at Full Moon Bay.

One childhood memory after another tumbled through her mind. More often than not her memories involved boring gatherings with boring guests. Their front door had practically revolved with the comings and goings of visitors. There were some fond memories, some of them involving Carl. Most of the time, she and her older—perfect—brother argued whenever they'd gotten within twenty feet of each other, but there'd been a few times when they'd connected.

Other memories involved her childhood best friend, Gail Gilbert, who had lived next door. At least they'd been best friends until junior high when Mrs. Gilbert had decided to send her daughter to Bayfield for school for what she'd believed would be a "better, more well-rounded" education. As soon as Gail had made better, more well-rounded friends, she'd dropped Grace like a hot potato. At the time, it'd stung that Gail wouldn't even look at Grace on the few occasions their paths had crossed, but it was all water under the bridge at this point.

"Grace?" The almost shrill sounding voice came from next door. "Grace Andersen, is that you?"

Grace glanced toward the Gilberts' and found Gail's mother heading up her sidewalk from the street. "Hello, Mrs. Gilbert."

"I heard you were back home," she said, crossing her lawn to stop at the hedge separating the two yards. "I just didn't know if I should believe it."

"Whaddya know," Grace said, keeping her distance from the smug woman who had never failed to point out to Grace's mother that the Gilbert house was nearly three times the size of the Andersens'.

"How long will you be staying on Mirabelle?"

"Not sure," she hedged. "Probably most of the summer."

"Oh, that's wonderful. Gail comes every year over the July Fourth holiday week and she'll be so excited when she finds out you're here."

Naturally. Now that skinny stick Grace Andersen had become famous Grace Kahill. "Tell her I said hello." Grace waved as she climbed the steps of her father's wide front porch, effectively cutting off any more conversation.

For a moment, she stood at the ornately carved front door, not sure whether she should knock, ring the doorbell or simply walk inside. It might be her childhood home, but the only time she'd come back to Mirabelle since she'd left had been for her father's retirement party and her mother's funeral. In the end, she knocked and waited.

Within a moment or two, footsteps sounded from inside and the door swung wide-open. "Grace! I thought I heard someone out here," her father said, pushing open the storm door. "For heaven's sake, since when do you knock at your own house?"

"Since it ceased being my house?" She shrugged and smiled.

"You have me there." He held out his arms.

As she hugged him, she couldn't help but notice he'd lost some weight. "How are you, Dad?"

"I'm managing. Some days are better than others." He gave her a weak smile as he drew her inside and closed the door. "Have you talked to Carl yet?"

"No." She hadn't been able to get herself to call her older brother. Not only were they several years apart in age, but so much time and distance had created an even bigger gulf between them.

Carl had been the good child. The straight-A student. The apple of their mother's eye. He'd been able to do no wrong. Grace, on the other hand, had never been able to do anything right. If she wasn't getting Cs, she was getting into trouble with teachers and coaches. As far as her mother was concerned, Grace had a tendency to flirt too much with the wrong sort of boys and not enough with the right ones. While her mother had insisted Grace take choir, Grace had wanted to join the basketball team. Grace wore too much makeup, dressed too strangely and swung her hips too much when she walked.

By the time she'd turned sixteen, Grace had simply quit trying to please her mother. Perhaps that's why modeling had drawn Grace in so thoroughly and completely. *She* may not have been perfect, but her body had been.

So much for that.

"Carl will be disappointed you haven't called," her dad said, reining in her thoughts.

Not likely. "I'll call him in the next couple of days."

"Well, come on in." He motioned toward the kitchen.

If her mother had been home, they'd have gone directly to the living room to visit, but Pastor John Andersen had always been a kitchen man, as simple and relaxed as Grace's mother had been formal and proper. Though he was retired now and doing only an occasional wedding service, her father had been a soft-spoken preacher, a kind dad and as far as Grace had known, an affectionate and loving husband.

As Grace walked down the slightly uneven hardwood floor of the main hall, she glanced from living room to formal dining area. Even less had changed in the interior of the home than the exterior, but surprisingly the rooms didn't look the slightest bit dated. Jean Andersen had, by design, decorated with timeless antiques she'd collected through the years. Her father, she noticed, had kept things as immaculate as when her mother had still been alive. Except for in the kitchen.

Her eyes widened at the sight of the mess that had accumulated. Her mother would be rolling in her grave if she could see the state of her domain. Dirty dishes were stacked in the sink and on the counter, mail and newspapers lay haphazardly across almost every flat surface, and a distasteful odor came from the garbage can.

"Dad?" she said. "You look like you could use some help around here."

"Oh, I know, honey. Can't seem to stay ahead of everything."

Stay ahead of it? He wasn't close to keeping up. "Do you mind if I pick up a bit?"

"You don't need to do that. Carol said she was going to come by tomorrow with a few meals. She usually stays for a while and helps me clean."

If that wasn't motivation enough for Grace to clean, she didn't know what was. Carl's wife, Carol, was as picture-perfect as Carl. That match had been made in heaven as had its offspring, their two children, Nikki and Alex. All Grace had heard through the years in phone calls with her mother was Carl this and Carol that intermixed with Nicole did this and Alexander did that. There was little doubt that Carol was the daughter Jean Andersen had always wanted.

Her father glanced around and sighed. "I guess I'm not as good as your mother was at keeping things organized."

"Why don't you sit over there at the counter and we can talk while I straighten up?" Grace started in on emptying the clean dishes from the dishwasher. "When did you eat last?"

"I think I had some cold cereal for breakfast."

"You think?" No matter. It was already after lunchtime. She opened the cupboard and found some soup. It was better than nothing. "You hungry?" She showed him the can.

"Now that you mention it, I could do with a little something, but I can do that." He opened the can, dumped the contents in the bowl, and set it in the microwave, dribbling broth everywhere.

"Sit down, Dad. I'll get it for you when it's done."

"What about you?" he said, sitting with his hands in his lap. "You going to join me?"

"I'm good. Thanks."

"So you got in yesterday. All settled?"

"Pretty much."

"Caught up with any old friends, yet?"

"No, and I'm not sure I have much of an interest."

"We've had a lot a new folks moving to the island in the past couple years. I think there's a group about your age."

Lovely.

"Some good people in that mix. Some...not so much."

That was about as negative as her father ever got when it came to assessing people. If he didn't like someone, chances were you'd never know it.

"So in which group is Sean Griffin?"

"Sean? Have you met him?"

"Yesterday. I'm boarding my horse at his stables. He was a bit...abrupt."

Her father chuckled. "Yep, that's Sean. Impatient. I'm not sure he's entirely adjusted to the pace on Mirabelle."

"Where's he from?"

"Your neck of the woods, I think. L.A."

What in the world had brought him here of all places?

They continued chatting about nothing of consequence while she finished putting away the clean dishes and then began piling the dirty ones into the dishwasher. When the microwave dinged, she set the hot soup in front of her dad and picked up the kitchen. By the time she'd finished, the dishwasher was full again, but at least the counters were clean.

She went through the mail, recycling all the junk and setting the bills and other correspondence in one neat pile. "This is the important stuff," she said, making sure he was paying attention. "So you need to go through this soon, okay?"

He nodded. "All right, dear."

Nearing the bottom of the stack, she ran across a recent photo of her mom and dad. They were sitting at a table, his arm was around her shoulder and their heads were tilted toward each other. It was rare to see Jean Andersen smile so widely.

"That was taken the night before she died," her dad said as he came to stand next to her. "We were playing cards at the Engebretsons' town house, and she'd just won a game of hearts by shooting the moon in the last hand."

Meaning she'd just forced twenty-six points onto all of her other teammates. Not an easy thing to do. God, it'd been a long time since Grace had played cards.

"It was a good night." He ran the tip of his index finger over the photo.

She glanced at him and his melancholy expression clawed at her heart. How could her father have so loved a woman with whom Grace had never really gotten along? It just didn't make sense. "It'll get easier, Dad."

He smiled wryly. "You know how many times I've said that exact thing to other people looking to their pastor for advice?" He shook his head. "It's hogwash." He sighed. "I still wake up every morning expecting to see her lying next to me."

The phone rang, piercing the sudden quiet.

She answered. "Andersen residence."

"Well, I'll be darned. This little Gracie?"

"Yes," she said, smiling with the realization that this man's voice sounded familiar. "This Doc Welinski?"

He chuckled. "That it is."

"How have you been, Doc?"

"I've been great," he said, pausing. "So sorry about your mom."

"Thank you."

They chatted for a few minutes about her plans. "Enough of that," Grace said finally. "I imagine you wanted to talk with Dad."

"That I do. Need to get that man moving again. Thought maybe a round of golf might do a world of good."

"Sounds like a great idea." She handed the phone to her father. "It's Doc Welinski."

"Willard? What's up?"

Grace put her father's lunch dishes in the dishwasher.

"No, no," her father said. "Not this afternoon. I'm too tired." Her father paused, presumably while Doc talked. "I know, I know. I'll get there. Just not today." Another pause. "Thanks for the offer." He hung up the phone.

"I think it would do you some good, Dad," Grace said gently. "To get out a bit."

"Next week." He patted her cheek. "It's good to have you home, Grace."

"It's good to be home, Dad."

CHAPTER FOUR

"SEE YOU TWO IN THE MORNING." Sean walked through his clinic waiting room after his last appointment of the day.

"Have a good afternoon, Doctor," replied Donna, his office manager.

"See you later, Dr. Griffin," his nurse, Kelly, said, smiling.

No matter how many times he asked them, he couldn't get those two to refer to him as Sean. Donna, a stout woman in her late fifties, had insisted it wasn't proper in a medical clinic to call the doctor anything except doctor, and Kelly, a pretty young—too young for Sean—redhead who'd moved to Mirabelle only last summer, wasn't about to cross Donna no matter how much she wanted to flirt with Sean.

Sean left the clinic and headed toward home. Although being the only physician on the island also meant being on call 24/7, limiting his clinic hours to mornings during the summer tourist season left him afternoons and evenings for his new business venture.

He reached the top of Mirabelle's hill and headed straight through the residential section toward the outer edge of town. After walking through the main gate to his property, Sean nodded at Eric, his stable manager who, along with a couple other wranglers, was taking a group of tourists out on trail ride through Mirabelle's state park land.

"Everything going okay?" Sean asked, stepping onto his front porch.

"Yes, sir," Eric answered. "Had two full groups this morning and have another two scheduled this afternoon."

"Great." As the line of horses left the main yard, Sean opened his front door, stepped inside and immediately stumbled over a pair of shoes left smack-dab in the middle of the hall. Austin's shoes.

He glanced around. It'd taken him several months to get this house exactly the way he'd wanted it, updated and refreshed, neat and ordered, but he'd finally managed. It had taken Austin less than a week to wreak havoc.

The kid was like a tornado. He'd thrown his sweatshirt over a chair. A pair of his socks were lying on the floor in the family room. An empty pop can sat on an end table, along with several sweat rings from other drinks. A cell phone, personal music device and both chargers were strewn across one of the kitchen counters. An empty milk carton sat next to the kitchen sink along with several dirty dishes and the jar of peanut butter and there were bread crumbs scattered everywhere.

Only three months. You can do it.

After changing out of his doctor garb for his preferred mode of dress—jeans and a T-shirt—he rapped on Austin's closed bedroom door. "Austin, time to get up."

No response.

"Austin?"

Still nothing.

"Austin."

"What?" came the surly response.

Sean took a deep breath and tried to let it slide. "It's after noon. You can't sleep the entire day away."

There was a long moment of silence. "I'll get up in a minute."

Sean went to the kitchen and set about making himself a sandwich for lunch. Once he pulled out the bread, he realized it'd be just as easy to make two sandwiches. A few minutes later, as he was sitting down at the table, Austin shuffled into the room. "I made you some lunch," Sean said, nodding at the plate opposite him.

Austin glanced from Sean to the plate and back again. "I'm not hungry."

Seemed like this kid was bound and determined to make this difficult no matter what Sean did or didn't do. "Suit yourself."

Austin opened the refrigerator door and searched around. Then he poured himself a glass of milk. A moment later, he reached for the plate. "I guess I'll just take this to my bedroom."

"Nuh-uh." Sean held down the edge of the plate. "If you're going to eat, eat here."

Austin sighed and shook his head. "Whatever." Reluctantly, he sat and started to eat.

They sat in awkward, uncomfortable silence. Sean racked his brain for some way to make a connection to this young man. His son. How weird was that? Surreptitiously, he watched Austin. The kid propped one elbow on the table, tilted his head to the left and used a napkin in a side-swiping motion. His mannerisms were too similar to Sean's to be coincidence. This kid was a Griffin, through and through. Somehow, someway, he had to make a connection.

"Look, Austin, I don't know what Denise told you about me, but, for what it's worth, I didn't know you existed until she called me a couple weeks ago."

"Yeah, well, I didn't know you existed, either," he said. "So that makes us even."

"You don't need to be such an—"

"Is this what you woke me for? To talk?" He rolled his eyes and pushed away from the table. "Get real, okay? You're not my dad. I don't have a dad. I don't want a dad. And if I ever did want a dad, I sure as hell wouldn't want you." With that, Austin stalked off toward the front door. "I'll meet you outside."

No longer hungry, Sean threw away what was left of his sandwich. Then he put their dishes in the sink and tried to recall what Arlo had said that first day about Austin. The kid had a right to be angry, and Sean needed to be patient. Unfortunately, patience had never been his strong suit. He took a long, deep breath, went outside and found Austin waiting for him on the porch.

The kid glared at him. "So now what?"

This was going to be a damned long summer.

"So now we find out what you can do around here," Sean said as cheerfully as he could manage.

The crew was out on the first of the afternoon trail rides, so for now it was relatively quiet in the yard. The only activity amounted to Arlo rigging a carriage until Grace walked into the yard and headed for the barn.

Suddenly, Austin's demeanor changed. "Who's that?"

"Grace Kahill. She's visiting for the summer and boarding her horse here."

"Damn."

You could say that again.

Dressed in tight, low-slung jeans, a straw cowboy hat and tall riding boots, she looked good. The bandanna around her neck was a nice touch, too. She went into the barn, came back outside with her horse and started brushing him.

Sean cleared his throat and, pulling his gaze away from Grace, pointed to the row of saddles hanging in the back. "Okay, Austin. Let's see what you got. Saddle this bay."

The sullen, obstinate teen suddenly turned nervous and unsure. "I don't know to saddle a horse."

That didn't make any sense. "But you can ride, right?"

"Sure. Been on plenty of trail rides and stuff on family vacations."

Family vacations? In other words, he didn't know diddly about diddly squat with regard to horses. "Your mom said you knew horses."

"What can I say? She lied. So what else is new?"

Shit. "I don't have time to teach you. And neither does Arlo or any of the rest of the crew."

"Well, good news for you," Austin said. "Now you have an excuse to send me home."

"I didn't say I was going to send you home."

"That's what you want though, isn't it?"

Sean had had about all he could take. "Look. There's enough to do around here to keep you plenty busy." He pointed to one of the barns. "Take that wheelbarrow and shovel over there and muck out all the stalls in the livery barn."

"Are you serious?"

"Very. Dump your loads into the manure spreader."

"Yes, sir." Austin mock-saluted and took off for the barn.

Arlo shook his head as he came toward Sean.

"Might as well spit it out," Sean said.

"Seems to me you're setting up one helluva confrontational relationship with that boy," Arlo said under his breath. "You sure that's what you want?"

"What I want is to not be a father."

"Too late for that."

"Dammit!" Denise had said he was a chip off the old block. "When I was his age I was *running* a trail riding operation, not working at one."

"But is that what you want for your son?"

"He could do worse," he said, watching Grace bring a pad and saddle outside and setting them over the nearest rail fence.

"I raised two boys here on Mirabelle," Arlo said. "Made 'em work here at the stables every summer. They helped take care of the horses every winter. And you know what?"

Sean waited.

"Neither one of 'em ever comes to the island to visit. Oh, they came down to Florida last winter. Couldn't wait to see me and Lynnie once we were off the island. But Mirabelle? They don't want anything to do with this place." Arlo started heading toward the livery barn. "Seems to me there's an opportunity here for you two. What's made of it is entirely up to you. Not that young man."

Sean stood alone in the yard. Arlo was right, of course. It was up to Sean to take the first step in forging a relationship with Austin and to make whatever relationship they developed worthwhile. Still, he didn't know where to start. How the hell could you forge a relationship with someone who didn't want anything to do with you?

SO THE KID WAS SEAN'S SON. *Interesting.*

Grace had tried not to eavesdrop while she was brushing Louie, but with the rising voices, it had been difficult not to absorb a few of the somewhat startling bits of information.

She set Louie's pad on his back, getting ready to saddle him for a ride and watched the boy attempting to muck out a stall. He'd stalked past her a few minutes earlier without the slightest acknowledgment of her presence and went into the first stall with an empty wheelbarrow and a shovel.

"How you doing, Grace?" Arlo said, his tall, bony frame ambling by her. Other than the fact that his short beard was much more gray than she remembered, he'd barely changed all these years.

"I'm fine. You, Arlo?"

"Good." He grinned. "I'm always good. You should know that."

Arlo went into the massive livery barn, took two of his Percherons—a matching pair of dappled grays—out of their stalls and brought them outside. Then he started prepping one to be hitched to a shuttle carriage that took groups of passengers around the island, most often from the Rock Pointe Lodge or Mirabelle Island Inn into town, or vice versa.

"Need some help?" she asked.

"If you're offering." He cocked his head toward one of the horses. "I got Pat here, if you can take Mike."

"Sure." Holding off on saddling Louie for the moment, she led him into the stall Austin had already mucked out. Then she came out to the yard, patted Mike's neck and whispered a few words to him as she attached his bridle and collar. Spreading the leather traces along his back, she was careful not to entangle them. It was a good thing she was tall. They were big horses.

"I want to thank you for sticking your neck out with Sean and agreeing to board Louie," she said as she adjusted the crouper. It'd been so long since someone had her back that she'd almost forgotten what it felt like, but Arlo had always been that way. Ready to stick up for her at a moment's notice.

"Ah. No worries," he said. "Sean might seem a bit gruff, but he's all bark and no bite."

"Could've fooled me."

"That's the point, isn't it?"

"And the boy," she said softly. "Sean's son?"

"Ayep."

"Came to work here for the summer, but he doesn't know a thing about horses?"

"That so surprising?" Arlo considered the boy as he straightened Pat's traces. "I seem to recall a certain young gal who once upon a time didn't know her bits from her reins."

She chuckled. "Too true."

She and Arlo hitched Mike and Pat to the carriage, and he climbed into the driver's seat. They both glanced at Austin. He'd dumped his first load into the spreader and was working on his second. The way he tried to keep from stepping in anything was like a poorly written comedy sketch. Either he had no clue what he was doing or he had an extreme aversion to horse manure, possibly both.

"The way I see it, somebody around here oughta take that boy under his—or her—wing," Arlo said. "Lord knows I don't have the time."

"Subtle, Arlo." She smiled. "Real subtle."

"Whatever you're going to do, do it quick, huh?" He made a clicking noise and tapped the reins, setting Pat and Mike off and out of the yard.

Grace glanced at Austin. He was sidestepping the manure as if it were acid. She couldn't help laughing.

The kid glanced at her and scowled. "Oh, that's real mature."

"It's just horse shit. It's not going to jump up and bite you."

"Easy for you to say. You like horses."

"What are you doing here, then, if you don't like horses?"

"Like I had a choice."

Man, did he look like a younger version of his dad. "My name's Grace."

"Austin."

"So, Austin, you've never mucked out a stall before, have you?"

"No." He looked angry, frustrated and in need of a friend.

Funny, that's exactly the way she felt these days.

Before thinking better of it, she opened the stall door. "Well, first off you need to change shoes." She pointed to a pair of rubber boots by the barn door. "Wear a pair of those and then you don't need to worry about stepping in anything."

He glanced toward the door. "Whose are those?"

"Probably Arlo's, but he won't mind."

Grudgingly, Austin pulled on the barn boots.

"While you're over there grab those gloves." She indicated the pair on the shelf above the boots. "So you don't get blisters."

He came toward her, looking at least a little bit better prepared.

"Now you're ready to get to work."

She showed him a better way to hold the shovel and before she knew what she was getting herself into she'd changed out of her riding boots and into her Wellingtons and was helping him take another load out to the spreader. In no time, they'd finished mucking out all the stalls in the livery stable and she'd shown him how to use the spreader in the back pasture.

On their way to the barn, she said, "So you really don't know anything about horses?"

"Nope."

"Bet your dad took that real well."

"He's not my dad." Austin frowned. "Technically, I guess he is my dad, but I didn't know it until a couple weeks ago. I thought my mom's husband was my real dad. Turns out he's not."

Unbelievable. "So Griffin deserted you and your mom?"

"No. He never knew she was pregnant. She's got all kinds of excuses for keeping that a secret. They were splitting, and he never wanted to have kids. I guess she thought she was doing them both a favor."

"So Griffin just now found out you're his son?"

"Yeah. Weird, huh?"

"What are you doing here now?"

He looked away. "My mom and…Glen are getting divorced. She's got enough on her hands with my younger brother and sister."

"She sent you here?" To get rid of him. That had to have hurt.

"Yeah. For the summer. Just for the summer." He sounded as if he was making excuses for her. "So now Sean's mad at me. Sent me in here to muck out the stalls."

Some small part of her took perverse pleasure in this upset to Sean's life. Why, she had no clue. The man simply drove her crazy. Then there was the fact that she felt a kind of affinity toward the kid, an outsider, like her. "How 'bout I teach you to ride?" Grace offered.

"Can you?"

"I can try. I grew up here on Mirabelle. Used to work for Arlo. I can teach you how to saddle a horse, how to feed them, brush them. You name it."

"Why do you want to help me?"

"Because I have a feeling it'll bug your dad," she said, grinning. Any enemy of Sean's was a friend of Grace's. "Time to teach you everything you never wanted to know about horses."

CHAPTER FIVE

"THIS IS RIDICULOUS," GRACE muttered to herself as she flipped off the bedcovers. First hot, then cold, then hot again. To the bathroom. To the kitchen for a drink of water. Night after night after night. She'd been on Mirabelle for more than a week and she wasn't able to sleep any better here than in her Hollywood Hills home. And she'd used the last of her pain medication.

Rolling out of bed, she glanced out the window. Below, the lights of Mirabelle's small village center twinkled, and the lake, black as the clear night sky, stretched as far as the eye could see. A full moon glittered on the surface of the abnormally still lake. On a night like this the view from Full Moon Bay would be amazing, but then the views from there were always amazing.

Her favorite spot on the entire island, Full Moon Bay, was north of Rock Pointe, the lodge and resort area her brother owned, Henderson's apple orchard and even the lighthouse. A gem of sugar-soft sand accessible only from the main road by a narrow deer path, no one but the locals knew of the bay's existence. When she was little, Grace had gone there to hunt for agates, and when she was older, for bonfire parties with friends. She'd skinny-dipped more than once in the shallow waters of Full Moon Bay, and, in fact, had lost her virginity there to some boy from Chicago who'd been there on vacation with his family. Funny, but she couldn't even remember the boy's name.

As much as she would've loved seeing the bay after all these years, the idea of hiking to the deserted northeast end of Mirabelle alone in the pitch-black stillness of the night sounded a bit bizarre. Instead, she walked into the bathroom, splashed water onto her face and patted her skin dry. Glancing through her window toward the barns behind her house made her think of Louie. Was he adjusting to Mirabelle any better?

The hell with it. She pulled on a sweatshirt and sweatpants, remembering that even after a hot day the nights on the island could get chilly, and slipped out the back door. She flashed on the possible complication of being discovered by Sean or one of his stable hands, but quickly dismissed that risk. She'd snuck into the Duffy's barns on many occasions when she'd lived here. Besides, what was the worst thing that could happen if she did get caught?

IT WAS PAST MIDNIGHT.

Sean sat in front of his computer screen in his office off the kitchen working up a new shift schedule for the stable operations. He'd already taken care of the livery schedule, prepped the day's bank deposit and gathered and emailed off the last two weeks of hours to his payroll accountant. All that after taking care of the carriages that had come rolling into his yard after the last of the shuttle runs around the island.

He finished the schedule and then stood and stretched. He was done for the night, and Austin still wasn't home. Granted, it was Friday night and he'd said it was okay to stay out late, but he'd made it clear to Austin that curfew on this island for sixteen-year-olds was midnight on Friday and Saturday. Sean had checked with Garrett.

His hands stuffed deep into his front jeans pockets, he walked outside and onto the wide, wraparound front porch, staring out into the night and hoping he was going to see a tall, lanky teenager coming toward him any minute. More than likely, Austin had made some friends and simply lost track of time. But what if he'd been scrambling around on the boulders along the shore? What if he'd slipped and fallen into the water? Sean didn't even know if the kid could swim.

The longer he stood there, the madder he got. *The little shit. No wonder Denise wanted to get rid of him.*

No, that wasn't fair. The truth was he couldn't blame the kid for acting out. Rebellion was probably in his genes, and Sean knew exactly from which side it'd come.

He paced the length of the porch and glanced out over the pastureland. Finally, he'd found a purpose for the money that had been put in a trust fund when his mother had passed away. Buying this old farmhouse and the one hundred plus acres of land along with the four barns, more than sixty horses and ten carriages would've made his mother happy.

Unlike the rest of the island with its Victorian gingerbread charm, the only quaint thing about this farmhouse was that it had been painted red with white trim to match the barns. Sean was okay with that. In fact, he rather liked this old house. With its wide-open rooms and simple design, it wasn't far off the mark of something he'd build on his own, given the chance.

He especially liked the fact that his property was at the outskirts of town, although as such, it was dark here. For Austin's sake, Sean had left every light on inside the house, as well as outside. He'd even left the floodlights on by the barns, hoping the kid would find his way.

He was starting to wonder if he was going to have to call Garrett Taylor when he caught some movement near the road. A shadowy form took shape. It was Austin, and he seemed to be taking his sweet time making it up to the house.

"Hey," Austin said sourly, as he came close.

Questions swirled around in Sean's mind, one after another.

What have you been doing all this time? Who have been with? Have you eaten supper? He settled for, "Where you been?"

"Around."

That tipped the scale, and Sean's badly worn patience snapped. "You couldn't take the time to answer your cell phone?" He'd called Austin's number no less than four times and had left two messages. "I need to know where you are, so you need to answer your phone when I call. And you're past curfew. I expect you to follow the law on this island."

The kid rolled his eyes. "Or what? You gonna send me back to Mom's?"

"That's the second time you've mentioned that. Maybe that's what you want, huh?"

Austin didn't say anything.

"Stay. Don't stay," Sean said. "I don't really care one way or another, but if you decide to stay, then you'd damned well better not make any trouble on this island. It's my home and the people here are important to me." He took a breath. "Get this through your head right here and now. Tow the line or leave."

Austin glared at Sean. "You're not my dad, okay? Not really. So you can't tell me what to do."

"That's the way it's going to be?" Anger, frustration, and concern all battled inside Sean for dominance. "Well, then, fine. Go," he said. "You think I really care what you do, or when you do it?" he said, anger pushing through.

"Figures." Austin glared at Sean. "You're just like Glen. I don't know why I thought you might be different."

"What's that supposed to mean?"

"I can't go home, okay? If I do I'll have to go to juvie. The judge agreed to waive detention only if I came here."

Denise had definitely not said anything about a judge, court or juvenile detention. She'd said he'd gotten into some trouble, but Sean had been too blindsided by the whole deal to ask for specifics. "What did you do?"

"What difference does it make?"

"I want to know."

Austin hesitated. "Broke a teacher's car window."

"Why?"

"Because he's a dick." He looked away. "He told our class that we could skip the final if everyone was getting Bs by the last week of school. We did it, but then he made us take the test anyway."

"So a teacher's a jerk and you're in trouble. Was it worth it?"

"Hell, no. I'm stuck here for the summer, aren't I?" Austin pushed past him on the porch and went into the house.

"Wait a minute." Sean followed him inside. "We need to get something straight."

He stopped, but didn't turn.

"This is working ranch, not a playground. I don't care if you stay out until curfew every damned night of the week, but you've had enough time to get settled. No more sleeping in until noon. You stay here, you work here just like everyone else."

"Whatever."

"No, not whatever. I don't want to hear the word *whatever* the rest of the summer. Understood?"

Silence again.

"Understood?"

"Yes!" the kid hissed through clenched teeth.

"Good. If you're going to live in this house, you're going to have to live by my—" Sean clamped his mouth shut.

Had he really just said that? Had he really just said all of that…that crap? He sounded like his own father. All the words, fighting words, had spilled out of his mouth as if he and Austin had been sparring for years.

The kid stood quiet and sullen, as if he'd heard it all before, as if nothing Sean said could cut him any deeper than he'd already been cut.

See? You were right, asshole. This was why you had no business being a father.

Sean took a deep breath. "Tomorrow you start work for real around here. Seven a.m. Okay?"

"Yeah." Austin walked away, slammed his bedroom door and a few seconds later the lights went out.

Sean shouldn't have been so hard on him. He could've at least given the kid more time to adjust. Too late. If he went and apologized right now the kid would laugh in his face. Better to let the dust settle.

He went around the house, shutting off lights, inside and out. He flicked off the yard floodlights and noticed a dim light on in the livery barn. *Now what?*

Stalking outside, he crossed the yard and opened the barn door. One light was on in a storage room and a rear window had been propped open with a stick. How had that happened? Those windows didn't even open. On his way through the barn, he glanced into the stalls. All the horses were quiet except for the Friesian. He was wide-awake and alert and sticking his muzzle toward Sean inquisitively.

"Still on West Coast time, boy, or what?" Sean stopped and glanced at the horse. Since Sean had seen him earlier in the day, someone had brushed and braided his mane. His coat looked even softer and shinier than it had that afternoon, if that was possible.

Hay rustled in the stall though the horse hadn't moved.

Sean went still. "Who's in there?"

More rustling sounded before a head popped up over the gate. "It's me."

Grace. A curry brush in one hand, she leaned her head against her horse's neck.

The first thing he noticed was that she'd traded in her tight jeans for baggy sweats. Hot on the heels of that observation was that all of the tenseness she'd seemed to be carrying in her body since the first day he'd met her was nearly gone. She looked as relaxed as a person could get, and while a part of him hated to destroy the moment, the last thing he wanted was for people to come and go on his property as they pleased.

"You know," he said, softly. "Some people might call this trespassing."

"I haven't been sleeping well." She looked away. "Brushing Louie…calms me."

"So that gives you the right to sneak into my barn."

"Sorry." She didn't sound, let alone look, very apologetic.

At a loss, he glanced toward the back. "Those windows stick. According to Arlo, they haven't been opened for years."

"There's a trick to it," she said. "Tap the upper right hand corner and they slide like a dream."

"You know this because…"

She took the brush and ran it down the horse's shoulder. "When I was a kid, I used to sneak in here at night."

"Troublemaker, huh?"

She wouldn't look at him. "You could call it that."

She'd likely been all kinds of trouble when she'd been younger. Probably still was. Why that turned him on, he hadn't a clue.

"Look," he said, switching gears, "I don't know what kind of deal you worked out with Arlo, but I meant what I said the other day about you taking care of your horse on your own. Arlo doesn't complain much, but he's not as young as he used to be."

"Don't worry about it. Arlo won't have to lift a finger to help me, and I plan on helping him out as much as I can."

Grace's horse rubbed his forehead against her and then settled his head on her shoulder. "Besides, I enjoy caring for Louie." She wrapped her arms around her horse's neck and smiled.

Suddenly Sean understood why people paid top dollar for pictures of this woman. Her blue eyes sparkled to life, her cheeks rounded with delightful fullness and her lips glistened with pure, sensual joy. Despite her face being devoid of makeup, she was without a doubt the prettiest thing he'd ever seen on two feet.

Their gazes caught, and as if she sensed his gut-level, very male reaction, her smiled slowly faded. Still, he couldn't seem to tear his gaze from her mouth.

He had to get out of this barn before he remembered exactly how long it'd been since he'd kissed a woman. That little peck he'd given last year to Missy Charms, the owner of one of Mirabelle's gift shops, in an effort to test the waters of their friendship didn't count. That kiss had fallen flat from both ends. Grace, he had a feeling, would be a whole different story.

Married, he reminded himself.

"For what it's worth," she murmured, "I'm sorry about causing a hassle over boarding Louie that first day we met."

Now *that* apology was sincere. "Arlo should've told you it wasn't his business any longer and just to set the record straight." He paused. "I wouldn't have made you send Louie home."

"So your bark *is* worse than your bite."

"Don't tell anyone, though, okay?" Clearing his throat, he turned toward the barn door. "By the way, you're a little old to be sneaking through windows. Next time you feel the need to visit your horse in the middle of the night, try the door."

"Does that mean I have your permission to trespass?" she asked, the remnants of a smile clinging to her voice.

"For now," he called over his shoulder. "But be careful,

Grace. You never know who you might run into while you're lurking around a man's property in the middle of the night."

"That a threat or a promise?"

He stopped in his tracks, felt a strong stirring in his groin and smiled to himself. Too bad he couldn't act on this sucker punch of an attraction he was feeling toward this woman. "Aren't you married, Grace?"

"Not anymore," she whispered, sounding almost breathless.

He turned to find her partially hidden in shadows, making it tough to discern her thoughts. "What's that supposed to mean?"

"Jeremy filed for a divorce last year." She ran her fingers down one of the braids on Louis's mane. "I signed the final papers just before I came to Mirabelle."

Was it his imagination, or did her gaze just travel all over him only to linger for a split second longer on the growing bulge in his jeans? Now he remembered how long it'd been since he'd kissed a woman, touched a woman's naked skin, let alone had sex. Too damned long. And he wasn't going to be able to rely on a set of vows to keep his head clear and focused.

"Consider this fair warning. Think twice before starting something with me, Grace. I'm not sure you'll ever be ready to give what I want from a woman."

"Which is?"

"Nothing short of happily ever after."

Surprisingly, she didn't look the slightest bit shocked by his admission, and that made him want her all the more. Before he could put into action every shocking thought running through his mind about exactly what he wanted to do to

Grace, he stalked out of the barn. He wouldn't have thought it was possible, but his summer had just gotten a hell of a lot more complicated.

CHAPTER SIX

"THERE," GRACE SAID, LEANING back from the gardens in the front yard of her father's house. Her left side was aching from use, but it was a good ache. "What do you think, Dad?"

Her father shook his head. "It's different. Pretty, I suppose."

"You suppose?" She laughed. "I guess I deserve that for trying to add some color to the front yard with some pink and purple impatiens. You want me to get rid of them and put in Mom's double whites instead?"

"Good heavens, no. That would be a terrible waste." He climbed the front porch. "Let's go in and have some lunch."

"I'm right behind you." Grace brushed off her garden gloves, slipped off her muddy shoes on the front porch and followed her dad inside. "I just need to wash up."

She headed into the powder room off the kitchen and lathered her grimy hands. Somehow, she'd managed to get dirt all the way onto her elbows. She glanced in the mirror. Even her cheeks were smudged with garden soil.

That a threat or a promise?

From nowhere her encounter with Sean in his barn the previous night popped into her head. What in God's name had she been thinking flirting with the man?

That he was as different from all the male models, photographers and designers in her world as night from day. That he was available and she was divorced and a good, old-fashioned romp in the hay might be exactly what she needed.

And then to be ceremoniously shot down. *Ouch.*

Only she wasn't buying it. Not entirely, anyway. True, she didn't have much experience with this kind of thing of late, but it seemed to her that Sean Griffin's mouth had said one thing and his eyes had said quite another.

Men looked at her all the time. She was used to, almost immune to, a lingering show of appreciation. What she'd seen in Sean's eyes had been different. He'd looked at her as if she'd been the only thing that existed in his world in that moment, as if he'd needed her like air or water, as if he was burning up inside and she was the only thing that could soothe him.

His heat had transferred to her as if his naked skin had been pressed against hers. All she'd been able to think about as she'd stood staring at him from Louie's stall was what it might feel like to have his hands on her, to have him over her, inside her. Nothing sweet or tentative would've sufficed, either. She'd wanted rough, needy, fast.

Grace laughed out loud.

Since the accident, she'd assumed she was all but dead from a sexuality standpoint. If she was honest with herself, the years before the accident hadn't been all that exciting, either. Her marriage to Jeremy had been more of a convenience than anything, and sex with a friend simply hadn't worked for Grace.

Jeremy had been the epitome of discretion with his romantic affairs, but Grace had never had the urge, let alone the need to seek any satisfaction outside of their marriage. It was surprising, really, considering how sexual she'd felt while living on Mirabelle, but something had changed in her after moving to California. She'd lost herself in her work, and she wasn't entirely sure that had been for the best.

Last night, though, had proven without a shadow of a doubt that the old Grace Andersen was still locked someplace deep inside. She was, after all, as hot-blooded as any other woman. So what was she going to do about it? She was divorced, footloose and fancy free. Sean Griffin had said he wanted happily ever after, but would any man really turn away from the offer of a casual fling? She imagined kissing him and placing her hands on him. *His hands on her.*

Bam. Reality crashed down. She would never be getting naked with a man. Not with this body.

"Grace?"

She jumped at the sound of her dad's voice.

"You okay in there?"

"Yeah, Dad. I'll be out in a sec."

Forget it, Grace. It's not going to happen.

Sloughing off all thoughts of the previous night—and of Sean—Grace dried off her hands and went into the kitchen. She and her dad made turkey sandwiches together at the center island. Feeling hungrier than usual, she used two pieces of whole grain bread, rather than having it open-faced, and slathered on some mayo. They'd just sat to eat when the front door opened.

"Dad?" The sound of a man's voice came from the foyer. "You home?"

Carl. Even after all these years she knew her brother's voice better than her own.

"In the kitchen, Carl," her father called.

A moment later, he walked into the room, his brow furrowing as he looked at her, almost as if he didn't recognize her. Then a slight smile slowly spread across his face. "Grace."

"Hello, Carl."

"I heard a rumor you'd moved back onto the island and I couldn't believe it. That's all they can talk about down at Duffy's and the Bayside."

Figures.

An awkward silence filled the air. A hug seemed too familiar. A handshake too distant. One thing was certain. He seemed to have aged even since their mother's funeral.

"Well, give each other a hug, for crying in the beer!" their father said, laughing.

Grace stood and they hugged briefly.

"How are you?" Carl said as he stepped away, his gaze traveling quickly down to her left shoulder and back again. "I mean…well, you know what I mean."

"I'm great," she said, evading the issue.

"You look good."

Better than at Mom's funeral is more than likely what he meant. "Thanks."

"So what's going on? Why didn't you call or something? Let us know you were coming."

"Honestly, it all came about so fast. One day I was looking at houses with a real estate agent and the next day I was making arrangements to come here. I called Dad to let him know I was coming."

"Well, that explains it." Carl glanced at their father. "I haven't talked to you in weeks, have I?"

"Nope."

"Sorry, Dad. It's been crazy busy at the resort." He glanced at Grace. "How long can you stay?"

"At least for the summer. After that, your guess is as good as mine."

"We didn't get much of a chance to talk at Mom's funeral."

He hadn't acted as though he'd wanted to talk, and she hadn't been physically up for staying much past the funeral. "Yeah, well, it was bad timing."

"Is there ever a good time for death?" he said, his gaze turning suddenly troubled as he ran his hands through his thinning hair. His hairline was receding and his temples were graying, and suddenly even she felt so much older just being his sister. "Are you staying here with Dad?"

"I told her she should, but I guess I understand her wanting her space."

"Three months is a long time, Dad. I'm over at the Schumacher's old place."

"How's it working out?"

"Good, so far. It's kind of out of the way of things. I like that. I'm boarding my horse at Arlo's and I wanted to be close to him."

"It's not Arlo's anymore," Carl said.

"No. That was a shocker. Dad says you and Sean Griffin are friends?"

"Yeah. Good friends." Carl glanced sideways at her. "Why?"

"He seems like a jerk, that's all."

Carl laughed. "He can be a little gruff at times."

"But he's a good man," their father added.

Carl glanced at her as if he was he was trying to find the right approach for asking her something. When had he become so diplomatic? "Carol wanted me to ask if you could come to brunch in a couple weeks."

"You mean a Sunday brunch?" she asked, surprised.

While she'd been growing up, Sunday brunch at the Andersen household had been a ritual of epic proportions. The food had seemed never ending, and the company boring. Their mother had routinely invited a different family from the island during the off-season and vacationing friends and relatives during the summer. Invitations to their home had been sought after, something Grace had never understood.

"You still have brunch?" she asked. "Even though Mom is gone?"

"Actually, Carol took over the tradition from Mom some years ago."

"Bet that went over like a lead balloon." She remembered too late that their father was there. "No offense, Dad."

"None taken," he said. "Your mother was actually glad Carol took over the reins."

"If you'd been around a little more," Carl said, "you might've noticed how fragile she was getting these past couple of years."

Well, there was no resentment in that comment, Grace thought sarcastically.

"Carl, that wasn't necessary," their father said.

"No, that's fine, Dad." Grace shrugged. "You were all Mom needed, Carl. I figured that out by the time I was eight."

"Hey, hey," their dad said, trying to smooth things over. "You two sound like kids again."

"Sorry," Carl said. "We only do brunch once a month these days. Should I tell Carol you'll be coming next time?"

"Doesn't sound like you want me there."

"Dad's coming. Right, Dad?"

"Yep. I'll be there."

That didn't answer her question, but she wasn't feeling like pushing it at the moment. "Yeah. I'll be there."

"Just in case you don't remember, our house is up the hill from the Rock Pointe Lodge."

"I know where it is."

"Funny." He headed for the front door. "All these years you've never been there."

"Funny," she whispered, watching him as he walked angrily away. "All these years you've never invited me."

Her father glanced at Grace. "He's been under a lot of pressure lately. His lodge's business has been busier than heck, and Carl...well, he's just not himself lately."

Like the last year had been a cakewalk for her. "It's okay, Dad. Carl and I will work it out."

Or not. She wasn't sure it made a difference to her one way or another.

"I WANT TO SEE YOU TONIGHT," Sherri Phillips said, her voice sounding low and soft over the cell phone. A bedroom voice.

Standing at the window of his home office, Carl stared out over the bluff toward the twinkling lights of Rock Pointe Lodge resort. His office door was firmly closed, but even so the prospect of getting caught had his heart racing and his palms sweating. That was likely part of the thrill, though, wasn't it? The forbidden nature of this—for lack of a better word—relationship.

"You shouldn't have called," he whispered back. "What if someone finds out?"

"Carl Andersen, Mirabelle's golden boy, having an affair? No one would believe it."

There was some truth to that. But still… "I told you what happened was a mistake."

One too many martinis had probably led to more than a few mistakes in the bars of this world, but Carl had never believed it could happen to him. He was a good husband and father, an upstanding citizen, an honest businessman. His entire life he'd always done what was right.

Even so, one thing had led to another, and before he'd known it he was in the men's bathroom joined at the hips with the single and sexy owner of Mirabelle's only hair salon. Although he vaguely remembered throwing a few bucks in the condom machine, it had all happened so fast part of him wasn't even sure it hadn't been a dream.

"I know. I get it," she said. "But I keep thinking about

what happened. We're hot together, Carl. You have to admit that."

It had been wild. Crazy.

"I want you—need you—so bad," she said. "I can taste you. All of you."

Oh, man. He felt an almost instantaneous hard-on. For the first time in a very long while he'd felt desired. Alive. Powerful. He was used to taking charge at his business, but this was something entirely different. This was heady and exciting. Still… "I don't think I can get away."

"Try," she breathed into the phone. *"Hard."*

Suddenly, he was racking his brain for an excuse to leave this house. There was only one problem. In all the years he'd been married, the only time he'd ever gone out alone after dinner had been for an emergency at the resort or to meet the guys for a basketball game or a beer at Duffy's. And in all those years, he'd never once cheated, never touched let alone kissed another woman or suggested any kind of inappropriate behavior. Until last week at the Rusty Nail. Now, he couldn't believe he was actually having this conversation. What was he thinking? That he'd already cheated on Carol once. What difference did one more time make? This time he would be totally lucid. This time he could make sure it wasn't a dream.

Great. You're a real prince, Carl.

"I promise we won't need much time," she said. "I'm already hot and…bothered."

He raked a shaking hand through his hair.

"Make up an excuse. You said yourself you're not appreciated at home." She paused, chuckled quietly. "And you *know* I'll appreciate you."

He never should've started talking to the woman with the reputation for going through men the way his resort went through hand towels, never should've spilled his guts over too much vodka. "I can't—"

"Carl, your marriage has been in a slump for years. You never know, this might spice things up between the two of you."

That sounded like a damned convenient excuse to him, but a part of him couldn't help but wonder if there wasn't some truth to the comment. He'd actually had sex twice with Carol since the incident at the Nail, and that was more sex than they'd had the entire previous month.

"The back door of my house will be open the rest of the night," she said. "I'll be waiting upstairs."

A sound came from the hall. The linen cabinets. Carol was putting away clean clothes.

"She's coming," he whispered. "I'll get away if I can. But we are not making a habit of this. Understand?" Quickly, he disconnected the call. Then he went to the computer at his desk, and opened the first spreadsheet available.

"Carl?" After a short rap on the door, Carol stepped into the room. Light from the hall poured into the dark. "Isn't that hard on your eyes? Working at your computer in the dark?"

"Yeah, I suppose. Wasn't thinking." Avoiding her gaze, he flicked on the desk lamp as she walked into the room carrying a laundry basket.

"I washed your sweater for you." She set the full basket down, took the knit cardigan off the top and hung it over his chair.

"Thanks." She cared more about the laundry, this house, the kids, than she did him, but then everything had always been so simple to Carol. Eat, sleep, be happy. The kids had been her life, keeping this house, her job, and she'd been good at it all these years. Sometimes he wished she was a little more adventuresome, a little less satisfied with her life. Maybe, though, he was dissatisfied enough for both of them.

He and Carol had started dating before either of them had turned sixteen. They'd gotten married right out of high school. He'd been a virgin before his wife, and all these years, she'd been the only woman he'd ever touched until last week. Was it any wonder their sex life had gotten stale? Was it wrong to want something more, to get excited about something, anything? To want to feel alive?

"Are you all right?" Carol said. "You look a little pale."

"Yeah. I'm fine." He looked away, afraid his gaze would give something away. Then he took a deep breath, glanced at her and shrugged. "Sean called a few minutes ago. He asked if I could meet him at Duffy's for a beer. I was thinking maybe I'd…"

"I was just going to read for a bit." She shrugged. "I'll probably be asleep by the time you get home."

"Okay. Good. I'll be going then."

She came toward him and gave him a quick peck on the lips. "See you in the morning."

"Yeah." He watched her leave his office. "I'll try not to wake you when I get home."

Easy. That had been so damned easy.

CHAPTER SEVEN

SEAN CRACKED OPEN his eyes a moment before his alarm went off. Since he'd never been one to pop out of bed at the drop of a hat, he'd been waking at five every morning to give himself some time before heading out to make sure they were ready for the first carriage rides at seven and trail rides at eight. If anything went wrong, he still had plenty of time before his morning appointments at the clinic.

As Sean lay in bed, cool and comfortable, he thanked his lucky stars that Arlo and Lynn had had the foresight to install central air-conditioning. The uncharacteristically hot temperatures Mirabelle had been experiencing weren't intolerable along the shore, but the stables were in the center of island, surrounded by woods that all but stopped any of the cool breezes coming in directly off the lake.

But while this big bed was comfortable, it sure was feeling lonelier than normal. Nights usually weren't the problem. By the time he made it to bed, he was usually too tired for anything but sleep. Mornings, though, were a different matter altogether.

It'd been a long time since he'd woken next to a woman's warm body and spent a lazy morning talking, cuddling and making love. Without warning, Grace entered his thoughts. What would she feel like to snuggle up against? Bony, most likely. She was a little too skinny for his taste. He preferred a woman with some meat on her frame, but she sure did have nice, long legs, the kind that could wrap around a man like—

Whoa. That train of thought wasn't doing him any good. Before his thoughts could wander again, he climbed out of bed and, having slept in the buff as usual, pulled on a clean pair of boxers. Then he padded down to the kitchen and poured himself a cup of strong coffee. What had he done before these machines had timers?

He glanced out the patio door just as the sun rose fully above the horizon. The first of the morning rays hit the horses grouped near the pasture gate, bathing their coats in a warm, golden glow. What a beautiful sight, the dark chestnuts and bays mixed with dappled grays and paints. Tails swishing. Manes blowing in the faint breeze. He couldn't believe it. The dream he'd had since he'd been about sixteen years old had finally come true. He owned a ranch.

A noise in the front yard drew his attention. He walked into his office and glanced out the window. "Well, I'll be damned." Grace really was serious about helping out Arlo.

She had Pat and Mike out in the yard and was brushing them both down, getting ready to hitch them to Arlo's carriage. Grooming those two big draft horses was going to take some time, and, if the sheen on her arms and face was any indication, she'd already worked up a sweat. She seemed to favor her left side a bit, as if in pain, but still she was out there, working away. Maybe high maintenance had been an unfair assessment of Grace Andersen Kahill, after all.

The phone suddenly rang, shattering the silence. Startled, Sean picked up the receiver before glancing at the caller ID. "Hello."

"Sean? Wow, you answered. From now on, I'll remember to call at ungodly hours."

"Vanessa." His sister, the middle of the three siblings, routinely phoned a couple times a year. More often than not, he wasn't up to the conversation and would let her calls go to voice mail. Most of the time, he eventually remembered to call back. "How are you?"

"All right. The kids are driving me crazy. But what teenagers don't drive their parents crazy?"

Reluctantly, he tore his gaze away from watching Grace work out in the yard. "And Steve?"

"He's good. Great, as a matter of fact. He finished his MBA and took a new job. Better hours, less overtime. More pay, even."

"Sounds like a win-win."

"How's the ranching business?"

He chuckled. "Good. Glad I bought the place. Did you tell Dad?"

"You kidding me? I'll let you have that pleasure."

It was too bad, really. Their father hadn't always been an ass. Oh, he'd always been a perfectionist workaholic, but their mother had done a good job of evening him out. Then she'd died and their father had been left to his own devices.

"I left the hospital a couple months ago," Van said.

It took a moment for that comment to register. "What? Did something happen?"

"Yeah, I suppose you could say that. I realized the kids weren't getting any younger and life is too short for sixteen-hour workdays. So now I'm teaching at UCLA. Gives me more time with the family. I'm even coaching Connor and Alexa's soccer teams, if you can believe that. You're not the only one with the balls enough to step off the Griffin treadmill."

"How did Dad take it?"

"How do you think?"

Badly, of course. "Is he still talking to you, at least?"

"Only because I make him."

"Are you happy, Van?"

"Getting there. What about you? Find a wife yet?"

He chuckled as he recalled an unusual moment of closeness he'd experienced with his sister in a previous phone conversation. He'd just moved to Mirabelle and had been feeling lonely as hell, and it'd felt surprisingly good to pour out his guts to her. She'd reinforced what he'd already known. He needed someone with whom to share his life. What would his sister say if she knew he was starting to envision none other than Grace Kahill in that role?

"Naw," he said. "No wife yet." He took a deep breath and decided to jump in with both feet. "But I do have a son. His name's Austin."

"Oh, my God! That makes me an aunt. How old is he?"

Sean explained the situation.

"How are you doing with the whole…dad thing?"

"Not very well, to be honest." He chuckled a bit before going into the details. It felt surprisingly good to unload on someone who knew him well enough to immediately understand the impact on his life. She understood how Austin's existence had thrown him.

"You'll figure it out, Sean. I know you will. And you'll be a good dad. You know what *not* to do." She paused. "Sorry, but I have to run."

"It's good to hear your voice," he said. "Thanks for not giving up on me."

"Pain in the ass or not, you're the only baby brother I've got."

As he hung up the phone, loud funky techno music sounded from down the hall. Austin's cell phone was going off in his bedroom. Unfortunately, his son was a hard sleeper. The snippet of sound kept repeating over and over. And over again.

Oddly enough, the noise didn't bother Sean as much as he would've expected. Shaking his head, he went down the hall and knocked on the door. "Austin, wake up. Austin!"

"Yeah." There was rustling in the room and then the cell phone went blessedly silent. "Okay. I'm up."

"You want eggs?"

"No, thanks."

He had to give Denise credit for at least one thing. The kid could be polite when he chose to be. Five minutes later, as Sean was sitting down with a couple of sunny-side up eggs, some toast and a full glass of orange juice, Austin came shuffling into the kitchen dressed in clean jeans but a rumpled T-shirt. Without a word, he grabbed a bowl out of the cabinet, filled it with cereal, poured in milk and then sat at the table. By the time he nearly finished his second bowl, he was starting to wake up. Somehow, someway, Sean had to break the ice with this kid. They couldn't sit across from each other in stony silence for the rest of the summer.

"I can make some time today," Sean said. "Teach you a few things about horses."

"Not necessary."

"You want to muck stalls the rest of the summer?"

"No." Austin glanced up from his bowl. "Grace is teaching me everything she knows."

Grace? No kidding. So that's what he'd been doing every afternoon. "Like what?"

"I don't know. Lots of stuff. She worked here for Arlo when she was my age, so she knows a lot."

"Have you learned how to saddle a horse?"

"Yep." Austin finished the last of his cereal and stood.

"Great. After you're done with breakfast, go out and help Eric get the horses ready for the first trail ride of the day."

"Okay." He dumped what was left of his milk in the sink and set his bowl in the dishwasher.

"Afterward, find Arlo. He said he needs help on some of his carriage runs today."

Austin turned and glared at Sean. "Why can't I go out on the trail with the rest of the crew?"

"Because I'll bet some of our customers will have logged more time in a saddle than you have."

"That's not fair."

"This isn't about what's fair. This is about what's safe. When I think you're ready, you can not only go out on the trail, you can lead. But not today."

"Whatever." He stalked out of the house.

Sean had a feeling he was going to hate that word before the summer was over. He stacked his dishes in the machine and poured himself another cup of coffee. No wonder his father had made so many mistakes. Being a dad was the kind of thing that would push anyone to his limits, and if there was one thing Richard Griffin had never been it was patient.

"AUSTIN?" GRACE KNOCKED ON the front door to Arlo and Lynn's old house. She was having difficulty thinking about the place as belonging to anyone other than the Duffys, maybe because the exterior still looked exactly the same as when she'd been growing up.

When no one answered, she knocked again, cracked the door open and called out, "Austin, are you here?" He was supposed to have met her ten minutes ago out in the livery barn, and he hadn't stood her up once since they'd started working together.

The coolness of air-conditioning hit her in the face and, unable to resist after all this time in the heat, she stepped fully inside, reveling in the crisp, dry air surrounding her. In one fell swoop, the changes Sean had made in the front rooms registered.

He'd turned the dining room into an office with a massive wraparound desk and had knocked down the wall between the living room and kitchen to create one large family room

area. Unable to resist wanting to see what other changes he'd
made, she stepped farther inside and glanced around. There
was no doubt a man lived in this house, and it wasn't because
it was messy. On the contrary, the rooms appeared uncluttered
and spotless. Still, Sean had clearly made his mark on this
house.

The high ceilings had been redone in a warm honey-gold
knotty pine and every light fixture had been updated. The
gold linoleum she remembered from in the kitchen had been
replaced with slate-colored tiles. The floral wallpaper Lynn
had been fond of had been completely stripped from every
room and replaced with solid earth-toned paint. A dark olive-
green in the roomy kitchen and a lighter version of the same
tone in the new, larger adjoining family room. Tan in his
office. Dark gray in the bathroom.

And if colors weren't enough to prove the masculinity of
the new owner, all one had to do was look to the furniture
and other decor. A dark leather sectional replaced the Duffys'
mauve sofa and matching recliners. The rooms were accented
with heavy wood side tables and metal lamps. The framed
artwork consisted mainly of framed photographs of horses
and landscapes. Then there was the massive plasma TV holding court in the family room.

A series of bronze horse sculptures on the bookcase caught
her eye. She picked one up and examined it. Rather than a
clean, modern design, these sculptures were quite detailed.
They were beautifully made, most likely by the same artist
and quite possibly expensive.

"Got those in Montana."

Grace spun around to find Sean, dressed only in a pair of
jeans with a towel draped around his neck, standing by the
hallway leading toward the bedrooms. As if he'd just stepped
out of the shower, his hair was wet and droplets of water
still clung to the smattering of hair on an otherwise smooth

and muscular chest. "I'm sorry," she managed. "Did I wake you?"

"No." He poured himself some coffee and then stuck the cup in the microwave. "Had to get cleaned up. A kid threw up on me this morning."

"Really?" But then, she remembered, they had all kinds of kids coming to the stables for trail rides.

"Par for the course. Some kind of summer bug going around." He took his coffee out of the microwave, and she couldn't help but stare at his lips as he took a sip. He had such a beautiful mouth. "Want something to drink?"

"No, thank you." Knowing if she stared at him much longer, she was going to forget why she'd come here in the first place, she turned and set the horse sculpture back by the rest of the set. "These sculptures are beautiful."

"One for every summer I worked on a ranch. Turns out that artist has made quite a name for himself since then."

"You have a good eye."

"Not so sure about that. I just liked the accurate details."

She noticed an old photograph of a woman around Grace's age in a relative place of honor on the nearest shelf. Curious, she picked up the frame and studied the woman's face. Sitting in the grass, she looked happy, blissful even, as she stared at the photographer. In the background, unfocused, were several children playing.

"My mother," he said softly. "My dad took that picture on her birthday. About a month before she died. I was eight."

"I'm sorry." That seemed so young to lose a mother. A part of her softened toward him. "How did she die?"

"Complication from an ectopic pregnancy."

"And your father never remarried?"

"God, no. He got lucky once. I can't imagine him ever finding another woman who would've put up with him."

Like father, like son? Smiling to herself, she set the photo down and turned to find him rubbing the towel across his chest. The motion drew her gaze to the nicely defined muscles in his upper arms and shoulders. Forget about his lips. What would that chest feel like?

He turned and caught her staring. "I can put some clothes on if I'm making you uncomfortable."

In truth, she liked looking at him far too much. A swath of dark curls peeked from under his arms and a dark line of hair ran south from his navel. It was the first time she'd seen him without a baseball cap, and she'd be damned if his closely cropped brown hair didn't have just enough curl in the strands to make her fingers itch to want to feel their softness.

"Then again." He smiled. "Maybe you like me just the way I am."

Oh, my God. Here I go again. Flirting.

"I'm sorry." She held up her hands. "But don't make this something it isn't."

"Well, maybe you should enlighten me, then." He didn't make one move toward her, and still Grace felt cornered. "What is...*this* between us?"

"Nothing. Nothing at all."

"Hmm. That's funny. Because the other night in the barn, I'd have bet you were coming on to me. And now—"

"I know this isn't much of an excuse," she said, stepping backward. "But I was tired the other night. A little out of my mind. You were absolutely right, though. I am not what you want. Never will be. So let's just...back up a bit." She took a deep breath. "I was looking for Austin. He was supposed to meet me in the barn."

"He went on a carriage run with Arlo." Despite Sean's slow smile, his gaze felt like a high beam light, searching out every deep, dark part of her soul. He knew she was lying through her teeth. "He'll probably be home in a few minutes."

She backed up farther, keeping her distance from him. "In that case, I'll wait for him in the barn."

"Grace."

She stopped.

"Austin told me you're teaching him the ropes around here."

"Yes." She straightened her shoulders, preparing for a fight. If he told her no go with Austin, she swore she was going to hit the man.

"Thank you for taking the time."

So he was human. "No problem. We haven't worked together much, but he seems like a good kid."

"I wouldn't know."

"Well, maybe you should find out."

"And just how would you suggest I go about doing that?"

"By spending time with him."

"He doesn't want to be around me."

"Oh, I think he does. You just have some ice to break through first."

"I'll keep that in mind."

Grace spun around and barely kept herself from running out of the house.

SEAN WATCHED GRACE HIGHTAIL IT out to the barn as if a wolf was at her heels. Not too far from the truth, he supposed, given the way he was feeling at the moment, not to mention what he'd said, the way he'd looked at her. He sure hadn't disguised the fact that he'd been ready to devour her in one big wolfish bite.

She's wrong for you, buddy boy.

He'd worked hard to slough off his privileged childhood to become a simple man with simple needs, and Grace didn't strike him as the type of woman who would be satisfied with anything simple. Besides, she hated Mirabelle. That's why she'd left all those years ago. Why in the world she was back was anyone's guess, but he'd put money on her not being here to stay.

She sure did like horses, though. He remembered her working up a sweat when she'd been brushing Pat and Mike that one morning. Not only that, but she'd been working with Austin.

So what if Arlo was right? What if Grace was the one woman who could make Sean's life even more perfect?

He glanced around, trying to imagine the sound of her voice, her laughter, her touch on this house. On him. It didn't come easily. He'd gone a long time without anything remotely soft or feminine in his life. Probably since his mother had died. Even Denise, Austin's mom, had been a relatively stoic, methodical woman. The truth was, though, Denise had been the one who'd been wrong for him. How many times had he thanked his lucky stars that she'd left him for Glen?

What if Sean had been looking for the wrong kind of woman his whole life? What if Grace with all her complications was perfect for him?

CHAPTER EIGHT

GRACE WAS, FOR THE FIRST TIME she could remember in a long, long while, starving. She still wasn't sleeping well—she'd had the nightmare again last night—but at least her appetite had returned since arriving on Mirabelle.

One thing at a time, she thought to herself as she came down the steps. After glancing through the refrigerator without any success, she dug through the kitchen cupboards, looking for something to eat. Nothing. At least there was nothing she wanted to eat. She could call Newman's, she supposed, and have more items delivered, but she had a doctor's appointment, anyway. She might as well stop at the grocery store beforehand to pick up a few things. Besides, she couldn't avoid the village center the entire summer.

Gathering her hair under a baseball cap, she wrapped a light scarf around her neck, slipped on sunglasses and took off down the sidewalk. When she came to the edge of the hill she glanced down on the town. "Well, I'll be damned," she muttered. She'd known things had changed, but she hadn't realized just how big those changes had been.

Prominent signs indicated there was a community center with both an indoor and outdoor pool, not to mention an eighteen-hole golf course. She remembered her parents talking when she was kid about a small contingent of locals pushing for those exact improvements. How in the world the residents had come to a majority consensus was beyond her, but apparently, the island was thriving.

Main Street was bustling with activity, much the way it had been during the summers of her childhood. Horse-drawn carriages clip-clopped down the streets, families on bikes zipped down the roads and tourists wandered along the sidewalks munching on ice cream cones and cookies. The town center was almost exactly as she remembered. Maybe things hadn't changed as much as she thought.

Keeping her gaze averted from the many tourists she passed along the sidewalk, she managed to slip unnoticed into Newman's. Immediately upon entering the store, she slowed and glanced around. This was not the grocery store she remembered from her childhood. With updated lighting and shelving units, a gourmet coffee bar and a brand-new deli with an amazing array of prepared items, this store would've given any of those she'd frequented in L.A. a run for their money.

The place was crowded with both tourists and locals. As she grabbed a few things along an impressive aisle filled with organic products, her gaze was drawn to a pregnant blonde about her own age pushing a cart with two toddler boys sitting in the center. When one of them stood and reached over the side, she said softly, "Nate, you have to sit down while you're in the cart."

"Crackers," he said, still reaching.

"Good idea." Smiling patiently, she grabbed two boxes, opened them both and handed one to each of her sons. The woman seemed to be enjoying having her hands full, but the dark circles under her eyes said she was also tired.

"Missy!" A black-haired, classically featured woman carrying a grocery basket came quickly down the aisle and passed by Grace. She planted a kiss atop the head of each boy in the cart and then turned to the mom. "You coming to Duffy's tonight?"

Locals. Even when Grace was growing up, she'd often

heard the adults talking about going to the pub for happy hour. Even Grace's parents had been Duffy's regulars.

"Mmm, I don't know," the blonde said. "Jonas is getting back from D.C. tonight, but I might make it later—"

"You won't be coming." The other woman laughed, and then slyly said, "At least not at Duffy's."

Grace smiled to herself.

"I miss him," said the blonde. "And the boys haven't been sleeping well. I think they're both teething."

One of the boys stood and reached for the dark-haired woman. "Sawah. Up!"

The dark-haired woman nabbed him from the cart and kissed his cheek. "How 'bout I babysit the boys for you this afternoon so you can catch a nap?"

"Would you?"

"I'll take them to the flower shop with me. Brian can help." She switched around groceries from her basket into the cart and vice versa, and then took off toward the front with the cart and the boys. "Come get them later!"

"Will do!" The blonde glanced at Grace and smiled. "What would we women do without good friends?" Then she threw a few more things into her basket and went into the next aisle.

Grace stood there for a moment, not wanting to run into either one of them again, then slowly finished her shopping, stuffing everything into a backpack before heading outside.

For some reason, that conversation had made her more than a little melancholy. She missed Suzy. Maybe even Amanda. The fact that Mirabelle had seen a recent influx of younger people surprised her. What could have possibly drawn them here?

Sighing, she hurried across crowded Main Street and went inland a couple blocks to the small brick one-story medical building that had been built before she'd been born. The waiting area looked as though it had recently been updated with granite countertops, new carpet and paint, not to mention computer screens, phone systems and copy machines, but Donna Albright still sat behind the reception center.

The middle-aged woman glanced up and put her hand over her chest. "Oh, my goodness. Grace Andersen."

"Hello, Mrs. Albright. How have you been?"

"Oh, I'm fine." She handed Grace a clipboard filled with paperwork. "Why don't you just sit right over there in the waiting area and fill out a couple of these forms. I'll let the doctor know you're in."

Grace took a seat, filled out and signed the various forms. Then she sat silently, passing on the magazines on the table. The last thing she wanted to read about was fashion or celebrities and their lives.

It was only a few moments before a nurse came out to the front, took Grace's paperwork and showed her to an examination room. "I'm Kelly Moser," she said as she took her blood pressure. "And what's the reason for your visit today?"

Grace had become ridiculously private since the accident. "Just a routine checkup," she lied.

"Oh, good. Glad you're not under the weather." She flushed as she handed Grace a hospital gown from a drawer at the base of an examination table. "You may need to put on this gown."

Over my dead body.

"I'll let the doctor know you're here." Kelly went out into the hall and closed the door.

Grace tossed the gown onto the counter just as a gentle knock sounded. The exam room door opened, and she froze as Sean Griffin walked into the room.

Dressed in pressed khaki pants and a short-sleeved, sky-blue polo shirt with a stethoscope draped around his neck, he looked nothing like the cowboy at the stables, let alone the bare-chested man she'd found in the farmhouse the other day. God help her, she wasn't sure which version of the man she found more appealing.

"What are *you* doing here?" she asked.

"Aside from owning Mirabelle Stable and Livery," he said, smiling, "I'm the only doctor on the island."

"What happened to Doc Welinski?"

"He retired a couple years ago."

Just like Arlo. Again, she should've known. Sean saying the other morning at his house that a kid had thrown up on him took on an entirely different meaning.

"So what are we here for today?" He glanced down on his paperwork. "There isn't much on your chart to go on."

The thought of unzipping that compression shirt in front of him, showing him her body, doctor or not, had the room spinning around her. Suddenly, she couldn't breathe. Couldn't move. Couldn't focus.

"Grace?" He reached out and touched her hand.

"Oh, no." She drew back and stood. She'd live for now without medicated creams and pain meds. "I'm not talking to you of all people about medical issues."

"Whoa, whoa, whoa," he said softly, almost as if he were talking to a skittish colt. "I know you were in a car accident some time ago, and while I don't know the extent of your injuries, I'm here to help."

"I don't think so." She headed for the door.

"Grace." He reached around her and held the door closed. "I'm a doctor."

"Well, I don't want to be your patient." He was so close she could smell his skin, his hair, the subtly sweet scent of hay mixed with the spice of a man's shampoo. So close there was nowhere else to look but into his eyes to find a color there almost bluer even than her own.

"What's going on? You came to see me, remember?"

"No. I came to see Doc Welinski."

He narrowed his gaze. "So you'd see the old Doc, but not me? Why?"

"Because…I knew him my entire childhood. Because he was sweet and friendly. He cared." And because he was old and didn't mess with her heartbeat, not to mention her senses, the way this man did.

Her gaze flew to the dark chest hairs curling through the V-neck opening of his shirt, and she had to take a step back. It was either that or lean into him, and that would've been a disaster. It was as if this man had flipped a switch on her long-dormant libido, and she was running wildly out of control.

"Grace," he whispered, "if you're in pain, I want to help. Let me."

"No." The very last thing she wanted from this man was medical advice, and the ache she was feeling at the moment low in her core was definitely not pain.

"All right then." He removed his hand from the door. "You know where to find me if you change your mind."

"Never going to happen."

FROM HIS OFFICE WINDOW, SEAN watched Grace stalk up the hill toward the residential section of town, but it didn't look as though she was headed toward her rental. More likely her father's home. The day was already unseasonably warm for this time of year, so she had to be uncomfortable in those layered tees and especially with that scarf around her neck. Why didn't she take it off?

Her head bent in concentration, her arms crossed, she looked like a woman with a lot on her mind, and he didn't blame her. He'd been unprofessional with her at their every encounter. That was one of the drawbacks to being the only doctor on a little island. He saw most everyone in a medical capacity at one time or another.

If he'd known he was going to be seeing her as a patient, he would've never let their previous conversations get so far out of line. Then again, his reaction to her had been in every instance so deep and elemental, he wasn't sure he'd have been able to control himself one way or another.

He'd had plenty of patients in the past that had been shy about their bodies, but awkwardness in front of a doctor didn't make sense with Grace, a model, someone who was used to baring her skin for all the world to see. If he had to guess, he'd say she was hiding an injury. But what kind?

A knock sounded on the door. "Dr. Griffin?"

"Yeah, come in."

Donna opened the door. "Um…what happened with Grace Andersen?"

"Kahill. Her last name's Kahill." He turned away from the window. "She hadn't realized Doc Welinski had retired."

"Oh, that's odd—"

"Not really." For reasons he didn't understand let alone want to examine, he felt protective of Grace. "She's been gone a long while and she knew Doc well. She doesn't know me at all."

"But—"

"Is that her paperwork?"

She nodded. "Did you want me to bill her?"

"No. Just leave it all here."

She set everything on his desk. "That was your last appointment for the day."

"Great. Thank you." As Donna left his office, Sean's cell phone rang. It was Carl. "Yeah," he answered. "What's up?"

"Can you get away for lunch?"

For a moment, Sean wondered if this invite had anything to do with his failed appointment with Grace. But, no, that wasn't likely. "Sure. Now works best."

"Meet me at the Bayside."

Stuffing his phone in his pocket, Sean flipped through Grace's paperwork. She hadn't filled out a single line of her medical history, but she had signed a release form. He could get all the California medical records he wanted with that little piece of paper, and he found himself very much wanting to find out as much as he could about Grace Kahill.

For a moment he considered the possibility, and then he walked through the office, handing the papers to Donna. "If Ms. Kahill makes another appointment, then you can send in this request for her medical records. For now, though, hold on to everything."

By the time Sean made it to the Bayside Café, Carl was already sitting in a booth by the windows overlooking the pier. The restaurant was packed with both tourists and locals all ready for one of Delores Kowalski's famous Wisconsin cheddar burgers. Having already had enough of those sandwiches to clog his arteries, he ordered a tuna salad on whole wheat with coleslaw.

"So how you been?" Sean asked as their waitress left with their orders.

"All right. You?"

"Busy."

They talked for a while about business and then Carl said, "If you're free on Sunday, Carol wanted me to ask you over for brunch."

Several times over the last year, Carol had invited Sean to join them for Sunday brunch. Sean didn't have the heart to tell her straight out that he didn't do traditional.

"I know brunch really isn't your thing, but Bud and Laurie Stall are coming," he added, "along with their kids. Might be nice for Austin to make that connection."

There, he had a point. The community center manager and his wife had three sons, two of them about Austin's age.

"And I'm wondering if you wouldn't mind talking to Dad. I don't think he's sleeping well."

Sean would always regret that he'd never seen Jean Andersen at his clinic, but she'd always gone to the mainland for her regular doctor appointments, even during the time when Doc Welinski had been practicing on the island. Sean couldn't help but think that some doctor somewhere had missed something in her medical history. He hadn't been able to be there for Jean. He was going to do his best to be there for John.

"Maybe he should come in to the clinic," Sean suggested, "so I can give him a thorough physical."

"He says he fine. Doesn't need a doctor. But you know—"

"I'll come, Carl," Sean said. "Have stethoscope, will travel."

"Thanks, Sean."

Their food was delivered and as soon as the server left Carl asked, "So how are things with Austin, anyway?"

"Teenagers are…interesting, but you already know that. Nikki and Alex are such good kids, though. What's your secret?"

"I can't take credit for them." Carl chuckled. "Carol's a good mom. She takes care of everything. So I guess what you need is a wife."

"Tell me about it," Sean said before realizing what he'd let slip.

"You serious?" Carl narrowed his eyes. "You're thinking about settling down?"

"I've been alone long enough, Carl." He'd never told anyone on the island that was his secret hope, but there it was. What would Carl say if he knew Grace had got him wondering? "If the right woman walked into my life, I think I can safely say I'd get married in a heartbeat."

"Careful what you wish for. Marriage isn't all it's cracked up to be."

"Oh, come on, Carl. Your life is perfect."

"Looks can be deceiving."

"What are you saying?"

"That marriage doesn't solve everything. You can be just as lonely with someone as you can be without."

LATER THAT DAY, AROUND HAPPY hour, Sean opened the door to Duffy's Pub and the familiar smells of Italian cooking and beer, as well as the sounds of loud conversation, laughter and music infused him with a sense of belonging. He squeezed his way through the crowd and located Missy and Jonas, Jesse and Sarah, the island wedding planner, and Garrett by the bar on the far side of the room.

"Hey." He stood next to Sarah and ordered a beer from the college kid tending bar. "This place is crazy tonight."

The locals usually stayed away from the most popular tourists haunts on Friday and Saturday evenings, but these days Duffy's was crowded even on weekdays.

"We can blame you two for that." Jonas nodded at Garrett and Jesse over the rim of his beer glass. "It's that deck you guys built this past spring. The tourists can't get enough of this place."

With an unobstructed lake view, Duffy's deck had turned into the perfect spot to watch the sunset, and the outdoor area heaters would likely prove the space comfortable from mid-May to mid-September.

"Sorry, guys." Garrett shrugged. "But it was worth it. Erica's business has about doubled this season from last."

"Well, I happen to like the deck," Missy said, nudging Jonas.

"Maybe we should build a locals-only deck," Jesse said, grinning before he took a swig from a bottle of water.

"How's the house coming?" Sean said, glancing from Jesse to Sarah.

"It's not." Sarah wrapped her hand around Jesse's waist. "The work on the old Draeger mansion is keeping Jesse busy."

"Make hay while the sun shines." Jesse grinned. "When things slow down in the fall, I'll get the exterior shell up. Then I'll work on the interior over the winter."

"Hey!" Sarah said, excitedly. "How's the whole Dad thing going for you?"

Sean chuckled and took a swig of his beer. "You guys can complain all you want about having babies and young kids, but a teenager takes the cake."

"I can wait for those teenage years," Garrett muttered.

"Well, I think he's exactly what you needed," Missy said. "You were entirely too content on your own, Sean."

"And what's so wrong with content?"

"Nothing." Missy smiled. "But happy is better."

Erica, Garrett's wife and Duffy's owner, came out of the kitchen and sidled up next to her husband. He planted a kiss on her neck and smiled. "You smell like garlic."

"So what else is new?" She wrapped an arm around his neck.

It wasn't often that Sean felt like a third wheel, but this moment, standing next to these couples, he'd never been more aware of his unattached status. "How's Hannah liking Madison?" he asked, suddenly missing their only other single friend who'd recently moved off Mirabelle.

"Loves it," Sarah said.

"She's tutoring over the summer and found a job teaching third grade in the fall," Missy added.

And Erica finished with, "She and her college professor are talking engagement."

Figures.

Sean felt a pair of hands on his back a second before Sherri Phillips appeared by his side. No one in the group would be pleased to see her, but Sherri wasn't daunted. "You promised me a dance last time we were here. Remember, Doc?"

He remembered the night. Not the promise. "Sorry, Sherri, guess I forgot."

"Come on, Sean. Just one." She tugged on his arm. "Then I'll leave you alone the rest of the night."

Maybe it was time to set her straight once and for all. In private. He set his beer on the bar and followed her out onto the dance floor. At least a current rock song blared from the jukebox and not some slow dance. Unfortunately, the floor was crowded and getting worse by the minute.

"Why is it you always look like you need a cut," she said, coming close and running her hands through his hair.

He grabbed her hands and pulled away. "Thank you, but my hair's just fine the way it is."

"I'll take care of your hair...and more...anytime you want."

"Sherri, I think it's time we talk." He stopped dancing. "I've been on Mirabelle for a while now, and you don't seem to be getting the message that I'm not interested. Not now. Not ever."

"How do you know until you try?"

"I don't need to try to know, so stop wasting your time on me, okay? I'm sure there are much more likely suitors." He left her on the floor and went back to the bar. By the time he grabbed his beer, Sherri was already dancing with a tourist, probably a fisherman here for a weekend with his buddies.

"So..." Missy said, raising her eyebrows at Sean. "What's going on with you and Grace Kahill?"

Figures again. What was it with women always trying to match up people? "What do you mean?" he asked, playing dumb.

Jonas shook his head and took a drink of beer.

Garrett laughed.

"Ooh," Missy said, smiling. "So that's the way it is."

Strange that he'd once wondered if he might be romantically attracted to Missy. She'd seemed the perfect match for him in so many ways, and there had been a mutual sort of connection between them, no doubt. Once Jonas had reappeared in her life, though, Missy's feelings had been made crystal clear to Sean. She loved Jonas. Just to make sure, though, Sean had kissed her once. As he'd expected, there'd been nothing, no sparks, no chemistry between them. He cared about Missy the way he cared about his sister. When he thought of Grace, on the other hand, Sean felt something altogether different than brotherly affection.

"I think I saw her in Newman's today," Missy said. "She's beautiful. Even with her hair stuffed under a baseball cap."

"Was that her in the aisle when I snatched the boys from you?" Sarah asked.

Missy nodded.

"She better be nice to you," Sarah said, glancing at Sean. "Or I'll take her out."

As the only doctor, Sean had already saved a few lives on this island, including Sarah's son, Brian. He supposed it was only natural she was a bit protective of him. "I'm telling you guys, there's nothing going on between me and Grace."

"That's not what Arlo says." Garrett grinned.

"All conjecture on his part. Trust me."

"I think she's lonely," Missy added.

That made two of them.

"Arlo said—" Erica slammed her mouth shut the moment she glanced up.

Sean followed her gaze to find Carl coming into the pub.

"Damn," Missy mumbled.

"Saved by the brother." Sean laughed.

The moment Carl joined them, the conversation turned to generalities, and it wasn't long before Sherri rejoined their group. "Well, hello, Carl," Sherri said. "Where's Carol tonight?"

As straitlaced as men got, Carl only glared down at her. "On the mainland with the kids."

"Well, you know what that means," she said, dragging him onto the dance floor. "When the cat's away…"

"Just think, Jesse." Sarah raised her eyebrows at her husband. "She coulda been all yours."

Jesse whistled. "Dodged that bullet, didn't I?"

"I feel bad for her," Missy said. "I think she just needs friends."

Jonas smiled gently. "And if I wanted to be…just friends with her?"

Missy grinned. "Now why would you want to do that?"

He laughed and threw his arm around her shoulder. "You got me there."

"That woman comes near you," Erica said softly as she glanced at Garrett, "and you'll likely have to issue a warrant for my arrest."

CHAPTER NINE

THE PARTY. AGAIN. DAMMIT ALL to hell. She hadn't wanted to be here the first time around let alone have to dream about it at least weekly for months on end.

No. I do not want a glass of wine.

The sushi is fabulous.

Not hungry.

Then what do you want, Grace?

I don't know. Faceless people surrounded her, laughing, talking and drinking wine. I don't know.

Can't fix this for you. Go home.

Home. Fine.

For the thousandth time, Grace climbed slowly—oh, so slowly—into her Bugatti, leaving Jeremy encircled by his friends. A large saucer-moon glowed in the sky as she put on her seat belt and sped down the road.

Music. Loud. Louder.

Cat. Out of nowhere. Black cat.

Brakes. Don't hit it. Can't—

Skidding off the road. Past the guardrail. Rolling. Once. Twice. Airbag. Can't see anything. Down. Down. Hit something. Hard.

Fuel. It smelled like fuel.

Oh, my God.

Half in, half out of consciousness. Have to...get off the seat belt. Can't move. Can't...

Then her feet were stuck in sand. On a beach. A bonfire

close and coming closer. She could feel the heat on her skin. Getting hotter. Couldn't move.

Laughter, loud and boisterous. The party.

Jeremy. Where are you?

Here. He stood and watched.

Soon she couldn't move her legs, her hips, her hands, her shoulders. Somehow the sand consumed her, turning even her neck as stiff as a board, and she watched helplessly as the fire came closer and closer.

Let me go! She struggled. The heat hit her face, singed her hair, penetrated her skin. No. No!

Grace's eyes flew open and, panting, she stared into the dark. A ceiling came into focus. The walls of a bedroom. Quickly, she sat up and reoriented herself. Her skin felt clammy from sweat. Her face hot, her throat dry. But she was on Mirabelle. She'd just had that same damned nightmare she'd been having since the accident.

Part reality, part surrealistic nightmare of things she couldn't remember. She'd never seen the flames the night of the accident. She'd passed out. But somewhere in her subconscious, she remembered the heat. The pain. She'd woken two days later in the hospital. Delirious. And that was when the real nightmare had begun.

She reached for the glass of water on her bedside table and downed every drop before padding into the bathroom. "Forget about it," she breathed into the still darkness. "Let it go."

But as she stood in the bathroom, the nightmare tripped through her memories. The faces. The flames. The horribly helpless feeling of being unable to move. Sometimes it was sand keeping her immobile, other times wet cement. Sometimes she was at the ocean, other times at the pool at their house or a photo shoot.

She didn't need a rocket scientist, let alone a therapist to interpret her dream. In her subconscious, she knew every one of those faces in her nightmares had worked, traveled and partied with them. Models, designers, photographers, makeup artists. She and Jeremy had made each and every one of their careers. And still, she'd woken every single time from her many surgeries in the hospital alone and unable to move so as not to disturb the skin grafts. All of those people had used her, even—especially—Jeremy.

Never again. Grace was all burned up.

Going to the barn to brush Louie wasn't going to cut it tonight. What she needed was a nice, slow cool down. Full Moon Bay. A hike to the northeast side of the island was exactly what she needed. Grabbing a flashlight, she set off out the door. Half an hour later, she was shining a beam into the woods looking for the path to the water. Even in daylight, the path would've been nearly impossible for someone unfamiliar with the island to find, but Grace had once known these woods like the back of her hand.

"There it is," she whispered to herself, thrilled that she'd walked right to it. She took off down the path. Fifty or so feet off the road, the woods seemed to close in on her, but she kept on going, determined to reach the bay. An owl hooted forlornly in the distance, sending shivers along her spine.

What's the matter with you? You did this a million times when you were a kid. There were no bears on this island, she reminded herself. No wolves. The worst she might encounter was a raccoon.

Something rustled in the forest, but she made herself go on. Soon, the light of the moon became visible. She was almost there. In no time, she stepped through the edge of the forest and out into the wide-open bay.

She stopped, flipped off her sandals and walked toward the water. Everything looked exactly as she remembered it. Not a thing had changed. Not the massive white pine towering near the lake. Not the boulders bunched together at the shoreline. Even the sand felt the same. Warm. Soft.

Grace took a deep breath and felt all the tension slide off her shoulders. Then she climbed onto a large flat rock near the edge of the sand and stared out over the moonlit water. As waves lapped gently to shore, she hung her legs over the edge of the rock and dug her feet in the sand, the softest of any Mirabelle beach.

As a child she'd come here hunting for shells or agates, her heart carefree, and a part of her yearned to live all over again the simplicity of life on Mirabelle. Picking raspberries in the summer. Sledding down the hill south of the bay. Skinny-dipping in the frigid waters.

She chuckled to herself, remembering how she and Gail used to dare each other to stay in the water as long as possible. Lake Superior only warmed enough for swimming once in a blue, blue moon.

Curious, she tested the water. It was warmer than she'd expected, but then everyone had been talking about how unusually hot this summer had been. She glanced around. The bay was surrounded by thick woods. Anyone swimming in the water would be clearly visible to anyone on shore. But then that would be half the fun of it. The risk of getting caught. Skinny-dipping during a full moon was the riskiest of all. And the moon didn't get any more full than on a night like this. Did she still have the balls?

"THIS PLACE SUCKS. I WANT TO come home."

From the desk in his office, Sean could hear Austin's cell phone conversation with Denise. The boy's bedroom door was open and he'd probably forgotten that Sean was working late again just down the hall.

"Arlo's okay. Grace is really nice." Pause. "No. No, Mom.

Sean's pretty much a dick." Pause. "No, Mom, it's not my fault. He's a dick."

Not wanting to listen to anymore, Sean shut off his computer, went into the kitchen and started making noise. It was late and he knew he'd sleep better if he did something to appease the emptiness in the pit of his stomach. He poured himself a bowl of cereal and was leaning against the counter eating when Austin came into the room. "How's your mom?"

"Fine."

"Your brother and sister?"

"Mmm," he grunted.

Something had to change between them and fast. "Look, Austin. I'd like things to be better between us. What do we do to get there?"

Austin didn't say anything as he opened a cabinet and took out a bag of chips.

"I'd like to start over," Sean said, trying to be honest. "I'd like to look at this summer as an opportunity. To spend some time together. I'd like a chance to get to know you."

"Why? What's the point? I'll be gone in a couple months."

"That's more time than we've ever had together."

Austin turned. He didn't look receptive to much, but at least Sean had his attention.

"We lost sixteen years," Sean said. "I, for one, don't want to miss another day."

For a moment, Austin's stern expression cleared. It seemed he understood, possibly even wanted the same thing. Then, suddenly, he shook his head and snorted softly. "I don't believe it. Not for one minute. You never wanted to be a dad, remember?"

"Who told you that?"

"Mom."

"That was a lot of years ago. Things change."

"If things changed so much then explain to me why you haven't gotten married? Had kids?"

That point was going to be difficult to dispute. "Okay. So I didn't *think* I wanted to be a dad. If you knew my father you'd understand. He sucked. I didn't want to make the same mistakes."

"So then you should be glad that I'm letting you off the hook." Austin started to head out of the room. Suddenly, he turned. "You don't want to be a dad, and I don't want or need a dad. You stay out of my way, and I'll stay out of yours. I'll do your lame job at the stables, go home at the end of summer, then we're done with each other." He went down the hall and slammed his bedroom door.

Well, that had gone over well.

After that, the last thing Sean wanted to do was try to sleep. A late night walk would clear his mind and give the house a chance to clear the malevolent vibes emanating from Austin's bedroom. A bright moon lighting his path, he strode out of his yard and down the path through the thick woods, his head down, his feet beating out a pace born of anger. Anger mostly directed at himself. He was failing miserably at this fatherhood thing. After a short while, his adrenaline subsided, his pace slowed and his head began to clear.

The path suddenly dumped him out onto one side of Full Moon Bay and he stopped the moment his feet hit the sand. Glancing into the clear night sky, he took a deep breath and felt his shoulders relax. Nights like this were why he'd moved to Mirabelle. The stars were so bright in the black sky, they almost didn't look real. You never saw a sky like this living in Los Angeles.

A soft, warm breeze smoothed over his face as he glanced out over the water. Waves lapped onto shore. Crickets chirped in the bushes behind him. And…someone was swimming in the bay.

What? This late at night? The moon illuminated the water as if it were closer to twilight rather than midnight. Still, he squinted, not sure if he was seeing properly. Sure enough, arms came up, one after another, stroking and stroking. The person was coming toward shore, not thirty feet from him.

Suddenly, the person was standing in the thigh deep water and walking the rest of the way toward shore. In profile, it was immediately clear that this person was a woman, definitely a woman. And if the small but perfectly formed breasts, the fullness of her lips, her high cheek bones and her long, graceful neck were any indication, a beautiful woman at that.

Oh, hell. He knew that poise, that elegant posture.

Grace. It was Grace.

She'd nearly hit dry sand before he realized she was buck naked. Her wet hair hung low down her back, allowing him an unobstructed view of her entire profile. He was off to one side of the bay, hidden in the shadows of the trees, but he knew he should leave, give her privacy. Still, his feet seemed stuck in quicksand. He couldn't believe what he was seeing. She'd gained weight since coming to Mirabelle and the body before him was nothing short of stunning. Long shapely legs. Beautifully curved backside. And shapely breasts, the proportionate fullness for her lithe frame.

She arced her neck back, squeezed the water from her hair, and a shot of desire ripped through Sean like an instantaneous transfusion of heat. She might not be the sure thing he was starting to think about for his future, but she sure would do for now. An involuntary groan rumbled in his throat.

Her head turned, as if she suddenly understood she wasn't alone, and her gaze landed on him. For a split-second, if even, she seemed startled. Then, as if recognizing him, as if entirely unconcerned by the fact that she was naked, she relaxed.

Still, he couldn't take his eyes from her.

"Hello, Sean," she said softly. "Enjoying the view?"

"I didn't know you were here," he said. "And then when I realized…I…I should've left. I'm sorry, but you are… *Grace,* you are…perfect."

"That's what they tell me." Then she turned toward him, affording him a full frontal view of her exquisite body.

He couldn't help himself. Involuntarily, his gaze traveled from her ankles up her trim calves and lingered for a moment at the apex of her shapely thighs before traveling higher. That's when the breath whooshed from his chest in an almost painful thrust. A large scar—a burn scar, he knew—covered one side from her upper abdomen across the side of one breast and on to her shoulder and upper arm. The bandannas and scarves, the jackets and long-sleeved shirts. No wonder.

Oh, my God. He swallowed.

All he could think about was the pain she must have endured. She'd most assuredly spent months in a hospital recovering from that massive of a burn. The skin graft surgeries. The physical therapy. One couldn't be a doctor as long as he had without witnessing pain, and burns like hers—what had most assuredly been third-degrees burns—were some of the worst. The wound had to stay bandaged, but the bandages themselves created almost unbearable pain to the first- and second-degree burns surrounding the third-degree burns. There was no relief.

Their gazes locked and for a moment, the softness, the vulnerability in her eyes threw him. Then she spoke and he realized he'd been mistaken. "Now what do you think of the view?" she asked, an acidic edge to her voice.

There just might not be a vulnerable atom in this woman's body. "Is that from the car accident?"

"You can find it online if you want the details," she said, bending to step into her shorts. "It's all there." She slipped her arms through the sleeves of what must've been some type of compression garment and zipped it up the front. Then she tugged a sweatshirt over her head. No one looking at her would have a clue what all that fabric kept secret.

"Is it still painful?" he whispered.

"That's none of your business." She shook out her hair.

"If there's anything I can—"

"You're not my doctor. I thought I made that perfectly clear the other day in your clinic." She grabbed her sandals, walked past him and headed toward the path. "And there's one more thing I don't need. Your sympathy."

HER HEART RACING, her breathing shallow, Grace walked through the woods for as long as she could keep her feet under control. The moment she was sure she was far enough away from Sean that he could no longer see her, she ran. She ran as fast as her lungs would allow. She ran and kept running, on and on.

Other than Jeremy and her doctors in L.A., Sean had been the only man to see her scars since the accident, the first man to see her entirely naked. Oddly enough, she hadn't been the least bit mortified at being discovered, at least not initially. In fact, he'd caught her so completely off her guard that she'd not only forgotten all about her scars the moment she'd caught Sean's face in the moonlight, she'd actually felt a sudden rush of desire pooling low and deep. If he'd been closer, she may very well have reached out to touch him, to kiss him. But the moment she turned, the longing in his eyes turning to disgust had been almost too much to bear, squashing her desire.

Forget him. He doesn't matter.

But he did matter. His reaction mattered.

She reached her yard, but didn't bother slowing down until hitting the back porch. Stumbling up the steps, she grabbed the railing and drew in as much air as she could.

"You run faster than I'd expected."

She spun around. He'd followed her. "Go away."

"No." His shoulders rising and falling as he caught his breath, he climbed the steps and faced her.

"I don't want you here."

"I'm not so sure about that."

"Well, be sure. Be very sure about this. I'm not interested."

"Have you always been this tough? Or did Kahill, L.A., the modeling business, make you this way?"

"I am who I am. Period."

"You're not fooling me, Grace. I've been around enough people with severe injuries to understand…a little thing called pride that can make people—"

"Oh, it's not pride." Quickly, she looked away. "It is definitely not pride."

"Then what is it?"

"You wouldn't understand. Most people wouldn't."

"Try me—"

"Fear," she blurted out before she could stop herself. "Would you believe it's fear?" Had she really said that? Had she really been honest?

"Of what?"

"Fear that…all I am is a model. A woman with a perfect body that isn't perfect any longer." Oh, good God, it was out. The truth. The fear she'd been holding inside all this time. That the sum total of her being was that of a pretty face and body. Without it, she was nothing. "Fear that no man could ever be attracted to me…"

"Well, the man standing in front of you is very attracted. You can bank on that."

"I saw your reaction to my scars. You had me in bed until you saw them."

"That's true. In a way. But nothing turned me off. Your

scars... The average person hasn't a clue what you went through. I know, at least I can imagine, what it took for you to come back from that injury."

"I saw your face. You were disgusted."

"No, Grace. Not at all. The only thing stopping me from taking you in my arms right this moment and carrying you to bed is the wall you've just put between us."

Was it possible he was being honest? Only one way to know. "And if I lower that wall?"

"I'm not sure you can."

Do you still have the balls, Grace?

Her heart racing, she stepped toward him, came to within inches of his face. His breath buffeted her cheeks, his gaze seared her skin. "Try me."

Slowly, purposefully, he moved toward her.

Her instincts screamed to pull away before it was too late, but she held her ground. She had to do this. She had to know if he truly wanted her, scars and all.

When his lips touched hers, Grace felt the sensations all the way to her toes. His touch was soft, tentative, as if he were afraid he might hurt her or frighten her away.

"I'm not a china doll," she said against his lips. "I won't break."

He groaned and slanted his mouth wider over hers. His tongue slipped between her teeth, tasting, exploring. He hadn't been lying. He did still want her.

Grace felt her body tighten with expectation. "Touch me," she murmured. "I want to feel you touching me."

Pulling her with him, Sean backed up, turned the knob on the door and kicked it open. Then she was against the entryway wall, Sean pressing against her, his leg between her thighs, his hands holding up her arms. He kissed her mouth, her neck, her face and he felt so good, so right.

Until fear crept in. Along with panic. He'd seen her scars

from a distance by the generous, forgiving light of the moon. But up close. Seeing. Touching. Under harsh light. She could never let that happen. It was never going to happen.

"That all you got?" she whispered, stiffening in his arms.

His answering chuckle was low and deep and almost tender against her throat. "You are something, you know that?" He let go of her and backed away. "This is a small island, Grace, and I've got the rest of the summer to tear down that wall. This isn't over yet between us. I promise you that."

Then he was gone, and it was all she could not to follow him.

CHAPTER TEN

"DR. GRIFFIN?"

Sean glanced from the computer screen at his clinic desk to find his nurse standing at the door. "Yes, Kelly."

"Those medical records you requested earlier this week arrived by courier."

"Thank you. I'll take them." Quickly closing out the patient record he'd been updating, he opened the package.

Almost a week had passed since the night he'd seen Grace at Full Moon Bay and kissed her on her porch, and during that time he'd seen neither hide nor hair of her. That hadn't stopped him from going ahead and ordering all of her medical records.

While he was no burn expert, he knew from what he'd seen at Full Moon Bay that she'd been injured severely enough to possibly still need care. That explained why she'd made an appointment with his office. He didn't blame her a bit for leaving upon realizing Doc Welinski had retired, but Sean would've considered himself negligent, knowing how stubborn Grace could be, if he didn't do everything he could to make sure she got whatever additional care she might need. And that required reviewing her medical history.

"Close the door when you leave, would you, Kelly?" He pulled out the large stack of files. This was going to take some time. "And hold my calls."

"Will do."

The moment she closed the door, he pored through Grace's

files one after another, learning, understanding. There were charts, X-rays, CT scans and MRIs. All of it he absorbed clinically, unemotionally, as a doctor, but when he got to the pictures of her burns in their original state right after the car accident, his gut turned. "Oh, my God, Grace," he whispered in the quiet of his office.

The pain had to have been unbearable, not from the third-degree burns—those had likely been deep enough to have destroyed most if not all sensation in the immediate area. It would've been the first- and second-degree burns surrounding the worst of the injuries that had hurt the most.

He called the L.A. extension included in the files and left a message for Grace's primary burn care physician. Surprisingly, the doctor called Sean within the hour.

"Dr. Griffin, it was good to get your message. I have to admit I've been a little worried about Grace."

"That makes two of us. Do you have time to answer a few questions?"

"Absolutely."

A long while later, Sean wrapped up the conversation. "So if I understand correctly, the only real concern you have at this point, given she's likely stopped physical therapy, is a possible loss in range of motion if she favors her left side too much."

"Exactly. She's also probably running low on pain meds and the medicated creams I've prescribed. She hasn't called for any refills."

Knowing Grace, she planned to never talk to her L.A. doctor again. Sean got the details on the various prescriptions, thanked the man and disconnected the call, satisfied with his understanding of Grace's history.

No doubt, she'd passed the worst of her ordeal, but what she'd gone through had been nothing short of hell, and she'd done it alone. From what her doctor had said, Grace's husband had been MIA. Only one friend and her assistant had spent any time at the hospital with Grace. She was strong, stronger than he'd given her credit for, and resilient. A diva, she was not. Not even close.

She was, though, likely to be angry at him for having these records. The doctor in him empathized, understood, but he'd done what needed to be done. He'd stand by his decision.

The man in him, on the other hand, couldn't help but feel a twinge of remorse at his actions. The more he got to know Grace, the more he wanted her in his arms, in his bed, in his life, but that didn't give him the right to delve unasked, unwanted, into her private life.

Somehow, someway, he'd find a way to make this right, and until then he was going to learn everything he could about burn recovery. For now, he called Henderson's drug store and put in an order for several different types of medicated creams. He'd figure out a way to get them to her later. It was the least he could do.

"DID YOU CALL THE SUPPLIER directly?" Carl asked.

As he listened over the lodge phone to his maintenance supervisor complaining about several warping patio doors at the townhome complex, his cell phone vibrated. He glanced at the incoming number and ignored the call.

"They should be under warranty," he went on with his employee. "But it's possible they weren't properly installed. Call Jesse Taylor this time. He does the best work on the island, and he might be able to make room for us."

Carl hung up and checked his cell phone. Sherri hadn't left a message, but that was the third time she'd called that morning. Suddenly, the side door to his office opened and he swung around in his chair to find Sherri, wearing sunglasses and a large, floppy hat, slipping in from the hallway.

"What are you doing here?"

She flipped the lock. "You wouldn't answer my calls, so I thought I'd drop on over."

"You can't come to my office like this. Someone could've seen you."

"I was very discreet." With a sly smile on her face, she pulled off her sunglasses and walked over to his main office door and locked that one, as well.

"I couldn't answer your calls because I'm working. It's been a busy morning."

"Well, then I'm just what the doctor ordered." Dressed in a short skirt, strappy tank top and a paper-thin T-shirt, she came deliberately toward him. "A little break."

Damned if he didn't get an immediate boner just watching her cross the room, her gaze focusing solely on him. "I told you I didn't want to do this," he said, remaining in his desk chair. "We can't do this."

"Oh, baby, come on," she breathed. Coming to stand behind him, she smoothed her hands down his crisply ironed dress shirt. "You probably won't believe this, but I don't do this all the time. I promise this will be our special secret. No one would believe it anyway."

He pushed her hands away. "I am not going to have an affair."

"You deserve this, Carl," she said, hopping onto his desk and causing her skirt to hike high up on her thighs. "All your life you've been the model son. The loving husband and father. Isn't it time you do something for yourself?" Then she spread her legs. No panties. Nothing under that skirt. And she touched herself.

He groaned, unable to take his eyes off what she was doing. "Are you sure you locked both of those doors?"

"Positive," she purred.

As he stood and stepped toward her, she ran her hands along the length of his erection and unzipped his pants. She was like a drug, heady and addictive. "This is the last time," he said as forcefully as he could manage. "Don't ever come to my office again. Don't call me. Don't contact me. This is it."

Her eyes darkened as she smiled.

"I mean it."

SUNDAY BRUNCH AT THE ANDERSEN house had never been a casual sort of affair. When she'd been little, her parents and their guests had worn suits and dresses. As time had gone by, the attire had grown slightly less stuffy, but had never become truly casual. So what in the world was Grace going to wear?

Passing by the makeup case she had yet to open since she'd arrived on Mirabelle, she headed directly into her closet. What was the point in primping anyway? She showered daily and used deodorant. Everything else seemed superfluous. It wasn't like anyone was going to see her up close and personal.

Except that Sean already had.

Her thoughts flashed on that night at Full Moon Bay, that kiss back at her house. She'd managed to avoid him since then, but he was right. This was a small island. She could pretend to ignore him and the feelings he stirred inside her, but the truth settled with a sick feeling in her gut. Sean Griffin had ignited something inside her, a slow burn of awareness, and she had no clue how to snuff it out.

Enough. You're not having sex with that man and that's all there is to it.

Even worse than the desire, though, had been the fear that had bubbled to the surface, a fear so strong it threatened to immobilize her. She was more than just a pretty face and a once-perfect body. She had to be. Somehow, she'd find a way to prove it to herself.

Fanning her hot face with a pad of paper, Grace put Sean

out of her mind and flicked through hangers, looking for something cool to wear to Sunday brunch at Carl and Carol's house.

Although she'd showered, her skin already felt damp with perspiration and she hadn't even stepped outside yet. Having to wear the heavy compression fabric made matters worse. Her body felt as if it couldn't breathe. *She* was beginning to feel as if she couldn't breathe. Once upon a time this tight-fitting fabric had felt comforting. Now it was starting to feel confining. Maybe it was time to stop wearing the damned thing.

Once her scars had *matured,* her L.A doctor had said. Then the threat of her scars spreading to healthy skin would be over. Couldn't come soon enough as far as Grace was concerned. In any case, she was sick of wearing long-sleeved shirts and capris. What she needed was a dress.

She ran her hands along the heavy fabrics and expensive trims of the clothing she'd brought with her from L.A. Why in the world she'd brought all this stuff with her was anyone's guess. Even if she could wear any of these clothes from her past life without the impact of her car accident plainly visible, she realized with a sudden shock of surprise, she had no interest. They were all too provocative, too…not really her.

Was it possible they never really had been her? What she wanted now was simple and classic. No tricks or flattery. No embellishments or shocking lines.

Selecting the simplest dress she could find, something that also covered all her scars, she drew it over her head, tried zipping it and found it too tight. Laughing, she pulled the damned thing off. She'd gained more weight since being on Mirabelle than she'd realized. Apparently, she was stuck with whatever would fit for today, but for the next time…

"There's only one thing to do."

She snatched the pad of paper she'd been using to fan her

face, then reached for the pencil sitting next to the phone and started drawing as she'd seen Jeremy do a million times. She drew lines that would easily hide her scars, but not let the world know she was trying to hide anything. Once or twice she had to erase something that didn't look right, but by the time she was finished, she loved what she was looking at, a summer dress she actually wanted to wear. Now to have it made.

Suzy.

Picking up her cell phone, she hit speed dial. The call was answered immediately.

"You ready to come home?" Suzy asked.

Grace chuckled. "Actually, I'm not. Guess I needed some R & R more than I realized."

"Tell me about it. I've got twenty seconds before I have to be in a video conference."

"You're working today? On a Sunday?"

"My, how quickly we forget. We're getting next year's spring collection ready. It's crazy here."

"Right." She had forgotten. "I'll be quick. I need a favor."

"Anything."

"If I send you a design, will you have one of your people put it together?"

"For real?"

"Yes—"

"Scan and email it to me. Pronto."

"I'm not sure if Mirabelle has a scanner." She hadn't thought that far ahead.

"What kind of place is this...Mirabelle?"

"No cars. Cobblestone streets—"

"Fudge shops and bed-and-breakfast inns. Yada, yada, yada. I remember. No wonder you were never happy in L.A."

"I was happy."

"No, Gracie, you were not."

She wasn't ready to think about that. Not yet. "I'll take a picture with my phone and send it to you. Oh, and add a half size—make that a whole—to my measurements."

"Sounds like Mirabelle is agreeing with you." Suzy chuckled. "Everyone's in the conference room, sweets. I gotta run."

"Talk to you soon." Grace disconnected the call and immediately sent off a photo of her design. Still looking for something to wear to the brunch, she stared at her closet. She had so many years invested in those clothes. So many parties and photo shoots. That life was gone. She was surprised to discover she really wasn't going to miss it all that much, and she'd stalled long enough.

Time for the Andersen Sunday brunch.

SITUATED ON THE NORTHEAST SIDE of the island, Rock Pointe bordered state park land and was, so to speak, the end of the road. Although Island Drive continued, circling the island only to end up again at the village center, there was nothing but miles and miles of trees—evergreen, oak, ash, maple and birch—between the point and Mirabelle's northernmost shore. Grace had explored pretty much all of it at one time or another while she'd lived on the island.

Rock Pointe Lodge was a conglomeration of buildings, rental units and activity centers. The main lodge, a massive stone-and-log structure, had originally been built in the early 1920s by a Chicago businessman with a penchant for salmon fishing and entertaining large groups. Some say the man had ties to Al Capone and that a booty of gold had been buried somewhere on the property, but no one with a lick of sense gave any credence to the rumors. Especially since every kid who'd ever grown up on Mirabelle, including Grace, had searched every inch of the woods surrounding the lodge ten times over without so much as a Buffalo nickel to show for their efforts.

In the early 1950s, the lodge had been sold and turned into a hotel. Since then, every owner had made his own mark on the place, including a variety of additions and improvements, but business had continued to wane and the resort had suffered the consequences—that is until Carl purchased the property.

Grace stood on the hill overlooking her brother's resort and marveled at the changes he'd made, improvements that her mother had proudly relayed through the years. First, he'd added a wing of additional rooms to the original lodge, as well as another wing housing a small indoor pool and hot tub. Next, he'd built a row of townhomes along the shore. His latest project had been several independent log cabins nestled in the woods overlooking the lake. Although the rustic flavor of the original lodge spilled over to all the new developments, the resort had apparently been updated with Wi-Fi and a small spa facility. With two restaurants, a small convenience store and its own marina, the resort was basically self-sufficient.

Carl and Carol along with their two kids lived in the house they'd built on the bluff overlooking the resort. Grace veered off the main road and started up the hill toward the large Victorian. Pale blue with dark blue trim, white spandrels and balusters, stained-glass windows and a gazebo off one end of the wide front porch, their home was as elegant as her parents' was plain. A perfect house for a perfect family.

She'd no sooner stepped onto the porch than the door swung open. Carol stood smiling with her arms outstretched. "Grace! It's so good to see you again."

Other than having added a few pounds and a few more wrinkles, Carol had barely changed. She still sported the same chin-length bob and wore the same—for all practical purposes—summer uniform of white dress pants topped by a solid pastel blouse. In the fall she favored brown and in winter black.

In green cargo-style capris and a couple of layered jersey tees, Grace felt distinctly underdressed and inadequate in Carol's presence. Some things never changed. "Hello, Carol." Grace forced out a smile and returned the brief hug.

Carol had grown up on Mirabelle a few blocks from the Andersen home. She'd started dating Carl before Grace had hit puberty, but Grace had never connected with her brother's girlfriend. While Grace had been out toilet-papering neighbors' yards and flirting with the tourist boys, Carol had been volunteering at the Chamber of Commerce and organizing fundraisers at church.

Carol and Carl, on the other hand, had gone together like vintage and handbags. They'd gotten married right out of high school, their father, of course, officiating. Exactly four years later, after Carl had graduated from college with a business degree, they'd come back to Mirabelle and purchased the failing Rock Pointe Lodge for a song.

"How are you feeling?" Carol asked in a conspiratorial whisper, a concerned expression on her face.

If there was one thing Grace hadn't been able to tolerate since her accident it was being treated like an invalid, and Carol looked as if she were going to pull out a chair for Grace and take her temperature. "Never better," she lied.

"Oh, good. We've been so worried about you."

As Carol closed the front door behind her, Grace's gaze caught on her reflection in the mirror over the side table in the foyer. So that's what she looked like without makeup. Hard to believe that woman had once been on the cover of not one, but four international fashion magazines in the same month. Self-conscious, she tugged her T-shirt higher on her neck and strode down the hall. *Might as well get this over with.*

The kitchen was a flurry of activity. Nikki, Carl's daughter and the oldest child, was at the counter chopping fresh fruit. A woman Grace had never met before was carrying plates into the formal dining room.

"Hi, Nikki," Grace said as her niece glanced up from slicing pineapple.

The young woman forced out a smile. "Hi." She didn't look any happier to be in here than Grace.

"Grace, this is Laurie Stall," Carol said, referring to the woman setting the table. "She owns an art gallery just off Main."

"Nice to meet you." Grace shook the other woman's hand. "I brought some caramel rolls." She held out the package. "Where should I put them?"

"On the buffet in the dining room." Carol waved her hand toward the adjoining room. "Next to the strawberry-rhubarb coffee cake."

Homemade coffee cake, no doubt. Grace had changed a lot through the years, but she still didn't cook. She brought her store-bought rolls into the dining room. "Need some help setting the table?" she asked Laurie.

"Actually, I'm almost done, but thanks."

"There!" Nikki announced holding out a large bowl of chopped fruit. "The salad's done. Now can I go outside now and wait for Galen?"

"Okay, off you go," Carol said with a smile.

Grace returned to the kitchen in time to see Nikki shoot out the rear patio door. "Can I help with anything?"

"Good heavens, no," Carol said shaking her head. "You're our guest. Why don't you go out onto the deck and relax?"

And Laurie wasn't a guest?

Grace looked more carefully outside and noticed a group of men sitting around a table. Her father sat under the umbrella, one hand wrapped around a glass of iced tea. Carl took a swig from a bottle of beer, a man Grace didn't recognize sat next to her father and there was another man with his back to Grace that she wasn't sure—

Sean Griffin.

CHAPTER ELEVEN

BEFORE GRACE COULD MOVE AWAY, Sean stood and turned toward the house, his gaze landing directly on her. A couple steps and he was in front of her, pulling a beer out of the cooler by the patio door. "I know," he said, softly enough that no one else could've possibly heard his exact words. "You weren't expecting to see me."

"What *are* you doing here?"

"I keep asking myself the same question. Generally speaking, I don't do brunches. I'm more of a pub guy." He flipped the top of his beer bottle. "But your brother and his wife have been inviting me since I moved to the island. Austin could do with meeting a few other teenagers and Carl was a little worried about your dad, so…"

"What's wrong with Dad?"

"Nothing as far as I can tell, but he won't come into the clinic."

Her father glanced up. "Grace!"

"Hi, Dad."

"Come on out and visit."

Well, that was that. She stepped outside, refusing to look toward Sean.

"Hey, Grace." Carl smiled and gestured toward the stranger. "This is Bud Stall. He manages the community center and golf course. And you know Sean, right?"

"We've met a few times," she said.

Sean glanced at her, his eyes intense, and her gaze flew

involuntarily to his lips. Lips she'd kissed. Awareness shuddered through her. Lips she apparently wanted to kiss again. *Get over it*.

"Why don't you join us?" Sean held out the chair he'd vacated. Suddenly, she realized, something had changed in the way he was looking at her. He was calm, almost respectful—

Her scars. Dammit. After seeing her at Full Moon Bay, he'd turned all doctor on her and she'd ceased to be just a woman. The last thing she needed was more pity. "No, that's okay. I think I'll go catch up with Nikki."

Carol came out onto the deck. "Does anyone need anything?"

"I think we're fine, Carol," her father said.

"All right, then. We'll be ready to eat soon." She stood behind Carl and brushed her hands along his shoulders.

Carl stiffened, as if her touch bothered him. Grace appeared to be the only one who noticed his reaction, but then everyone else on the deck was a man. She studied her brother for a moment. Trouble in paradise? Probably none of her business.

As Carol went back into the house, Grace left the deck and went off into the yard. Austin was throwing a Frisbee to Alex, Carl and Carol's son, and three boys Grace had never seen before, two of them teenagers. She exchanged waves with her nephew. "Hey, Alex." Her nephew seemed to have grown several inches since the funeral. "How are you doing, Austin?"

"Good," he said, smiling at her and then throwing her the Frisbee.

"Oh, no. You don't want me to play," she said, catching the disk. "I'm horrible at this." To prove her point, she whipped it to him, only to have the toy veer sharply to the one side and head toward one of the other kids. "See what I mean?"

It was a bit unnerving knowing Sean was behind her, keeping tabs, but she'd be damned before she'd give him the satisfaction of returning the attention. She wandered off to the side of the house and found Nikki sitting in a tree swing tied to a thick branch of an old maple and texting on her cell phone. Grace sat in the grass not far from the young woman and glanced into the clear blue sky. "Do you have to do this every Sunday?"

"Yes." Nikki rolled her eyes. "I can't wait to go to college in the fall."

"Where are you going?"

"University of Minnesota in Minneapolis, but any place is better than here," she said, pushing herself on the swing. "This island is so boring."

Grace laughed. "Tell me about it."

"So why did you come back?"

"I'm not really sure."

"Dad said you were in a bad car accident."

"Got divorced, too," she said, chuckling.

"That sucks."

Actually, that was one thing that had happened in the last year that *didn't* suck.

Two young men, one light, the other dark, and a woman about Nikki's age came into the yard and approached Nikki from behind. The woman put her index finger to her mouth, indicating Grace should be quiet, as she snuck up behind Nikki and pushed her, swinging Nikki into the air.

"Ahh!" Nikki screamed.

"You're such a girl," the young woman said, laughing.

Nikki jumped off the swing and turned to hug each of them in turn. "When did you guys get to Mirabelle? I was just expecting Galen."

"We got here this morning," the woman said.

The three glanced at Grace.

"I'm Nikki's aunt, Grace." She glanced from the young woman to the lighter-haired young man. "And you two look very familiar."

"I'm Lauren Bennett."

"Kurt Bennett."

"Ah! You're Sophie Rousseau and Isaac Bennett's twins."

"Do you know them?" Kurt asked.

"Of course. I grew up here on Mirabelle." Grace smiled and then quickly sobered as she remembered her mother calling to tell her years ago that Isaac Bennett, a DNR park ranger, had been killed in a raid on a fishing operation. "Sorry about your dad."

"Thanks," Lauren said.

"And you are?" Grace asked, glancing at the other young man.

"Galen."

"You, I don't know."

"I'm Natalie and Jamis Quinn's adopted son. They run the summer camp for kids on the other end of the island. We live in Minneapolis during the school year."

A camp for kids? "No kidding? Where that old lady used to live?"

"Yeah. That was Natalie's grandmother."

Lauren linked her fingers through Galen's, and Galen pulled her closer to his side. Young lovers. Oh, to be so innocent again. "Nikki, let's go check out the new laptop you got for college," Lauren said.

"It's in my room," Nikki said, glancing at Grace.

"Don't worry about me." Grace waved them away. "You guys are staying for brunch, right?"

"Yep."

"Then we'll catch up later."

"Nice meeting you," Lauren said.

Kurt and Galen nodded.

As she watched the kids run into the house, Carl moseyed toward her and plopped down in the grass. "Lauren's back," he said, smiling. "That made Nikki's day."

"Apparently."

"They've been best friends since they were toddlers. Sophie and Noah taking Lauren and Kurt to Rhode Island for the school years has been tough on Nikki."

"I gotta ask." Grace stopped swinging to whisper, "Are Lauren and Kurt Isaac's or Noah's kids?"

Carl chuckled. "That's what they call a million-dollar question."

Grace raised her eyebrows. "Bet the jaws started flapping when Noah came back to Mirabelle."

Grace had been in high school when Noah Bennett had left Mirabelle for parts unknown. A few months later, after having been practically glued to Noah's side for years, Sophie married the older Bennett brother, Isaac. Speculation had been that she was pregnant, but no one knew for sure which Bennett brother was responsible.

She flopped onto the grass and gazed into the branches of the old maple tree stretching out above their heads. "Do you remember that tree house we built back at Mom and Dad's?"

"We?"

"Hey! I helped. You know I did. Who was the peon to find scrap lumber for the door? Who stole shingles from the Henderson's toolshed for the roof?"

Carl laughed and shook his head. "I can't believe you didn't get caught on that one."

"They made up for it by pinning enough other things on me that I didn't do."

"True." He took a swig out of his beer. "Like when Noah

Bennett opened all the paddock gates and Arlo's horses started wandering around town."

Grace chuckled. "Arlo knew I didn't do that, but Noah's dad still came to chat with Mom."

"You sure weren't on good terms with Police Chief Bennett, that's for sure."

"Can't really blame him. I caused him enough headaches."

"Have you run into him since you've been back?"

"God, no, and I'm sure I don't want to."

"He's much more relaxed now that he's retired. You might even enjoy visiting with him."

"Wouldn't count on it." She leaned back and tugged out a few blades of grass. "How are things between you and Carol?"

Suddenly uncomfortable, he glanced away. "Fine. Why?"

"You seem a little tense around her."

"You can't be married for as long as we've been without a few ups and downs. You should know that."

Yeah, and sometimes the downs led to divorce.

"We'll be all right," he muttered.

"Lot of changes here on Mirabelle," she mused. "People selling their businesses. Retiring. New people moving onto the island."

"Mirabelle's doing pretty good these days."

"You should be proud. You've really built a good life here for yourself."

"It hasn't all been a bed of roses, I'll tell you that much."

"Oh, come on, Carl. You've lived a charmed life. You're the perfect husband. The perfect son. Me? I'm the troublemaking daughter."

"I'm not the enemy, okay? I grew up in the same house you did."

Suddenly, her brother looked so much like their father had

as a younger man. "I didn't mean to offend. You're just so much better at this hometown thing than I am."

"You think it's easy living here?"

"You're the golden boy. The son who can do no wrong."

"Mom and Dad have always loved me best, is that it? Grace, grow up."

"You have to admit Mom never fought with you."

"That's only because I never took her bait. Hell, while she was alive, I couldn't wait for September to roll around."

When her parents headed south for the winter.

"The off-season's peaceful for me in more ways than one."

"So how did you put up with it?"

"By accepting that she was always going to criticize. She was always going to tell me how to do things." Shaking his head, he chuckled. "She could walk into my lodge and, without fail, find the one dusty table in the lobby."

"I had no idea."

"Clearly, you were away too long."

"Well, I'm here now. I'm here if you need anything." She couldn't shake the feeling that there was more going on between him and Carol than he was letting on. "We're family. Families help one another through tough times."

He laughed, low and sadly. "If that isn't the pot calling the kettle black, I don't know what is."

She looked away. "I'm sorry for losing touch with you."

"Didn't you ever get homesick after you left?"

"Never."

"Your career kicked off pretty fast. I suppose you didn't have much time for getting homesick."

"I buried myself in work. Didn't have time to think of home."

"I remember not ever being able to get a hold of you. Seemed like you were always gone. Traveling."

She thought back to those years, to a life that now seemed so distant. "I lost myself in work. Literally. Forgot who I was." As she said the words, she realized for the first time how true they were.

His smile slowly turned into a sly grin. "So when are you going to tell me what's going on with you and Sean?"

He'd caught her off guard, and she didn't know how to respond.

"Oh, come on. The minute you walked out onto the deck, Sean tensed as if he'd touched a live wire. You walked out into the yard, and he couldn't take his eyes off you."

"You two are good friends."

He nodded.

"Then I'll be gentle with him."

"Grace, be careful. Honestly, Sean isn't as tough as he puts himself out to be."

Sean Griffin a softy? That'd be the day.

"Grace! Carl!" Carol called from the deck. "Brunch is ready."

"Be right there," Carl called as he hopped to his feet. "I mean it, Grace. Sean's here to stay. You'll be heading off to parts unknown when you decide you've had enough of us. Don't mess with him."

"THAT WAS THE BEST MEAL I've had since…well, since the last brunch you hosted, Carol." John smiled at his daughter-in-law.

"Thank you, John, but I did have some help." Carol glanced around the large table.

Somehow the adults had all sat in the formal dining room and the kids and young adults were in the kitchen. Sean had ended up sitting directly across from Grace. "Thank you, ladies," he said, his stomach feeling as if it was about to burst. "Everything was wonderful."

"Now, if you don't mind—" John was the first one to push away from the table "—I think I'll head into the living room and shut my eyes for a few minutes."

"By all means, Dad," Carl said. "Go ahead."

"You all right?" Sean studied the retired pastor. His color looked okay, but that didn't mean there wasn't anything wrong. If something happened to him on Sean's watch, he'd never forgive himself.

"I'm fine. Fine," he said, standing, but then he wobbled a bit and reached for the edge of the table.

Instantly, Sean hopped up and steadied the other man.

Grace took his arm. "Let me help you, Dad."

"Stood too fast, that's all." Even so, John wrapped his hand around Grace's arm and walked slowly out of the room.

"I'm going to check on him," Sean said. "To be on the safe side."

He followed Grace into the living room and perched on the edge of the coffee table as John sat on the couch and put up his feet. "Let's check your pulse." He wrapped his hand around the older man's wrist.

For a moment, he was intensely aware of Grace standing behind him, but then he redirected his focus to John. A few minutes later, he let go of John's hand. "You might need an adjustment to your blood pressure medication. Do you have a way to take your blood pressure at home?"

"Yeah, I have one of those digital thingamabobs."

"Take your blood pressure at breakfast, lunch and dinner for the next several days, make notes and then come into my clinic, okay?"

"Ah, that's not necessary. I'm fine," John said. "Just a little tired."

"Dad, we need to do this. Take your blood pressure and go to Sean's office. Please?"

"All right." John closed his eyes. "For you."

Sean stood and glanced at Grace. She looked worried. "Let's go outside for a minute." He drew her with him out to the front porch.

The moment the door closed, she asked, "Is he okay?"

"Well, without being able to do a thorough exam, I won't know for sure, but my gut tells me he's simply going through an adjustment period." He walked down off the porch and across the grass. "It can't be easy to suddenly find yourself without the woman you've been with for more than forty years."

"He doesn't want to do anything." She walked by his side. "Won't go out. Won't pick up his old hobbies."

"Minor depression isn't all that unusual for a man in his situation. If we can make sure he's sleeping and eating all right, get him out every once in a while, I think things will take care of themselves."

Before he knew it, they'd made it around the side of the house and into the backyard. Mirabelle, as well as the time she spent out of doors, seemed to be agreeing with Grace. The sun had highlighted her honey-gold hair and smattered her nose and cheeks with freckles. She seemed more relaxed than that first day she'd arrived on the island. Her gait was almost loose and her smiles came more easily.

"For what it's worth," he said, "if I'd known my presence would make you uncomfortable, I wouldn't have come today."

"You said it yourself. This is a small island. We're going to bump into each other whether we like it or not." She made her way to the edge of the bluff and stood looking out over Lake Superior and the resort below.

"Carl tells me you were both born here on Mirabelle?" Sean said, coming to stand next to her.

"Yep," she said. "My parents moved here when Mom was pregnant with Carl."

"I imagine that view was little different when you were a kid."

Suddenly, she spun toward him. "So this is the way things are going to play out between us? Small talk? Pretend like nothing has happened?" She stared at him, long and hard. "So be it. I can do that, but first let's get something straight."

"Okay."

"About what happened the other night. I want us to put it behind us."

"Sorry, Grace, but I'm not sure it's possible for me to just forget."

"Well, you're going to have to try. I don't want you treating me any differently because of…because…"

"Exactly what part of the other night are you referring to?"

"I don't want your sympathy, okay?"

Interesting. "You're talking about Full Moon Bay, aren't you? The part where I…saw you…"

She swallowed.

"I'm talking about what happened between us afterward. At your house. I'm not likely to forget the kiss anytime soon." He held her gaze. "What are you so afraid of, Grace? That you might make a connection? That a brick or two in your wall might tumble down?"

"I'm not afraid."

"Then you shouldn't need to avoid me."

"Maybe I don't like you. Or is that impossible for you to fathom?"

He laughed. "Oh, no. I'm sure there are plenty of people who can't stand me, but you don't know me well enough to dislike me." Then he turned and headed across the yard. He would've put money on her gaze following him the entire way. Oddly enough Carl was watching him from the kitchen window. Sean went into the house and found Austin, Alex and the Stall boys playing a video game in the family room. "Austin, I'm headed home."

"Okay," he said without bothering to look up. "I'll be home in a bit."

"Thanks for everything." Sean found Carol and Carl in the kitchen.

"I'm glad you finally made it here, Sean," she said, smiling.

Carl walked him to the front door. "So...you and Grace..." he said, pausing. "I think you should know she's not the person people usually think she is."

"I know that."

"I'm not so sure—"

"You ever known me to mess around with women, Carl?"

"No."

"Then what makes you think I'll start with your sister?" Carl sighed.

"Nothing's going to happen that she doesn't want to happen."

"Maybe that's what I'm afraid of," Carl said. "You're not as tough as you want everyone to believe, either."

SEAN SAT IN THE CORNER SEAT OF his sectional sofa later that Sunday night only half listening to the comedy playing out on the big-screen TV. What captured his attention more than anything was Austin. The young man laughed and Sean was immediately struck by how much he sounded like Sean's brother. Amazing. How those family traits had come through regardless of proximity.

The movie ended and Austin glanced over at him. "Did you like it?"

"Yeah, it was funny. Good suggestion."

Austin went on to describe his favorite part in the

movie and suggested another movie they might watch later that week.

"I'd like that," Sean said. Not necessarily the movie, but spending time with Austin. The connection was tenuous, but it was there. This was the first time the two of them had been around each other without arguing. "Did you have a good time at the Andersens'?" he asked.

"Yeah, it was okay."

"You getting along okay with Hunter and Matthew Stall?"

He shrugged. "They asked me if I wanted to go golfing sometime this week, but I don't have any clubs."

"You and I are almost the same height. You can use my clubs if you want."

"Thanks." Austin looked down at his hands. "Glen never let me use anything of his."

Sean held his breath. Was the kid actually going to share something significant? What was Sean supposed to say? Do? "I take it you and…Glen—" he started off softly "—didn't have all that great of a relationship."

Austin laughed. "Our relationship sucked. He was always on my case about grades and chores. My music or video games. My hair. My clothes."

Sounded damned familiar. "My dad was like that."

"No shit?" Austin focused on Sean as if intent on listening.

"Yeah." Why not share a bit himself? "If I didn't get straight As, I got grounded. If I missed curfew by just a minute, I got grounded. If I didn't keep my room clean—"

"You got grounded."

Sean chuckled. "I swear there were a few years I spent more time in my room than I did in school."

"Glen grounded me a couple times, but I hated it more when he took away my cell phone or laptop."

"Yeah, but did you ever have to take riding, tennis and golf lessons, just so you could play basketball?"

"No way."

"Way. In the end, I gave up b-ball, so I wouldn't have to do all the rest."

Back and forth, each one tried to up the other with more stories. In the end, Sean realized that he and Austin had more in common than genes, and Austin looked a little surprised to have made a connection.

"Sometimes," Austin said softly, "I think Glen knew all along that I wasn't his kid. That's why I could never do anything right."

Son of a bitch. Sean couldn't help but feel protective toward the kid. His son. Austin was his son. If Denise's husband had been there at that moment, Sean wasn't sure he wouldn't have punched the asshole.

"I keep wondering if maybe I'm the reason they're getting divorced."

"I understand how you might think that," Sean said. "But I have to believe that marriages aren't made or broken that easily. Glen and Denise are responsible for what's happened to their marriage. Not you. I'd put money on them being in this position with or without you."

"I suppose."

"Do you think Glen will keep in touch with you? I mean, after the dust settles?"

"I don't know and I don't care." Austin shrugged. "Honestly, I used to always wish that he wasn't my real dad."

"Bet you never thought that wish would come true."

"Weird, huh?"

"I used to wish my mom hadn't died."

They talked about Sean's mom and the circumstances surrounding her death for a little while. The longer they talked, the stronger their connection seemed to grow. Sean couldn't help but feel as if they'd turned a corner. He was almost afraid to let the night end, but he could tell Austin was getting tired. Sure enough, the boy got up and hesitated, almost as if he was thinking the same thing as Sean. What if tomorrow they were back to square one?

"Well, I'm going to bed," Austin said. "See ya."

For the first time since Sean had found out about Austin's existence, the thought of parenting didn't scare the hell out of him. He knew he still had a long way to go in learning the ropes of fatherhood, but if he and Austin had connected once, they could connect again.

"Good night, Austin."

After Austin's bedroom door shut, Sean flicked off the TV and all the lights in the house. Suddenly, the house felt too quiet. Not yet ready to call it a night, he went outside on his porch with a beer, took a deep breath of cool night air and listened to the crickets chirping in the nearby bushes.

As he leaned against the porch post, he noticed a dim light coming through one of the livery barn windows. Grace. No doubt the day at her brother's had left her feeling unsettled.

"Dammit," he muttered. "Not again."

He was about to step off the porch when he stopped himself.

Bad idea.

He downed his beer and went inside. There was only one outcome to joining Grace in the barn that was going to satisfy him, and he wasn't sure it was the right outcome for her. In fact, he was almost positive he was the last thing she needed.

CHAPTER TWELVE

"MR. ANDERSEN?"

Grace sat next to her father in the waiting area at Sean's clinic toward the end of the week following brunch at Carl and Carol's house. "That's us, Dad," she said, standing. It had taken some doing to get her father to take his blood pressure readings three times every day, but she'd finally managed to convince him that it couldn't hurt and might even help.

"Oh," he said, glancing up from the newspaper he was reading. "Oh, right."

They followed the nurse down the hall and into an examination room. Grace sat next to her father and waited while the nurse took his vitals and made notes.

"All righty, then. The doctor will be with you in a minute." The nurse smiled as she left the room.

Unaccountably nervous, Grace took several deep breaths. What in the world was she worried about? It was just Sean. He'd be examining her dad, not her.

A soft knock sounded on the door a second before Sean came into the room. Dressed in what appeared to be his doctor uniform, khakis and a knit polo shirt with a stethoscope draped around his neck, he looked clinical and professional, but nevertheless handsome.

"Morning, John. Grace." Sean glanced at each of them in turn before sitting down with some paperwork. "I'm glad you came in." He studied the notes, glanced at the computer screen at the desk and then finally turned to her father. "So what's your blood pressure been doing since we were at Carl's house?"

Grace handed him the notes she and her father had taken.

"Looks like we need to adjust your blood pressure meds." He wrote out a new prescription and handed it to John. "Start these new pills, but I want you to keep monitoring things a couple times a day. Call me in a couple weeks with the results."

"Okay." Her father nodded.

"And I've got one more prescription for you." Sean held her father's gaze. "Two times each week, you are required to—and this is important—golf, fish or play poker."

Her father chuckled. "That right?"

"Yeah, that's right. Doctor says."

"All right, Sean. I hear ya."

Sean glanced at her and she smiled. "Thank you, Sean—"

The exam room door swung open. "Doctor, we have an emergency out here."

"Excuse me." He shot out the door.

Grace followed to find a hysterical woman carrying a young, sobbing child in her arms. "Help us," the woman cried, clearly panicking. "He's swelling up like a balloon."

"Are you his mother?" Sean asked as he took the boy from her arms and quickly carried him into the nearest room.

"Yes," the woman said, following.

Grace and her father stood frozen in the hallway as Sean examined the boy, looking into his eyes, listening to his heartbeat. The boy couldn't have been much more than two. His mouth and face were swollen and his breathing was turning labored and raspy.

"Oh, God!" the mother cried. "You have to do something! Quick! He can't breathe!"

On hearing his mother, the boy squirmed and resisted Sean's efforts. The nurse reached out to hold the boy down, but Sean gently moved her aside.

"It's all right," Sean murmured as he brushed the boy's hair from his face. "What's your son's name, Mom?"

"Jayden," she managed on a half sob.

Sean then smiled at the boy and patted his small chest. "It's okay, Jayden. You're going to be fine in a minute. Relax. Breathe. Slowly. Good boy."

Grace couldn't stand it. She went into the room and put her arm around the woman. "It's all right. Your son will be all right."

"Did he fall?" Sean asked, the boy now sufficiently calmed that he could continue his exam. "Get hit?"

"No. We were just down at the beach, playing in the sand. All of sudden he starting screaming and raced toward me."

"Was he eating or drinking anything?" Sean studied a spot near the boy's mouth.

"Just apple juice," the mother said. "He was drinking a juice box."

Grace had never seen a medical professional operate in an emergency situation, but Sean was nothing if not calm, controlled and methodical. She had no clue how he managed such presence of mind under the circumstances. Her own pulse was racing as if the boy were her child.

"Could he have gotten stung by a bee?" Sean asked. "Did you see a bee?"

"No…I don't… Yes, I did see a couple of bees earlier."

"Anaphylactic reaction," Sean said, glancing at his nurse. "Epinephrine. Stat."

"What is it?" the mother asked. "What does that mean?"

"It means he's allergic to something. Most likely bees. It looks like he got stung near his lips." Sean glanced at the mother for the first time. "Does he have any allergies?"

"No. None that I know of, but he's only two."

The nurse raced in with some medical supplies and Sean quickly prepped a needle. "How much does your son weigh?" he asked.

"Um…" The mother panicked. "I can't remember…I…"

Grace squeezed the mother more tightly and whispered, "Sean needs to know your son's weight so he can give him the correct dosage."

The woman nodded and her face suddenly cleared. "Thirty-five pounds."

"That sounds about right." Sean prepped the needle, gave the boy the shot and smiled over at the mom. "Your son is going to be fine." He grabbed a blanket from the drawer under the table, wrapped the boy in it and handed him to his mother. "Now, I need you to sit here and wait for a little while to make sure he doesn't need another shot. Okay?"

She nodded and sat with her son in her lap. The boy was already breathing much more easily. After instructing the nurse to wait with the mother and son, Sean took Grace's arm and led her out into the hall.

"I'm sorry I butted in, I just—"

"I'm glad you did, Grace. Thank you." He followed Grace and her father out into the waiting area. "Okay. Go get those prescriptions filled," he said, as if saving a boy's life was an everyday occurrence.

"I'll do it right now, Sean."

"Oh, and one more thing." He disappeared into his office and came back with a small package. "Bob Henderson said some doctor from out in L.A. called in this prescription for you to be delivered here."

She took the package. Amanda or Suzy must've called her burn specialist. "Thank you."

"Remember." Sean smiled at her father. "Golf, fish and poker."

Okay. So Carl may have been right. Sean was more of a softy than she'd expected.

Her father chuckled, and they headed out the door. "Mirabelle's lucky to have that young doctor," her father said as they left the clinic and turned toward Henderson's drug store.

She might be sick of doctors, nurses, hospitals and such after what she'd gone through, but more and more she was feeling as if Sean was one doctor she could trust.

"YOUR BACK IS STRAIGHT. Heels are down." Grace smiled at Austin. "You look good."

"Thanks. It feels good." Austin smiled proudly as they rode their horses side by side down the trails through the woods bordering Sean's land.

"Can we gallop now? Finally?"

A natural with his horse, he'd done well with the trot and canter. Add to that the fact that his horse was well-trained and mild-mannered, and they had a nice long open field ahead of them, and Grace found herself saying, "Why not? Just before we head home."

"How do I do it?"

"You may need to press your feet against your horse's belly to get him going. Or you can try asking him for what you want. You'll figure out how to get him going. Once you do, lean forward, keeping your back straight. Stand on your feet and give your horse the reins. Like this."

She made a clicking sound. "Let's go, Louie." She leaned forward in her saddle as Louie swiftly transitioned from trotting to an all-out gallop. Louie had always been an easy ride, but he was the smoothest galloping horse she'd ever experienced. The wind in her hair felt wonderful as they flew across the field in no time. She might even go so far as to say she never felt better than when she was riding.

They reached the fence on the other side. Louie slowed

and she turned in her saddle in time to see Austin coming up behind her, a wide smile on his face as his horse came to stop next to Louie. "That was amazing," he said, laughing. "I think I'm starting to get this whole horse thing." He glanced over at Grace, suddenly serious. "Thanks."

"You're more than welcome."

"Can we do that again?"

She chuckled and, without another word, signaled to Louie to head back the way they'd come. She and Austin flew across the field. By the time they were finished and trotting back into the yard, they were both laughing. Grace found Sean leaning against a fence post near the field in which they'd been riding. Apparently, he'd been watching them. Austin seemed to turn expectant, as if he wasn't sure what kind of reaction he was going to get from Sean.

"Looks like you've been working pretty hard," Sean said to his son. "That saddle feeling pretty comfortable?"

Austin nodded.

"Okay, then. Go find Eric. Tell him I said you're ready to lead your own groups on the trail rides, and don't forget to take care of your horse at the end of the day. Diego's yours."

"For the rest of the summer?"

"Yep. Anytime you want to come back to Mirabelle, he'll be here waiting for you."

As if he didn't know quite what to say, Austin smiled and turned Diego around toward the riding stable. "Thanks, Sean," he called over his shoulder.

"Don't thank me." Sean glanced at her. "Thank Grace."

"Thank you, Grace," Austin called over his shoulder, a big grin on his face. "Again!"

Then she was alone with Sean, and despite the awkwardness between them, she had to say something. "That was a nice gesture. Austin has really taken to Diego."

"He's a good horse." His gaze followed his son.

"It's been fun working with Austin."

"Even though he is a bit on the angry side?"

"Can you blame him?"

"No. There's one thing that's for sure in this whole mess. Austin is blameless."

"Maybe you should tell *him* that."

"I'm getting there. We're working things out." He held her gaze. "It should be me thanking you for working with Austin."

"Not necessary, but you can do me a favor."

"What's that?"

"I'd like to let Louie do some socializing." She nodded toward the other horses grazing nearby. "Can I let him out into one of your pastures with a few of the other horses?"

"Sure," Sean said, walking with her as she crossed the yard. "He's been here long enough to feel comfortable." He nodded toward the pasture closest to them. "That's a good group there. Pretty calm and easy. He should do okay."

Grace loosened the cinch on Louie's saddle. Before she had a chance to straighten, Sean had reached around her and lifted away the heavy saddle.

"Thanks." She grabbed the pad off Louie's back, opened the gate and led her horse into the open area and unbridled him. By the time she came out to the yard, Sean had stowed away her saddle. She leaned against the fence and watched Louie and the other horses eye each other.

Louie glanced out over the pasture, blew loudly through his nose and his tail swished with excitement. There were ten or more horses interspersed throughout the pasture. A couple groups of three wandered here or there, grazing. A loner or two rested in the shade.

"There he goes," Grace said softly.

Louie whinnied and then trotted confidently out into the

field, his head held high, his tail catching the breeze and flying behind him.

"He's beautiful," Sean said.

In no time a group of three horses who'd been watching Louie with interest struck out side by side after him. Louie glanced behind him once or twice, noticed the others following him and kicked up the pace.

"They're all beautiful," she whispered.

Soon, the four horses were galloping in a loose line until Louie reached the crest of a hill, stopped and nodded his head several times. The others slowed to a trot and regrouped. Louie turned and met them nose to nose, and they caught each other's scents. Ears flattened and perked up. Tails swished. One of the horses sniffed at Louie's shoulder and Louie got a little excited, kicking out with his hind legs. The other one reared up and snuffled.

"I could stand here and watch them all day long," Sean murmured.

She glanced at him and was amazed to discover that the look on his face was as close to total contentment as she'd ever seen. "This is why you came to Mirabelle, isn't it? The horses?"

"The horses were part of it, I guess. Yeah. Honestly, though, I was looking for a lot more." He turned toward her. "I was looking for the perfect life."

"And you thought you'd find it on Mirabelle?"

"Yeah, but I didn't know that the first time I came here." He glanced out toward the field. "I was at a conference in Chicago. Met a woman. We…hit it off."

She grinned. "So to speak."

"She'd always wanted to go to Mirabelle and was planning a weekend here in between the conference and going home to Minneapolis. I had a couple days before I needed to get back to the hospital. So I went with her.

"We stayed at the Mirabelle Island Inn. She hung around doing spa stuff while I golfed and went riding. At the end of three days and nights, it was clear we had absolutely nothing in common other than the fact that we were both doctors." He paused. "Come to think of it, that's about all I ended up having in common with Austin's mom, too."

"She's a doctor?"

"Yeah. We met in med school."

"Fell madly in love—"

"Or so I thought."

"What happened?"

"I'm not exactly sure. Everything was fine until one day it wasn't." He shrugged. "I never wanted a family, and she was okay with that at first. Gradually, though, she started talking more and more about babies, a home in the burbs."

"You wouldn't reconsider?"

"No way. Being a parent…it's the biggest commitment you can make in your life, and if you mess it up, you mess up a child. I had the worst role model you can imagine. We weren't living, breathing, loving beings to my father. We were status symbols. Descendants. Doctors-to-be to carry on the proud Griffin name. Strike new medical ground and make him proud. I didn't know how to be a father, and wasn't willing to make the mistake of learning on the job."

"So now what do you think about having kids?"

"I'm going to miss him when he leaves at the end of summer. How's that for a turn of events?"

She smiled. "He's a good kid."

"What about you? You want kids?"

"I don't know. For some reason, with my career, I never thought of it as an option. A part of me, though, would like the same thing you want. And what Carl actually has. A perfect life."

"Yeah, he does have it all, doesn't he?"

She glanced at him. "So how did you eventually end up staying on Mirabelle?"

"There was a riding accident while I was here. A young boy got thrown from a horse right by the ninth hole where I had just teed off. The kid was lucky. Only broke his arm. I checked him out and got him down to the clinic."

"Was Doc Welinski still here?"

"Yeah. Ready to retire, though, he told me. Come hell or high water, he said he was heading down to Arizona for the winter with Sally McGregor."

"You've got to be kidding me. Sally?"

"Yeah. Why?"

"She was the meanest person on Mirabelle. What would Doc have to do with her?"

"She was dying. Had cancer. Doc wanted to go south with her. Help her enjoy the time she had left."

"I feel bad, now. We used to throw rotten tomatoes at her house."

"You mean *you* used to."

She laughed. "Yeah. Me. It was always me."

"Well, apparently, Sally softened a bit as she got older. A lot of people were pretty choked up around here when she died."

"So Doc talked you into staying?"

"He asked me if I'd consider it. I told him no way."

"What changed your mind?"

"Went back to L.A., back to the daily grind at the hospital and one day a few weeks later, a pregnant woman came into the E.R. Eight months along. Car accident." He looked away. "There didn't seem to be a chance of saving both her and the baby."

"You had to choose?"

He nodded. "Protocol dictated I save the mother, but my gut told me she wasn't going to make it. Instead, I saved the baby. The mother died, and the review board slapped my hands."

"Why?"

"Because I increased the probability of the hospital losing a lawsuit. Apparently, my own dad was the one who pushed for the reprimand."

"That's terrible."

"Par for the course, really. What tipped the scales for me was getting commended a few weeks later for—this time—following protocol and losing a patient. I might've been able to save him if I'd followed my instincts. Instead, I let the review board, and my dad, into my head. A couple days later, I just walked away from it all."

"You like being a doctor, though. Going by how you were with my dad and that boy with the bee sting."

"I do, actually. In spite of my father. Everyone in my family is a doctor. Father's a neurologist. Older brother is a renowned cardiologist. Older sister was on the cutting edge of stem-cell research, although she's teaching now."

"And you chose the E.R."

"A bit of a rebellion, I guess." He grinned at her. "You wouldn't know anything about that now, would you?"

"No, not at all." She chuckled. "So you ended up on Mirabelle, in the end."

"I knew it would drive my father crazy."

"That's an awfully big move just to piss someone off."

"It is, isn't it?"

"You must be very angry at him."

"For a long time. Not anymore." As he said the words, Sean realized for the first time that he had truly, finally reconciled himself to the way things were with his father. It was such a relief to have that settled.

She gave him a soft smile, and he was thrown for a moment, found himself thinking of the way she'd looked galloping on

Louie earlier. She was so graceful on a horse, so patient when she worked with Austin, so gentle with the horses. In truth, she looked as if she belonged at these stables even more than him. That realization stunned him. How could she seem to be so right for him and yet him be so wrong for her?

Tearing his gaze away from her, he glanced out into the field and watched Louie with the other horses, hoping to redirect his thoughts. One of the other groups of horses suddenly got curious about Louie and trotted over to check him out. In no time, all them were off again, galloping across the pasture with Louie at the front.

"Well, I'd say Louie's fitting in just fine," he said.

"He sure does look content," she said, her voice breaking.

He glanced at her, noticed her unaccountably tearing up, and softened. "And you're crying. Why?"

"Too bad it's not that easy for people to meet." She looked so lost, so alone, and he couldn't help but think of her spending all that time in the hospital alone recovering from her burns.

He stifled the urge to pull her into his arms and comfort her. "Next week is July Fourth," he said gently. "There are all kinds of activities around the island. Pick something and do it. I'll go with you."

"Not going to happen." She shook her head. "That's the busiest week of the entire summer on Mirabelle. This place will be crawling with tourists. If that isn't reason enough to stay home, there's always Gail Gilbert."

He chuckled. "What?"

She explained how she and Gail had been best friends until Gail snubbed Grace. It was clear those old memories hadn't entirely healed for her. "I won't be stepping foot in the village. Here and my dad's house. That's it."

"Have you always hated Mirabelle?"

"No, actually." She paused. "When I was little, I thought I was the luckiest girl in the world. To live on what seemed a fairyland. Mirabelle was the kind of place people wrote books about, you know?" Smiling, she glanced at him.

He didn't know what to say.

"A fantasy island. With our carriages and our quaint little village and our Old-World feel. I thought my father's church was the prettiest building on the island. On lazy summer afternoons when it was hot, I'd sneak inside, lie in a pew and stare at the windows for hours at a time. They built the church around the glass, not the other way around. Did you know that?"

"I had no idea." But it was clear to him from the sound of her voice, the way her eyes twinkled with memories, that she truly had, once upon a time, loved Mirabelle.

"The Rousseaus were the first to settle on Mirabelle," she said. "Marty and Sophie's descendants brought the stained-glass plates over from France several hundred years ago."

"I didn't know that, either."

"I used to think there couldn't possibly be a better place to live."

It sounded to him, almost, as if she still loved Mirabelle. "So you hadn't planned on leaving?"

"Not initially, no. I always figured I'd marry an islander and live here the rest of my life. Open a bed-and-breakfast inn and meet all kinds of fascinating people."

"What changed?"

"My hormones, I suppose." She chuckled. "I turned into a teenager. Almost overnight, it seemed. My mother and I fought constantly. It didn't help when I suddenly realized there was no one on Mirabelle that I wanted to marry."

"No one?"

"I dated Isaac Bennett for a very short while. He was several years older than me and quite the stick in the mud compared to his brother, Noah." She laughed. "Unfortunately, I couldn't get Noah interested in *me* to save my soul. He had eyes for one girl and one girl only."

"Sophie Rousseau," he said, supplying the name.

"There were plenty of boys to pick from during the summer, though."

"Fresh meat?"

"Something like that." She laughed. "But there was more to it, I think. I started realizing there was more to this world. A lot more. People. Places. When I started getting interested in fashion that was all she wrote. I knew I had to go to L.A."

"An overnight success, they say."

"Compared to a lot of other models, I suppose. Jeremy discovered me within a year after I'd left Mirabelle. I waited on his table in a restaurant. Everything happened so fast after that, I'm not even sure I could remember the sequence of events. I went from sharing a tiny studio with two other girls to basically living in five-star hotels in Milan, Tokyo, Paris and London. For several years, I worked 24/7. One day I passed out at a photo shoot. Jeremy took me to L.A., and that's when…"

"You married him."

"Seemed like the logical thing to do."

"Are you saying it was a marriage of convenience?" That surprised him.

"In a lot of ways, that's exactly what it was." She raised her eyebrows at him. "Is that so bad?"

"No, but why would you do it?"

"He asked me. His reasons were sound. We were good partners, close friends. Our careers came first and we accepted that. Together, we were so much stronger than we were apart."

"What if you'd fallen in love with someone else?"

"That wasn't likely to happen. My career has kept me far too busy to find the time to fall in love."

"So you've never been in love? Not even with Jeremy?"

"Never."

"Hard to believe."

"Why?"

"There had to be men falling over your feet."

"That doesn't mean they loved me. They didn't know me. Didn't care about me. Every man I've ever dated before Jeremy only wanted something from me. A reference. An introduction. A quicky just to say he did it with Grace."

"Seems hard to believe."

"When you lie in a hospital bed for weeks on end and only two people visit you on a regular basis and you pay one of them, reality crashes down pretty fast." She looked away. "Jeremy filed for divorce the day after the doctors gave their final prognosis. Scarred for life."

"Nice guy," he said, unable to keep the sarcasm from his voice.

"Actually, I understood his reaction. But all the others…"

"Friends who turned out to be not such good friends." He paused. This was as good a time as any to see if she needed any medical care. "So how have you been feeling lately? Any range of motion issues? Lingering pain?"

With a questioning look, she glanced at him.

"You favor your left side sometimes," he explained. "Hard for a doctor not to notice."

"I'm good, actually. Completely off pain meds and my left side is close to one hundred percent."

"If there's anything else—"

"I'm fine, Sean," she said, cutting him off. "But thank you. Reconnecting with my roots here on Mirabelle has been the best medicine for me. I may have been bored here while I was growing up, but at least it was real. Here, for most of the residents, I'm still just Grace Andersen. There's something oddly comforting about that." She turned to him and smiled. "So have you found everything you were looking for here on Mirabelle?"

"Almost everything."

"Almost?"

He looked away.

"You were serious about wanting happily ever after, weren't you?" she asked. "About wanting a wife?"

At the moment, it seemed like such an old-fashioned thing. "Is that so bad?"

"No." She smiled gently. "Not at all."

CHAPTER THIRTEEN

WITH PALE EARLY MORNING LIGHT emanating through the sheers on her bedroom window, Grace stood naked but for her thong panties and glanced down at the clean compression garment she'd set out to wear for the day. The damned things were supposed to help minimize scarring, but for her they'd become almost like a crutch. Or worse, a way to hide from the world.

This morning, though, she couldn't seem to make herself slip one on and zip it up. She wanted to breathe. She was sick of letting that damned car accident define her life, her dreams. It was time to move on, but how?

She couldn't go back to L.A. to see her burn doctor. She didn't want to leave Mirabelle. Today, in particular, she didn't even want to leave her house. It was the week of July Fourth and the island would be crawling with tourists, but in order to leave her compression garments behind, she needed a medical diagnosis.

Suddenly, the image of Sean in his clinic with that little boy who'd gotten stung by a bee flashed through her mind. His gentle way with her father. There was one person here on the island who could help her move on. Quite possibly in more ways than one.

"IS IT BROKEN?" THE YOUNG mother asked, a worried expression deepening the wrinkles on her brow.

"Well, that's what we're going to find out." Sean glanced

at the almost three-year-old girl. She looked at him with her big brown eyes as if he were a monstrous ogre. Every time he reached for her elbow, she flinched away.

"How 'bout we take an X-ray?" He smiled, trying to reassure her. "A picture of your arm to see what's wrong?"

"I can't believe it," the mother said, shaking her head. "We were just playing at the park. I was swinging her between my legs. Then all of a sudden, she cried out. Then she started holding her arm close to her body."

Sean knelt down, getting eye-level with the girl. "Does it hurt?"

"A little," she whispered.

He'd put money on the elbow being dislocated as opposed to anything being broken, and if he could just get his hands on that joint he could put things back in place. "Let's head down to the lab and get an X-ray." He stepped through the door.

The mother picked up her daughter and carried her out into the hall.

"You know—" He turned suddenly and, before the girl fully understood what he intended on doing, he reached for her elbow. Yep. Dislocated. "Let me try..." A quick twist... and...

The girl winced for a split second.

Done. "Can you move it now?"

Her pained expression cleared. She stuck her arm out and bent it back and forth.

"It's okay!" the mother said, surprised. "Doctor, what did you do?"

"Radial head subluxation generally presents itself in children between the ages of one and three. Affecting, more often than not, girls and their left arms."

The woman looked at him as if he were speaking Greek.

"A classic case of what they call nursemaid's elbow. Basically, a dislocation of the joint."

"How did you know without an X-ray?"

"Her symptoms are classic." He smiled at the little girl. "I don't think anything's broken, but we'll take an X-ray just to be sure." He filled out a form and handed it to his nurse. "Nurse Kelly will take it from here."

"Thank you, Dr. Griffin," the mother said. "You just saved what's left of our family vacation."

The girl wriggled out of her mother's arms and smiled at him.

Cute kid. He couldn't help but wonder what it might be like to have a daughter. "I think this calls for an ice cream cone to celebrate. Don't you?"

The girl nodded. Then, quite suddenly, she reached out and hugged Sean's leg. Both the mother and Kelly chuckled. Sean patted the girl on the head. He glanced up to see a woman in a large floppy hat and sunglasses watching him from the waiting area with a soft smile on her face. Grace. All covered up, or not, he would've known her a mile away.

"If you'll excuse me, I've got another patient."

His nurse took the mother and daughter down to the X-ray room, and Sean headed toward Grace. It was just the two of them in the waiting room.

"You love being the hero," she said, "don't you?"

"Maybe a little." He grinned. "What made you brave the July Fourth crowds, Grace?"

"Actually, it wasn't that bad out there." Her smile slowly disappeared. "I need a favor."

That sounded personal, too personal for the likes of the waiting area or an examination room. "Why don't you come on back?" He went down the hall and entered his office. Once she'd followed him inside, he closed the door. "Have a seat."

"I don't want to sit." She was nervous, edgy.

While she proceeded to pace from the door to the window, he perched on the corner of his desk and waited.

"I need you to look at my scars," she said softly. "And tell me if I can stop wearing the compression garments."

Knowing Grace, this was huge leap of faith she was taking with him, and he didn't know what to say.

"I know you're not a burn expert." She stopped and held his gaze. "But can you do this for me?"

"A month ago, I would've had to say no."

"But now?"

"Now I think I can make that assessment." He had to tell her the truth. "This might piss you off, but I ordered all your medical records, and I talked to your doctor out in L.A. I wanted to know what kind of additional care you needed, if any."

The burn specialist had said that most of his patients typically wore some form of compression bandages for six to nine months. Grace had been wearing hers for closer to a year so there wasn't much risk of misdiagnosis.

"How did you…?"

"You signed a release form that first time you came to the clinic."

Nodding, she turned away from him. "And what was in those files?"

"Everything," he said softly. "I read every piece of medical information from the time of the car accident through to your last appointment."

"So you saw…"

"For what it's worth, I care about you."

"So the medicated creams from Henderson's. They didn't come from my L.A. doctor."

"No. That was me. Grace—"

"It's okay." She kept her back to him, as if looking at him might be too much for her. "I get it."

"You do?"

"A month ago, I would've been angry. This would've felt like an invasion of my privacy. But I trust you, Sean. I trust your opinion. As a doctor. As a…friend. That's why I'm here."

He stepped toward her, came to within inches of her, could feel her body heat, smell her hair. For the first time in his career, personal feelings were interfering with his professional judgment. He didn't want to make a clinical assessment of her scars. He wanted to fold her into his arms and hold her. God help him, but he knew holding her would never be enough. In truth, he wanted to kiss her, taste her, lay her over his desk and—

God, what a pig he was. She'd come here, vulnerable and exposed, looking to him for help, and all he could think about was making love to her. He needed to be here for her. As a friend. As a doctor. For her.

"Grace?" he whispered. "I want to help."

She leaned against him, rested her head on his shoulder. "I wish I could forget it. Forget it ever happened."

"But you can't. You shouldn't." He put his arms around her waist and pulled her tight.

Suddenly, she stepped away from him and locked both doors to his office. Then she closed the blinds and paced. "No one…other than the specialist in L.A. has seen…I have to do this. Now. Before I change my mind." She started unbuttoning her shirt. First quickly, then slowly. Then she stopped altogether, revealing the underlying, skin-toned compression garment, and turned away.

He ached for her. Somehow, someway, he would keep this professional, clinical. Distant. For her sake and for his. "Let me get you a gown." He snatched one from the adjoining exam room and held it out to her. "Put it on with the opening in back. Leave your left arm out."

"I know." She took the robe from his hand. "I've done this more times than you can imagine."

"One last time, and hopefully you'll never have to do this again." He turned to leave the room.

"Don't go," she whispered. "If I'm alone…I might… This will only take a second."

He waited, keeping his back to her, and listened to the rustling of skin against cloth.

"There. You can look now."

He turned around and swallowed down the intense emotions drummed up by the sight of her looking so defenseless, so alone, in that damned patient robe. She was watching him, tense and alert, waiting for him—no, expecting him—to be repulsed.

He couldn't have faked revulsion if he'd tried with everything in him. What he felt for her in that moment was the most intense admiration and respect he'd ever felt for another human being. What he felt was a need, a want so strong, he didn't know how he could contain himself. What he felt was damned close to a little thing called love.

He was falling in love with Grace. She was everything he'd ever wanted and so many things he'd never known he needed. But she couldn't know. Not here. Not now like this. Maybe not ever. Giving her a half smile, he flicked on the lamp on his desk and turned the angle of the window blind to allow in the light without losing privacy. "Come into the light."

She stepped toward him and looked away. Like a skittish colt, she was trembling.

"It's all right, Grace," he said.

Now get this done for her. Clinically. Unemotionally.

He studied her scar, from the upper edges above her collarbone all the way down her side and arm, trying to forget this was Grace. The bright pink color from the photographs of her scars had faded. The color of the scar was close to her normal skin tone. He reached out and she flinched away.

"Grace, I just need—"

"I'm sorry." She couldn't seem to catch her breath.

"You don't need to be sorry." Gently, he ran his fingers along the scar tissue on her arm, near her collarbone, the edge of her breast. He lifted her arm and got a good look at her side. The scars felt smooth, soft and that was, ultimately, the determining factor. "You're all good, Grace. Your scars have matured. They won't spread. You can stop wearing the compression garments."

"That's it? You're sure?"

"As sure as I can be. But…" He pulled out his cell phone. "I'd like to take a couple pictures of just the scars and send them to the burn clinic in L.A. Is that okay?"

She nodded.

Carefully keeping the focus strictly on the scars, Sean clicked off four quick, close-up shots. He turned to his desk, pulled out her files and searched for her doctor's number. After sending off the photos along with a quick message, he turned. "Well, that's—"

She was gone. The patient gown was flung over one of the chairs, her clothes were gone and her compression garment was in the garbage.

"Good for you, Grace," he whispered even as he smiled. "Good for you."

WHAT IN HELL IS HAPPENING TO ME?

Her hands shaking, her skin a mass of ultrasensitive nerves, Grace raced out of the medical clinic as fast as she could. No doubt, Sean had attributed her clearly distressed state to his examination, but the undeniable truth hit her hard.

It was Sean, his proximity, his fingertips on her skin, his

breath on her neck, the warmth emanating from him that had her falling apart at the seams. All she'd been able to think about in his office was wanting to feel the full pressure of his hands on her, on her neck, her breasts, her stomach. She hadn't given a damn about how damaged her body might be. She'd wanted to feel his touch on her healthy skin, not her scar.

She'd gotten only a block away from Sean's office when the odd feeling of her breasts bouncing with every step made her stop. So strange. Her nipples rubbed against the fabric of her shirt, causing them to turn pebble hard. Her chest felt as if it had expanded to twice its normal size. And her shoulders felt free to move every which way without constraint.

She was free. Finally, she could start to move past the accident. Finally, she could start over. Her body, it seemed, was more than ready and willing.

SEVERAL DAYS LATER, WITH ARLO out on carriage runs and Austin out on a trail ride, Sean found himself alone with Grace in the livery barn. She was giving Louie a shower in the bathing stall. He was twenty feet away at the workbench, repairing a brake on one of the carriages. As distracted as he was by the sight of her bending over, though, her T-shirt wet, her jeans even wetter, he might as well have been in the direct line of water spray.

Those compression garments had to have felt restrictive and she'd worn them for months on end. He truly didn't blame her for wanting to stretch her wings a little bit, but the situation was made excruciatingly more painful for him by the fact that she wasn't wearing a bra. The wet fabric of her shirt conformed to every curve of her body like a second skin.

Bony? Not even close.

She'd just finished rinsing the horse when his cell phone rang. He pulled it out of his pocket and glanced at the number displayed on the screen. *Shit.* Since moving to Mirabelle, his phone conversations with his dad had been more like one-sided diatribes on how Sean was wasting his life in Hicksville, U.S.A.

"Someone you don't want to talk to?" Grace said. "I know the feeling."

He answered the call and held Grace's gaze. "Hello, Dad."

She raised her eyebrows at him.

"Sean. It's good to hear your voice."

Sean wished he could say the same. Trouble was that authoritative, judgmental sound hadn't changed an octave from the time Sean had been a rebellious, obstinate teen.

Grace motioned she would leave.

Sean put his hand over the receiver. "You can stay. Don't worry about it. This won't take long."

"You sure?"

"Positive."

She returned to wiping down Louie.

Truth was there was something strangely comforting about her presence.

"How have you been?" his father asked.

"Fine. You?"

"Good. Very well, in fact."

A long awkward silence hung over the line. Sean couldn't think of a thing to say.

Suddenly, his father sighed. "Enough is enough, son. You've made your point. I'm not in charge of your life. You want to be an E.R. doctor the rest of your life, so be it. Come home. We've got a spot waiting for you at the hospital."

"That's awfully magnanimous of you, Dad, but I'm quite happy where I am."

"You can't be serious. A family practitioner on a tourist

island? Putting on bandages and treating bee stings? The occasional head trauma from a horseback riding accident?"

As his father's voice rose, Sean was forced to hold the receiver farther away from his ear. Apparently able to hear the one-sided conversation, Grace glanced at him and frowned.

"For God's sake," his father continued to rant, "if that isn't a waste of your talent and intellect, I don't know what is."

The words to defend himself burned the tip of Sean's tongue. He wasn't curing cancer, but he'd saved several lives here on Mirabelle. He was making a difference, but what would be the point in defending his decision? His father would never understand. "It's my life to waste, though, isn't it, Dad?"

"No. It isn't. I didn't spend hundreds of thousands of dollars sending you to the finest medical school in this country to have you throw it all away on some…damnable midlife crisis. Most men get a fast car and a mistress. They don't throw their careers away for nothing."

Midlife crisis. That was actually funny. Even funnier was the fact was that his father had never paid for Sean's medical school. After undergraduate school, Sean had been so sick of his dad breathing over his shoulder and dictating what classes he was going to take that Sean had struck out on his own. It had taken him a little longer than his brother and sister, but he'd paid for med school on his own or with scholarships and student loans. Trying to remind the stubborn fool would get Sean nowhere.

"You're a Griffin and Griffins achieve. They don't subsist."

"Well, this Griffin just bought a horse stable," Sean bit out. "He's now a groomer, hay thrower and stall mucker. Chew on that." He turned to look out the window, hoping the view of his land and his horses moseying here and there might calm him.

Dead silence hung on the line for several long moments.

"You have the highest IQ in generations of Griffins," Sean's father finally said. "Don't you feel the slightest amount of remorse about your decision? You could be doing great things, Sean."

"I'll leave that to you, Van and Rick."

"What am I supposed to do with you?"

"Nothing. That's the whole point, isn't it? It's my life. Let me live it." Sean hung up the phone. He closed his eyes and waited for his erratic heartbeat to return to normal. When he turned, Grace was watching him. "Don't give me shit just now, okay?"

"Okay."

Sean turned back toward the window and glanced out at the pasture. "I wish I could say that he came from a poor family. That he worked his fingers to the bone to get where he is and that's why it's so hard to see me, from his point of view, blow an education. But he's a blueblood, through and through. From a long line of surgeons. One of my uncles became an attorney and he was virtually cast out of the family." Sean sighed. "The sad thing is that I actually liked working in the E.R. I like being a doctor."

"Why is that sad?"

"Because I gave it up for the wrong reasons. I gave it up *because* of my father. I came to Mirabelle because I knew it would drive him crazy. A small community. A family practitioner." Sean chuckled. "Part-time, of all things. Jab the knife in deep and twist."

"Is that why you bought Arlo's stable, too?"

That he had to think about. "I don't know. I don't think so."

Probably the only thing his father had ever done right, as far as Sean was concerned, was insist that his progeny learn to ride horses and ride them well. Although in the elder Griffin's mind this skill was likely a throwback to the genteel times of his own childhood, Sean had never complained. From day one, he'd loved working with horses.

"What would happen if your dad was out of the picture?" she asked. "What would change?"

He turned toward her.

"Could you honestly ever imagine leaving Mirabelle?" she asked.

"No."

"Well, you have your answer then, don't you?"

They stood looking at each other for a long, quiet moment, and suddenly the future Sean had envisioned for himself shifted and coalesced into him and Grace making a life together. Could that happen? "And you?" he whispered. "Could you ever imagine staying on Mirabelle?"

As if her thoughts were tracking along similar lines as his, she blinked and backed away. "I honestly don't know."

Then a carriage came into the yard and Arlo appeared in the barn door and the moment was gone. They stepped away from each other, putting a discreet distance between them.

"Sean!" Arlo called. "I could use your help here."

"Coming," he replied. "Well, if you do decide to stay on the island," Sean said, trying desperately to make light of what had just passed between them, "could you do me one small favor?"

She raised her eyebrows.

"Wear a bra?" He glanced down at her wet chest and smiled gently. "Personally, I think the natural look is amazing, especially on you, but you walk around like that much longer and you might just give Arlo a heart attack."

CHAPTER FOURTEEN

SINCE GRACE HAD ARRIVED ON Mirabelle more than a month ago, her days had fallen into an easy pattern. The mornings she spent at her dad's house, doing a little cleaning for him, a load or two of laundry or some yard work. Then she had lunch with him, ensuring that he had something healthy at least once each day, before heading to the stables to feed Louie, do some higher level training with Austin or help out Arlo.

She usually didn't get back to her rental home before seven. By then it would be time for a light supper, a shower and a quick check for phone messages and emails before heading off to bed to read or watch a little TV before falling asleep. Funny, but she hadn't used her treadmill or stationary bicycle once since she'd arrived on the island. There was a time this simple schedule would've bored her to tears, but she hadn't felt this content in years.

Finished with her shower and already in pajamas—it felt so good to not have to sleep with those damned compression garments—she sat down to her laptop and cell phone to find several messages waiting. Apparently, Amanda needed a call back tonight, so Grace dialed her number on her cell.

"Grace! I'm so glad you called."

"Hello, Amanda."

"I have some exciting news. *Vogue* called. They were happy to hear you're feeling better and wanted to talk to you about doing an exclusive. A back in the saddle type cover story. Isn't that great!"

No. It was, actually, one of the most ridiculous things Grace had ever heard. Those editors didn't care about her. To them she was a commodity, something to sell to readers. Grace's stomach pitched violently as she imagined a possible photo spread. There was something about the proverbial train wreck at which people couldn't help but gawk. When it came down to it, she was probably even more valuable today than at the height of her modeling career. "Tell them no."

"What?"

"I said tell them no, Amanda."

"Are you sure?"

"I'm not interested in getting back in the saddle. Not now. Not ever." These days, there was only one saddle she wanted to climb into and it had nothing to with modeling.

"Jeremy was the one who suggested it to them," Amanda said carefully. "He thinks it'd be good for you."

Jeremy. Grace laughed and shook her head. "Jeremy doesn't get a vote. Not anymore. Tell them no, please."

"All right," Amanda said softly.

"Anything else?"

"No. That was it. How are you liking Mirabelle?"

Grace's first reaction was to shut Amanda down and cut off the conversation, but that seemed harsh just now. "I like it. Thanks for asking."

"You sound relaxed."

Grace chuckled. "That obvious?"

"Yeah. You sound good."

Amanda had been working for Grace for more than four years, and Grace had held her at arm's length all that time. "Enough about me. How have you been, Amanda?"

Much to Grace's surprise, they talked for close to half an hour, and she would've continued their conversation if another call hadn't interrupted. "I'm getting another call. It's Suzy."

"You'd better take it. Talk to you again soon."

"Thanks, Amanda. In fact, thanks for all you've done for me over the years."

"It's been my pleasure, Grace."

Grace switched over to the incoming call. "Hello, Suze."

"I miss you. The dirty martinis at Eli's just aren't the same. When are you coming back?"

Off and on, Grace had been ruminating over Sean's question the other day about her staying on Mirabelle. She wasn't about to wonder about his intentions behind the question. Those thoughts were simply too confusing. "What if I don't ever come back to L.A.?" A brief silence hung on the line and Grace held her breath.

"You're serious, aren't you?"

"Yeah, I am."

"So I'm going to have to come to you, is that it? Where the hell is Wisconsin, anyway? Somewhere by Kansas?"

"You're in luck. You can let the pilot of the plane worry about that."

"So...tell me. Met any interesting men on Mirabelle?"

The question caught Grace off guard, and she hesitated.

"Oh, my God!" Suzy exclaimed, reading into the silence. "You *have* met someone, haven't you?"

"On an island the size of Mirabelle?"

Suzy laughed. "Tell me about him. If you don't, I will pester you to death."

Grace sighed.

"To death. I swear."

"He owns the horse stable."

"A cowboy? Be still my heart."

He was far from a cowboy, but there was no harm in letting Suzy fantasize. "And he's the island's doctor."

"A twofer. Grace, you dog. I didn't know you had it in you."

"Honestly, I don't know what's gotten into me."

"Does it matter? You are so due, sweets. Enjoy it."

"I'm not sure if I can."

"What? Since when—" She stopped, then as understanding seemed to dawn, she said softly, "Oh, Grace. If he's half the man you deserve, he'll want you exactly the way you are."

Scars and all? She could dream.

"How are you? Really?"

"I'm…getting there."

"Love the dress design you sent."

"Good." Grace smiled inside.

"I'm sending it off to you in four fabrics."

"Four?"

"Looks good in every case. I was surprised. Now I want something from you." She paused. "The designs for an entire line of clothing."

"What?"

"I want a collection. Clothing by Grace. Grace Couture. We'll decide on a label later. Coats, jeans, shirts, dresses, pants, blouses. Everything."

"A dress is one thing. An entire line…I'm not a designer."

"No. You've just lived and breathed the design industry for years. Don't tell me Jeremy didn't ever ask your opinion, and don't tell me you didn't give it. You know what to do. All you have to do is do it."

Grace's heart raced with uncertainty.

"Grace, my dear, dear friend, I have this feeling that this will make you happy."

Grace had loved imagining that dress, and she wouldn't have to leave Mirabelle to do this.

I don't have to leave Mirabelle.

The moment the thought entered her head she sucked in a breath. She didn't *want* to leave Mirabelle. She wanted to stay. She loved it here. She was home again.

"Okay," Grace said. "I'll give designing a line a shot, but I'm not promising anything."

THE NEXT MORNING, EXCITED TO start her day, Grace hopped out of bed. Ideas for a collection for Suzy were already racing through her head, but she needed to get them down on something other than scrap paper. She tugged a baseball cap low over her brow and slipped on a pair of dark sunglasses and a scarf before stepping outside.

Once again, it was hot out, and she was glad she'd slipped on a pair of shorts. The scarf, however, wasn't coming off. She'd given up her compression garments, but she'd probably never be ready for tank tops.

Keeping her gaze straight ahead and walking fast, she made it downtown and headed straight for Henderson's drugstore. They didn't have what she needed. She'd already been to Newman's enough to know they wouldn't have the right supplies. That left the gift shop across the street. Whimsy.

Grace stood outside and admired the window display. Someone had spent quite a bit of time arranging and rearranging each item for the proper presentation. There was a fanciful feel to every item for sale, from the birdhouses to the stationery, the wind chimes to the spice racks and vegetarian cookbooks.

Hopeful she'd find what she was looking for here, she went inside. Soft instrumental music was playing behind the register and a stick of incense burned at the front counter where a young college student with dreadlocks stood helping a customer. The place wasn't crawling with tourists, but there were a few moseying here and there. Grace kept her head down as she perused the aisles. Off to one side of the front counter, she located a section of art supplies, including Calligraphy pens and ink, molding clay, markers and sets of acrylic paints, but the spot clearly reserved for sketch pads was empty.

The sounds of female laughter erupted from the storage room. Through the strings of beads hanging in the doorway separating a back room from the front retail area, Grace caught sight of three women sitting at a small table eating lunch. Apparently, the area doubled as a break room.

"You can't be serious," the woman with short dark hair said. "They both cheated on each other?"

"On the same night?" asked the one with long blond hair. Grace had first seen that woman at Newman's.

"Yep," said the third one, the black-haired beauty who had offered to babysit the blonde's two little boys. "At their respective bachelor and bachelorette parties."

"Unbelievable."

"So they called the wedding off?"

"Yeah, can you believe it?"

The women laughed, and Grace felt a curious sense of melancholy. Since coming to Mirabelle, the only people she'd had any contact with had been men, Arlo, her father, Austin. And Sean. She missed conversations with women. She missed Suzy. Heck, she even missed Amanda.

Suddenly, the blonde pushed back her chair. "I need my water." She stood and came toward the door.

Grace quickly returned to looking through the art supplies just as the other woman reached the front. She glanced at Grace and cheerfully said, "Hello."

"Hi." Grace surreptitiously studied the other woman.

She was—there was no other word for it—cute, with a heart-shaped face and long blond hair, and looked to be about Grace's age. "Gaia, are you doing okay?" she asked the young woman at the register as she grabbed a bottle of water off the front counter.

"I'm good, Missy."

Apparently, she was the owner or manager, one of the new people her father had mentioned settling on the island in these past few years. Just then, a trim but muscular black cat slinked out from the back room, through the beads, only to wind itself through Grace's legs. Grace stiffened.

As the blonde turned around, she reached out to touch Grace's arm. "You okay?"

"Yeah. I'm just not…particularly fond of…"

"Cats?" The woman picked up the ball of fur and scratched under his neck. The resulting purr emanating from the animal was clearly audible. "This is Slim. He saved my life. Literally."

"A black cat who looked a lot like him almost took mine," Grace whispered.

"I'm sorry." The woman set the cat down in the back room. "Are you looking for something specific?"

"A sketch pad."

"Oh, that's right. I ran out, but it's been so busy today I haven't had a chance to restock. Why don't you come to the back and I'll get one for you."

"That's okay. I can wait here."

As the woman disappeared into the storage room, the other two women still sitting at the table glanced curiously at Grace.

"Here you go." The shop owner returned, holding out a thick pad of drawing paper. "Will this work?"

Grace felt the texture of the paper. It was a bit stiffer than it should be, but it would do. "It'll be fine."

"Anything else?"

"No, thank you."

"I'm Missy Abel." The woman headed over to the register. "You're Grace Kahill, aren't you? I've heard so much about you. It's nice to finally meet."

"Excuse me?"

"Sean's a good friend. You've come up a time or two."

What, exactly, did that mean? Had she been wrong to trust Sean? Grace snatched the pad of paper. "Thank you." She tossed a twenty onto the counter. "I don't need any change."

"But...but...Grace, I think you're misunderstanding."

"I'm sure I understand perfectly."

SEAN LATHERED UP A BAR OF saddle soap and rubbed down the saddle he was cleaning. He heard footsteps behind him and without turning he knew who he'd find coming into the barn. "Hello, Grace. What's up? Your feet sound angry."

"You're talking about me."

He turned. Man, was she angry. Had photographers ever gotten this side of her? If not, they'd been missing out.

"The gift shop owner. On Main." She came to stand outside the stall. "She said you talk about me all the time."

"Missy?"

"I want to know what you've said."

"Nothing. A big group of us get together for happy hour about once a week. They're good friends. They ask about you now and then. What you're like. How long you're staying on Mirabelle. That kind of thing."

"And what have you told them?"

He held her gaze. "As little as possible in as vague a way as possible."

She looked away. "The woman looked at me, as if...she knew about everything that's happened between us."

"That's because she knows me. Missy's a very good friend. And very intuitive. What I didn't say probably told her more than what I did say." He smiled gently. "I have no doubt that while you were in her store she read your aura and your love line and has already decided whether or not you and I will be spending the rest of eternity together." He was hoping the comment might garner a small smile.

Instead, she turned away. "I hate this island."

"Grace, I was kidding." Kind of. "Missy's a good person. They're all good people. I think it's time you come and meet some of the new people on this island. Come to happy hour. At Duffy's."

She didn't say a word.

"You can sit, have a drink and relax. You do still know how to do that, don't you?"

"I...I don't go out in public. For a very good reason."

"No one will bother you. In fact, the islanders get very protective of their own."

"That I believe. Except that I'm not one of their own."

"If you're with me, you will be." He tried another approach. "Did you know Missy is really a Camden?"

"One of *the* Camdens?"

He nodded. The Camden family, one of the oldest and wealthiest names on the east coast, was as close to royalty as it got here in the United States.

"Well, she doesn't have a face that's been plastered on the cover of practically every magazine ever made, that's for sure."

"True, but her face is known, and no one has ever bothered her here on Mirabelle." He tilted his head at her. "What happened to that spirited, defiant teenager, Grace?"

"I ASKED YOU NOT TO CALL ME again," Carl whispered as he closed his home office door.

This was the first time she'd contacted him since coming to his office down at the resort in the middle of the day, but she didn't like being ignored. That much was obvious. Since his cell phone had gone off several times after dinner, and he wasn't sure if she'd push as far as showing up at his house, he figured he'd better call her back.

"I tried not to call," she said. "I really don't want to make this difficult for you. But I can't stop thinking about us. What happened at your office."

Oh, man. The woman was every man's wet dream. But that's what she needed to be. A dream.

"There is no us," he said softly. "That's what I keep trying to explain to you. I meant what I said." He spoke gently, but clearly, hoping to get through. Sherri was proving to be unpredictable. There was no telling what she might do if she got angry. "What happened was a mistake." Probably, the biggest in his life.

"It didn't feel like a mistake to me," she said, sounding hurt and vulnerable. "No matter what you're telling yourself, there was a reason we happened. We've got something special. Give us a chance."

Maybe she was right. Maybe he deserved something better, more meaningful. If he had a woman who wanted him more, who needed him. Maybe then—

Who was he kidding? He was no monumentally great catch. He ran a good business. He'd managed to pay the bills all these years and put some money aside for the kids' college and retirement. But he was no Don Juan in the bedroom or otherwise. He was a homebody through and through. So marriage sex had gotten stale. What had he expected?

"No," he whispered. "We never should've happened to begin with. I got drunk. And stupid." He paused. "I know it was long time ago, but I made vows to Carol. I'm not happy I broke them." Not once. Not twice. Three times. "I'm trying to set this right. I'll never break my marriage vows again. With you or anyone else."

"Then leave her."

"Are you out of your mind?"

"No marriage. No vows."

For a moment, he entertained the possibility. Starting over.

Starting fresh. It'd be exciting. A new lease on life. He wasn't getting any younger, that was for sure.

Then he imagined actually walking out the door. They'd have to sell the house. Nikki was heading off to college, but where would Alex live? He couldn't do it. He couldn't break it all up. "I'm married," he said. "Carol. The kids. The house. My business. I can't just walk away from everything."

"People do it all the time, Carl, and you can't deny that we are good…very good…together."

There was no doubt the sex had been amazing. Even now, he was on the verge of a hard-on just thinking about the way she'd—

"No," he ground out. It was happening again. He was getting turned around. "I'll get away if I can, but please stop calling me." He disconnected the call, set the phone on his desk and rested his head in his hands.

A knock sounded, and Carol immediately opened the door.

Had she been listening?

"You all right?" she asked, clearly concerned.

No, she didn't have a clue, making him feel even worse. How could he have betrayed her? His wife. The mother of his children. "I'm fine. A little tired and I have a headache."

"Seems like you've been working a lot lately."

He hadn't been, not really. Just couldn't seem to get himself to come home, couldn't seem to face Carol for any longer than was absolutely necessary.

"Sean just called looking for you. He was wondering if you and a couple other guys wanted to get together for a beer tonight at Duffy's."

There it was. His excuse to get away had been handed to him like candy. "I'll call him back."

"Didn't you just get together with him last week?"

"Ah…" Carl's heart beat erratically as he tried remembering

where he was supposed to have been and when. "Yeah. We did have a beer. But he's got a lot going on. With his son living with him and all."

"Oh." She was looking at him funny.

Was she looking at him funny?

"In any case, if you're not feeling well, maybe you should go to sleep early tonight, instead of heading out."

"Yeah, but I'm guessing Sean needs to talk. A break might help the headache. I think I'll head to Duffy's."

His cell phone vibrated, but he ignored the infernal piece of technology. The sick feeling that she wasn't going to disappear peacefully roiled in his gut. Maybe he'd better fess up and tell Carol before she found out. Maybe if she heard it from him— He opened his mouth and then quickly looked away. Was he only out to clear his conscience?

Carol glanced at the phone and then at him. "Aren't you going to answer that?"

He closed his eyes. They didn't have a perfect marriage by any means, but Carol didn't deserve this.

"What's going on?" Carol said, her tone worried. "We haven't talked about the resort for a while. Is there something wrong?"

"Everything's fine at the lodge. Good, in fact. We're having one helluva busy summer. Just a bad day." He grabbed the phone and shut it off. "There was a couple who complained about their housekeeping service earlier today and I don't want to deal with it anymore tonight." That was a bald-faced lied, but he had to come up with something. "The night manager will just have to deal with it."

"That's what you're paying him for." She turned toward the hall. "I'm going to read for a while. Good night, Carl."

"Good night. See you in the morning." He followed her,

slipped out of the house, and dialed a number on his cell. "Sean? I'll be at Duffy's in a little while. There's something I need to do first…"

CHAPTER FIFTEEN

"I KNOW, GRACE, BUT IT HAS TO get done," Grace's father said from the kitchen. "There's no sense in all of her things collecting dust. She'd hate that kind of a waste."

"I'll take care of it, Dad." Grace headed down the hall. She would've much rather been at her own house working on her new designs for Suzy. The ideas had started flowing fast and furiously once she'd gotten over the initial shock of Suzy asking for an entire line, but her mother's closet had to get cleaned out.

"How 'bout we bring up a six-pack of beer and do this together?" Her dad reached into the refrigerator.

"Missing Duffy's?" Grace said. "I hear the locals still occasionally get together for happy hour."

He frowned. "You might have something there."

Grace had brought over several of the boxes she'd used to move over her things when first coming to Mirabelle. She now had them lined up in her father's bedroom. "Did you want to keep any of her clothes?" she asked the moment he appeared in the doorway.

"Don't think so." He popped the top on a bottle of beer and stood at the entrance of the walk-in closet he'd shared with Grace's mom. "Might as well take everything to charity. Unless you want something."

That wasn't even close to the realm of possibility. Although they weren't all that different in size, Grace and her mother had been vastly different in taste. Jean Andersen's style had been classic all the way. More often than not, she had chosen solid colors with a print mixed in here or there. Grace, on the other hand, had embraced new trends with a vengeance. Almost every penny of the money she'd earned working for Arlo had gone into clothes.

"Why don't you sit down?" She directed her dad toward the recliner in the corner. "You can manage the process."

Grace grabbed an armload of blouses and pants hanging at the front of her mother's side of the closet. None of the items looked familiar, so they must've been relatively recent purchases. After folding everything and stacking the articles in the first box, she went back for more. On the third trip, she ran into older clothes that Grace remembered from when she was a kid. "Why didn't she get rid of this stuff?"

"She always kept her favorites."

Grace chuckled as she held out a boxy flannel shirt in a red-and-black plaid. "I remember when I bought this for her one Christmas." It had been during Grace's exploration with the grunge look of the early nineties. Holey jeans, baggy shirts, camouflage jackets. All in all, not a successful look for Grace. "I think she wore this shirt once."

"It looked terrible on her," her dad said. "But she wanted to make you happy."

"And I so wanted her to be a hip mom." Chuckling to herself, she remembered going from the grunge stage to Goth. For three months she'd refused to wear anything that wasn't black. Even gray wasn't bleak enough. Black tights and boots. Black sweaters. She'd even painted her nails black. At various times, her hair had been colored pink, blue, black and platinum blond. She'd even gone through a piercing stage. First her nose, the upper edges of both ears and one eyebrow. Getting her navel pierced had been the last straw for her mother.

"Look at this." Grace laughed, holding out a red leather miniskirt she'd bought for her mom on an excursion to an outlet mall on the mainland. Once Grace had gotten her driver's license, she'd headed to those stores on a monthly basis. "I can't believe I ever thought she'd wear it."

"She did. One night for me." He grinned. "Along with silky underwear and high heels. Although none of it stayed on her for long."

"Eeew, Dad!"

"Your mother was far from a prude, you know?"

"Still…" Laughing, she folded the skirt and dropped it into a box. "Too much information."

Once she'd removed all the clothes and shoes out of the closet, she moved to the boxes stacked on the floor under where her mother's clothes had been hung. The first one was filled with old Christmas cards. She quickly flipped through the contents. "Did you want to look at this before I throw it away?" She showed the box to her father.

"No, I don't think there's anything special in there. She saved her favorite pictures, thinking she'd make something from them someday. Never seemed to have the time."

Grace threw the cards in a garbage bag and went on to the next item. A large square box, this one was packed with cards, letters and little trinkets her mother had received from Grace and Carl through the years. She set the box on the bed.

"What did you find?"

"Memories." She flipped through one thing after another. Cards for Valentine's Day, birthdays and Mother's Day. Home-made or store bought, her mother had kept them all. Little pins given as gifts. A baggie with a couple of baby teeth. "I remember making this," she said, holding out a little box made of folded paper, complete with a cover. Multicolored glitter that had glued onto every flat surface was falling off all over the place. "In third grade."

On top of that, her mom had kept the products from some of Grace's make-believe play. A menu Grace had made of supposedly French dishes for her restaurant, a list of salon services for, of course, a spa and the prices of shoes, purses and jewelry in her accessories store.

"I remember doing all of these. I was probably about eight."

"She loved listening to you play. You were so imaginative. So resourceful."

Each piece of paper brought her back in time. She remembered feeling carefree and bold, as if she'd been capable of anything. That was how she'd felt when she'd left Mirabelle. "Funny, how things change."

"That little girl is still inside you, Grace."

The offer for a cover story from *Vogue* flashed through her thoughts, but immediately she dismissed the possibility.

"I know she's there," her father said. "I can still see that mischievous glint in your eyes."

She kissed him on the cheek and kept digging in the box. The next few notes stopped her cold. Hate notes Grace had written to her mother in various fits of anger. She was embarrassed to show her father, but she had to know. "Why did she keep these?" she asked, holding them out to him.

He smiled slightly as he looked through them. "I don't know. Maybe to remember you were both human."

"I can't believe I was so mean."

"Passionate. At least that's what your mother called you."

"Sounds like she was making excuses for me and my bad behavior."

"Don't be too hard on yourself." He glanced into the box. "Looks to me as though there are ten times as many love notes as hate notes."

"We fought all the time. Why?"

"I'm not sure she ever understood you, Grace." He paused, as if he were remembering. "You were fearless, possibly even reckless at times, in how you lived your life. You left here when you were only seventeen, ready to take on the world. She was so frightened about all the bad things that could've happened to you."

"Every time I called, she'd get angry. Why couldn't I do this? Why did I have to do that?"

"But she always, always loved you."

The damage had been done, though. Eventually, Grace had stopped calling altogether. "I wish I could do things over again."

"Don't we all," her dad whispered.

She dug a little deeper into the closet and, much to her surprise, found a stack of fashion magazines under a shoebox. They were several of the covers Grace had done early on in her career. "She kept these?" Grace glanced at her father. "I thought she hated what I did."

"Never. When you started appearing in magazines, your mother got subscriptions to all of them."

"I didn't know."

"She knew exactly what time of the month they'd all be coming. Couldn't wait."

That seemed so odd, given that Grace and her mother had argued constantly over her career. The cover shot that had propelled her career to an entirely new level had also sparked the biggest argument between them. There it was, stuck in the middle of the stack. Grace on one of her first covers for *Vogue*. The electric-blue dress she wore had been specifically designed to bare more of her than it covered. These days, it didn't seem all that shocking, but this shot had been the first of its kind, pushing every possible limit of the day.

Grace stared at herself, at her old body. She couldn't believe she'd ever been so brazen. All her childhood, modesty in all things had been drummed into her head. Every shirt had to be buttoned up. No low necklines, short hems or suggestive makeup. Strange, how life had run full circle. She might be adjusting to life without compression garments, but she could no more wear that dress today than she could walk naked down the street.

Maybe her father had been right. Going through her mother's things hadn't been such a good idea, but now that she'd started, she couldn't very well stop in the middle, leaving her father's bedroom a mess.

Not quite ready to toss all those magazine clippings, Grace returned them where she'd found them and pulled out the shoebox that had been sitting on top. Inside she found a stack of old photos, flipped through them, and found her mother, looking quite the hippie, in many of them.

"Oh, my God!" She sat on the floor, the photos in her lap. Clearly, there was more she didn't know about her mother. "Tell me about her, Dad. Tell me everything you remember about her when you two were young."

He smiled and glanced off into space. "We met at an anti-war rally."

Unbelievable. She'd always imagined her parents as strait-laced, by-the-numbers conservatives, not radical statement makers.

The surprised look on her face must've registered and he laughed. "Now you ready for that beer?"

She grabbed a bottle and twisted off the cap. "I have a feeling we're going to need more than a six-pack."

"WELL, AUSTIN," GRACE SAID once they'd slowed to a canter, "I think I've taught you about everything I know."

The young man turned in his saddle. "You sure?"

"You've been a good student and you're a fast learner."

He'd proved to be good company, too. He was a natural with horses and Diego, Sean's chestnut gelding, had easily taken to Austin. Earlier that afternoon, Diego had been in a paddock off the riding stable. The moment he noticed Austin coming out of the house, he'd cantered over to the gate, clearly excited to spend time with the boy.

"So now what?"

"Now you spend time in the saddle and practice. The more hours you put in, the sooner you'll be as good a rider as the rest of the other trail hands."

"Will I still see you?"

Sweet kid. "I'll be at the stables almost every day. We can still go on rides together. I'll still help in the barn. You just don't need any formal instruction."

They continued in silence for a few moments.

"So what do you think so far of Mirabelle?" Grace asked.

"It's okay. Not as bad as I expected."

"Feeling homesick?"

"No," he said decisively. "Not anymore."

"Not missing your mom, sister and brother, stepdad, friends? At all?"

"I don't have any friends. None worth missing anyway. I talk to my mom every couple of days. I never got along with my dad—stepdad, I should say. Although now that he's getting a divorce, I'm not sure what Glen is to me."

Grace didn't know what to say.

"You grew up here on the island, right?" he asked.

"Yep."

"Did you like it here?"

She laughed. "No. I hated it. Pastor's daughter. Everyone watching me through a magnifying glass. I couldn't do anything right. Plus, the place was boring. At least in winter. In the summer, it was great. So many people coming and going. I loved the summers here."

"Where did you go to school?"

"They actually had a school here on the island. I think

it's still here, and a little bigger than it was in my day. Guess there are more families with kids."

"Did you like the small school?"

"Nope. Hated that, too. Same teacher for, like, four grades. Mrs. Gallant. This old battle-ax of a woman who smelled faintly of mothballs, and she walked like a…a…football player. Heck, she was big enough to have played center." Grace chuckled, remembering. "But now that I think about it…she used to sneak me her fashion magazines after she was finished reading them. Made me promise not to tell my mom. She even bought me a book once on fashion designing. God, I haven't thought about her for ages." She sighed. "Okay, maybe she wasn't so bad, after all."

"She still here?"

"Naw. I heard she retired a couple years ago and moved to North Carolina." It might've been nice to thank the woman for all she'd done for Grace.

"Are you glad you left?"

"I can't imagine my life having turned out any other way." Grace glanced at him. "Why so curious about Mirabelle and schools? You thinking about staying?"

"On Mirabelle? You crazy? Besides, Sean can't wait for me to leave, so his life can go back to normal."

"I wouldn't be too sure about that, if I were you." She could tell by his thoughtful expression that he wasn't sure about anything right about now.

CHAPTER SIXTEEN

"HOW ARE THE TRAIL RIDES going?" Sean asked as he approached Austin near the end of the workday.

Sean had just saddled Boss and was planning on taking a short ride before he headed to Duffy's to meet with his regular crew. He hadn't been out on Boss for weeks, and it was a gorgeous midsummer day. Big, fluffy white clouds dotted the azure sky and there was just the right amount of a breeze to keep the bugs away.

"Good. Great, as a matter of fact," Austin said as he finished releasing several of the horses into the back pasture.

"You getting along with Eric and the other hands?"

Austin nodded and closed the gate. "We're doing fine." Suddenly, he looked worried. "Why?"

"No reason." Sean shrugged. "Just checking in with you."

Austin looked more than a little relieved.

Guess they still had some work to do before his son felt completely relaxed around him. "Hey, Austin." A thought occurred to Sean and he mounted Boss. "Want to join me for a ride?"

Austin seemed to consider it. "Sure," he finally said. "Diego's still saddled. I'll get him."

A moment later, Austin and Diego met Sean and Boss at the trailhead. "Do you care where we go?" Sean asked.

"Yeah, actually," Austin said, excited now. "I've been hearing about a place called Full Moon Bay, but I can't find the path to the beach."

"That I can show you."

They talked about the Stall boys, the island, Austin's experiences this summer as they headed out through the trails on state park land. It was the most relaxed conversation Sean had ever had with his son, and he was grateful for the excuse of a horse ride. Without Boss and Diego, this might not be happening.

They hit Island Drive and galloped for a bit. Austin was not an expert by any means, but with practice he'd one day be a very good rider. A half mile or so down the road, Sean stopped and pointed toward the deer path. "Here we go. This'll take us to Full Moon Bay."

"How do you remember how to find it?" Austin glanced around. "All these woods look the same to me."

"Come here often enough and you'll know. Start by looking for that big tree." Sean pointed out a massive white pine across the road.

"Gotcha."

Sean slowly took Boss down the path toward the water. The moment they hit sand, he spotted, of all things, Louie meandering nearby at the edge of the woods, grazing. For a second, Sean's heart raced out of control. Had the horse thrown Grace?

No. Couldn't be. He glanced around the bay. There she was, sitting against the trunk of a tree on the other side of the bay. Her bare feet buried in warm sand, she was so focused on whatever was in her lap that she hadn't noticed them emerge from the woods.

The moment Austin drew up beside Sean, he called out, "Grace!"

She glanced up and waved. "Hi, there!"

Without the same reservations Sean had about disturbing

her peace, Austin hopped down from Diego. "What do we do with the horses?" he asked Sean, as if it was taken for granted they'd be stopping for a while.

"We can let them graze." He unbridled Boss and Diego and both horses wandered toward Louie.

Austin walked across the beach to join Grace. "What are you doing?"

"Mmm. Not much." She closed what looked like a sketch pad and set it aside.

"Is that a drawing pad?" He picked it up.

"Austin," Sean said. "Grace might not want you looking at that."

"Oh, sorry."

"That's okay." She smiled indulgently. "You can look at them."

He flipped through the pages. "These are tight. What are they for?"

"A friend of mine asked me to design her a clothing line."

"No shit?"

She laughed. "I was just putting the finishing touches on a hooded trench coat before I email everything to her." She paused. "So what do you think?"

"I didn't know you could draw like this."

"Neither did I until I tried."

"I like them." He closed the pad. "So are they going to make clothes from these? Stuff we'll be able to see in stores?"

"Maybe. It depends on whether or not Suzy likes them."

"Suzy's a friend of yours, I take it?" Sean asked, sitting down beside Austin.

"Best friend." She seemed so relaxed to Sean.

Austin glanced around. "This bay is awesome."

"It's pretty private," Sean said. From personal experience, he knew that occasionally a sailboat, kayak or fishing charter boat might pass by, but no one usually gave the small bay a second glance.

Austin hopped up, went down by the shore and started skipping stones into the water.

"May I?" Sean asked, referring to the sketch pad.

"Sure."

He flipped through the nearly full pad. He didn't know anything about design, but her drawings were remarkable. All of them flowing and imaginative, some whimsical, others elaborate. Some simple, others elegant. Still others classic. Some of her sketches had been filled in with colors, and others had been finished in only pencil. "When did you find the time to do these?"

"Here and there." She looked out over the water. "When they came to me."

"I thought you were a model, not a designer," he said, damned close to awestruck.

"So did I." She chuckled. "But I guess when you live with a world-renowned designer for as long as I did you pick up a few things."

"Oh, I think you're selling yourself short. Take me, for example. I don't have a creative bone in my body. Wouldn't know where to begin even after fifty years in close quarters with a designer. You, Grace, are very talented."

"Are you flirting with me?"

"For once, no." He kept looking through her designs. "I'm serious."

"Thank you."

He was surprised to find that his comment had actually meant something to her. Not wanting to read too much into it, he handed her back the pad. "For what it's worth, I'm impressed."

"You can be impressed later. That is, if Suzy ends up using any of my designs."

They sat in companionable silence for several long moments, both of them watching Austin skipping stones. Sean couldn't help but remember the night he'd encountered her here, skinny-dipping, the night everything had changed between them. The night his attraction to her had developed into so much more; respect, admiration, affection.

As if she were remembering their encounter as well and the memory unsettled her, she stood suddenly. "I need to go."

"We'll go with you," he said.

"Louie," she called, "let's head home."

The three of them returned to the stables together, talking and laughing, almost as if they were a real family.

GRACE TOOK LOUIE TO THE LIVERY barn, brushed and fed him and then went to her dad's house to use his camera to snap pictures of her designs and email them to Suzy. She hesitated for a moment, her finger poised on send. What if Suzy didn't like these designs as much as that simple dress? What if her friend was just being nice and trying to keep Grace busy? What if—

Stop it. This is business for Suzy. She's not going to produce a line of clothing to be nice.

Sean and Austin had liked her designs. In fact, the look of respect in Sean's eyes as he'd flipped through her pages had bolstered her confidence more than she'd expected. Granted, they weren't experts, but she'd enjoyed sharing a piece of her life with the two men who had become so important to her in such a short amount of time. Sean wasn't the only one who was going to miss Austin when he left at the end of summer.

Send the designs off. What will be will be.

A moment later, the email sent, she came out of her father's library as the front doorbell rang. Swinging the door wide, she found a much older and heavier version of the Doc Welinski she remembered. "Doc!" She grinned.

"Gracie-Grace." He came inside and hugged her. "What a sight you are." They chatted for a few minutes. "Now where's that father of yours?"

"Watching the early news. Go on back." She followed him down the hall.

As soon as Doc reached the family room, he said, "Come on, John, let's go."

Startled, her dad glanced up. "Go where?"

"It's local's night at Duffy's." Doc grabbed the remote, shut off the TV and winked at her. "Grace is even coming tonight, aren't you, Gracie?"

Not an easy way out of this. "Yep, that's a great idea. Come on, Dad. Let's go."

He glanced at the two of them. "You two are in cahoots, but, oh, all right." He sighed and hoisted himself out of his chair. "Only for a little while."

Doc had brought up his golf cart, so it was only a matter of minutes before they were down the hill, parked and walking toward Duffy's. Her dad's pace was slow, and with every step an internal war waged inside Grace.

You can't go in there. Sean will be there.

Go into the damned pub, Grace. What's the worst thing that could happen?

Someone could recognize you and stare at you like you're a freak.

Yeah? So what else is new?

Maybe—just maybe—Sean is right.

She'd worn a pair of very lightly tinted sunglasses, hoping that coupled with being out of L.A. might be enough that people might not recognize her.

"Excuse me." A woman brushed past her, her father and Doc when they were only a few feet from Duffy's. As the woman grabbed for the door handle to the pub, she glanced into Grace's face without the slightest hint of recognition.

So this is what anonymity feels like.

Emboldened, Grace followed Doc and her father inside. The place was crowded and other than a couple of men checking her out, no one gave her a second look. The glasses were working.

She glanced around, noticed a familiar dark head of hair sticking out above most of the crowd and craned her neck for a better look. Sean. He took a drink from a bottle of beer and laughed at something that had apparently been said by the woman sitting next to him. Surrounded by his friends, including Missy Charms Abel, the gift shop owner, he looked completely at ease, as if he belonged here. People nudged by her, some more forcefully than others, but she couldn't get her feet to move.

"Hey, you guys made it!" That was Arlo's voice.

Grace spun around to find Arlo and his wife, Lynn, coming in the door behind them. "Oh, my goodness, it's little Grace!" Lynn said, holding out her arms. "Look at you."

Lynn's face seemed as though it hadn't aged a bit, but her long hair had turned almost completely gray, a bright, natural silvery color. They hugged and chatted for a few moments before Doc motioned toward a table deep into the pub. "There's Dan Newman. Let's head over there."

"Grace, you coming?"

"I'll join you later, Dad, okay?"

As Doc, her dad, Lynn and Arlo squeezed through the crowd, Grace felt the urge to head outside. She was about to turn when Sean glanced her way, his gaze smoothly passing over her. Suddenly, his head snapped back to her and he smiled.

"Come here," he mouthed, waving her over. When she didn't move, he narrowed his gaze and without a word to his friends walked toward her. "You came," he said. "I wasn't sure you ever would."

She fought the urge to lean into him. "Doc stopped by the house to see if he could get Dad down here, so I tagged along."

"Glad you did." Then he indicated the light tortoise-shell framed glasses. "Are they real?"

"Clear glass."

"Well, they work. No one in here has a clue who you are."

"Your friends do." She found every person in the group he'd been with looking their way. "Sean...this was a mistake."

"No. It wasn't. You'll see." He ran his fingertips lightly, quickly along her cheek, and then he...kissed her. Softly. Sweetly. Quickly.

Stunned by his bold move, she couldn't speak for a moment, let alone move. She didn't know what to think, to feel. "What was that for?" she finally whispered.

"I wanted to touch you. I want everyone in here to know exactly what you mean to me."

Her first reaction was to call foul. She didn't know what she meant to him or what he meant to her. How could he possibly know? But the truth was that with one touch he'd placed a bubble of protection around her and all her misgivings dissipated. A kiss that had seemed so abrupt, so out of place, was suddenly the most right thing in the world. He had her back.

And her hand. Pulling her through the crowd, he led her to his group and drew her next to him. "Everyone. This is Grace. Grace, this is everyone."

There was a brief moment of stunned silence and then one of the women sitting on a bar stool said, "Hi, Grace. I don't know if you remember me, or not—"

"Missy," Grace said, reaching forward to shake the woman's hand. "I do remember you. I'm sorry about—"

"No worries." Missy waved it away.

While Sean got her a glass of white wine, everyone else introduced themselves. Jonas, Garrett, Sarah and Jesse. They said a few more people would be coming later, asked her a few mundane questions and then the conversation went on as before. She was at once accepted, but at the same time no one particularly special. In short order, she was chatting and laughing as if she'd known these people for months. Grace couldn't remember the last time she'd had so much fun meeting and visiting with new people.

A young woman came out of the kitchen and set a large basket of French fries, another basket of onion rings and a medium works pizza on the bar in front of Garrett. "You're a mind reader, baby," Garrett said, grinning.

"You can share," the woman said. "Or not. Up to you."

"Oh, he's sharing, all right," Jonas muttered, reaching around Garrett for a piece of pizza.

"Definitely," Jesse added, grabbing a handful of French fries.

The woman who'd brought out the food turned to Grace and smiled. "Hello, I'm Erica."

"Grace."

"Good to finally meet you. Gotta get back to work." She then went behind the bar.

As the group huddled around the food, Grace found herself next to Jesse. He took a bite from a slice of pizza and Grace noticed the scars on the back of his hands. Burn scars.

A rush of panic swept through her before she managed to calm herself. "Your hands," she said to Jesse. Not long before she'd come to Mirabelle, her father had told her about a fire that would've killed a young boy if not for a daring rescue by one man. "Did that happen to you here? On Mirabelle?"

"Mmm-hmm," he said, chewing.

"Were they painful?"

He nodded and swallowed. "But I'd do it over again in a heartbeat. Brian's alive."

So he was the man who'd saved the boy. "Badges of honor," she said quietly. Not at all like her scars.

"That's what Sarah says." He smiled as he held her gaze.

"You're a very brave man."

"Not really." He shook his head, self-conscious. "Anyone would've done what I did."

"No, they wouldn't," she said softly. She knew that for a fact. Jesse, already heading for a piece of pizza, didn't hear her, and it was probably for the best as a sudden burst of melancholy threatened to settle over her. The people whose garage she'd hit when her car had gone off the road had apparently watched as her car had gone up in flames. Other than calling 911, they hadn't lifted a finger.

"You okay?" Sean asked.

"Good. Fine." She shook off the memories of her car accident, reached for a crispy onion ring, and took a big bite. Sweet and savory exploded simultaneously in her mouth. Deep fried food did wonders to uplift her mood.

"Good, aren't they?" Sean asked.

"Amazingly good," she said, reaching for another one.

"Well, I'll be a son of a gun," a man's voice sounded behind her. "If it isn't Grace Trouble-with-a-capital-*T* Andersen, I'm a monkey's uncle."

She turned and found her gaze connecting with the stern eyes of an older, white-haired and mustached gentleman. On recognizing that menacing look, she backed up and bumped into Sean's chest. "Chief Bennett?"

He chuckled, the sound laced with something a tiny bit wicked. "That's me, but it's just Jim now. The illustrious title of police chief now belongs to this man here." He glanced at Garrett. "Better keep an eye on this one, Chief."

"That right?" Garrett eyed her.

"She caused even more trouble on this island than Noah."

"Why does that not surprise me?" Sean said, snickering.

Everyone laughed.

"I'm sorry," she said with as much sincerity as she could muster. "Forgive me?"

Chief Bennett chuckled. "Buy me a beer and we'll let bygones be bygones."

"Deal." She paid for a beer and handed it to him.

"So what was the worst thing she ever did?" Missy asked, grinning.

"Hmm, that's a tough one." Jim scratched his cheek. "We talking property damage or general mayhem?"

The circle surrounding her laughed even harder this time.

A vaguely familiar man came toward their group. "I think I remember her letting out all of Arlo's horses once upon a time."

"Noah?" she said, smiling. "Is that you?"

"Hello, Grace."

She shook his hand and then good-naturedly swatted his arm. "And you know darned well who let those horses out."

He grinned at his dad. "Sorry, Pop. It was me."

"Figures." Jim shook his head.

Grace couldn't help but smile as all her childhood shenanigans came back to her in a rush. Suddenly, Mirabelle felt like the best place in the world to grow up.

"Grace?" A woman moved to Noah's side. "Grace Andersen?"

"Sophie." Grace smiled. "It's good to see you. I met Lauren and Kurt at Carl's a few weeks ago."

"Hard to believe they're heading off to college in the fall," she said. "Good thing we have another set of twins at home keeping us busy."

Noah put a hand on her neck and massaged a shoulder. They spent several minutes catching up, and then Sean leaned over and whispered in her ear. "I don't mean to break up old-home week, but I'd like to show you something."

"Okay."

"We'll be back in a little bit," he said to the group as he set his own beer and her glass of wine on the bar. Then he took her hand and drew her through the crowd and out a side exit. On reaching the alleyway, he turned toward the shore. The moment they moved out from between the two buildings, the marina became visible. Boats, yachts and sailboats with their masts jutting into the black sky bobbed next to the docks. Lake Superior was black, even blacker than the sky, which was splashed with stars and a brilliant sliver of a moon.

"It's beautiful."

He came to stand behind her and wrapped his arms around her waist. Although the deck beside them was abuzz with activity, they stood quietly in the shadows. No one noticed them or seemed to care about their presence on the boardwalk.

It seemed the most natural thing in the world for Grace to close her eyes and let herself fall against him. He was only a few inches taller, so when she relaxed and leaned her head back, their cheeks touched, and she forgot herself in the perfect feel of his embrace.

He pushed her hair aside, exposing her bare neck. "I'm glad you came tonight," he said, running his lips along her skin, sending shivers through her center.

"Sean, what do want from me?"

"You make it sound like I have some kind of ulterior motive."

She turned in his arms. "Don't you?"

"It should be pretty obvious what I want."

Moonlight reflected in his eyes, and for a moment she nearly forgot that she couldn't—wouldn't—let anything physical happen with a man. Then it all came back to her. He may have seen her scars, but was he anything more than a doctor empathizing with a patient? Could this be anything more than pity? She stepped away. "I need to go."

"I'll walk you ho—"

"That's not necessary." She turned and walked away.

"Maybe not," he said, following her. "But I'm still going to make sure you get home safely."

They might've been silent as they walked up the hill, but the silence was charged with emotion. Finally, they reached her house at the end of the road. "Thank you," she said, turning toward him, "for inviting me to Duffy's. For introducing me to your friends. For…being so welcoming." She paused. "It means a lot to me."

"So polite. So distant. And so not what I want from you," he said, almost to himself. He looked into the sky as if he were trying to find the strength for something, and then he turned and headed for his property. "Good night, Grace."

She wrapped her arms around herself to ward off a sudden chill, but she couldn't make herself go inside until Sean was out of sight. Why, she couldn't have said. Then it dawned on her. Disappointment. That's what she was feeling. She'd wanted him to come inside. She'd wanted more than a kiss from Sean, so much more. So what had happened to the woman who had skinny-dipped at Full Moon Bay? What had happened to the woman who had kissed Sean with complete abandon?

She'd started to care about Sean, and somehow that realization was even more frightening than showing him her scars.

"I LOVE THEM."

Grace paced in her kitchen, holding her cell phone in a tight grip as she listened to what Suzy had to say about Grace's designs. "Are you serious?" she said. "You like all of them?"

"Gracie, I don't just like them, these designs are, quite simply, the best thing I've seen for a long time. You've put together a line that looks like…well, like you. Gorgeous and classically beautiful. Each piece, individually, seems simple, but when you put everything together, it's brilliant. Everyone will love it."

"So now what?"

Suzy laughed. "Would you hate me if I told I've already gone to Barney's?"

It was every new designers dream to get a foot in the high-end department store. "And?"

"They want an exclusive. And they want it now. They've already given me an order."

"But how do we—"

"Gracie, this is what I do, remember? I have manufacturing connections. We can be in business starting today. You just say yes and I take care of the rest."

"Yes!" She grinned.

"Then we're off and running. All you have to do now is start thinking about a spring and summer collection."

Grace felt like she needed to pinch herself. How could it be that the one thing she thought had ruined her life, the car accident, had actually been the best thing that could've ever happened to her?

"By the way," Suzy said, "how's your cowboy?"

"He's not mine." Grace smiled. "But he's fine."

"Does he have any friends?"

"Several."

"How big is that island?"
"Minuscule."
"Damn."

CHAPTER SEVENTEEN

IT SEEMED EVERY TIME SEAN turned around, Mirabelle was celebrating some holiday or festival. The standards, like Memorial Day, Independence Day and Labor Day marked the beginning, middle and end of summer. But the Mirabelle residents in an attempt to draw in tourists also celebrated Founder's Day in mid-June, Bastille Day in mid-July, the Blueberry Festival in early August and the Apple Festival in the fall.

Generally speaking, holidays meant nothing more than a lot of extra work for Sean, given the medical emergencies that seemed to pop up whenever a place got crowded and people started partying. By the time Blueberry Festival rolled around, the locals were starting to go a little stir-crazy, Sean included, and in need of letting off a bit of steam. More often than not, the islanders were out and about in full force, letting their summer help take the reins of their respective businesses for the day.

Sean spent a couple hours in the clinic in the morning and then went home to change. On his way out, he stopped to knock on Austin's door. "Austin?"

"Yeah?"

Sean opened the door. "Want to go down to the Blueberry Festival with me?"

"Thanks, but I'm meeting Hunter and Matt down there in an hour. We're going to get some lunch and then hang out."

Sean turned.

"Hey, Sean?"

"Yeah?"

"Thanks for giving me the day off."

"No problem. That's kind of the tradition on the island. Blueberry Festival is the one day all summer the locals take off."

"And I'm a local?"

Sean grinned. "You bet."

"You're still on call, though, aren't you?"

"No rest for the wicked." Sean smiled. "See you later."

"You know, maybe I will come with you." Austin hopped up. "I can hang around down there until Matt and Hunter show up."

"Great."

The Blueberry Festival was organized by Mirabelle's Chamber of Commerce, so along with the typical food stands and craft booths, there was also quite a bit of fundraising going on with a bingo tent, games for youngsters like a lollipop wheel and balloon toss, and, Sean's favorite, a dunk tank in which Mirabelle's most visible residents took turns getting wet.

"So where we going first?" Austin asked as they hiked down the hill.

"Dunk tank."

"Who's going to be in it?"

"The real question is who won't be?"

A few minutes later, Sean was standing in front of the tank with three baseballs in his hand. "You're going down," he said, grinning as he wound up to throw his first ball.

"I'll believe it when I see it." Garrett Taylor sat in the tank, dressed in swim trunks and a T-shirt. Somehow he'd managed to stay dry for the first part of his half-hour shift.

Sean threw the first two balls and missed by a hair.

"That all you got?" Garrett said.

"Get ready, Chief. I'm gonna bet that water's cold!" Sean let the ball rip and hit the target dead-on, making Garrett's seat disappear from under him and dropping Garrett into the tank of water.

He emerged from the water, laughing. "That, Dr. Griffin, was a big mistake."

"My turn." Garrett's brother Jesse was grinning from ear to ear as he gave the attendant a five-dollar bill.

"You want fifteen balls?" the young man said.

"Have to do my share donating to the Chamber of Commerce." Jesse chuckled and sank Garrett with his first ball.

"Just remember, bro," Garrett said, coming up for air, "you're going to get as good as you give!"

"I hate to break it to you, Garrett, but you had the worst arm on the south side." Jesse laughed. "We just let you pitch while we were growing up because we felt so sorry for you."

"I'm telling you, Jesse—"

Jesse's throw hit the target, dunking his brother again, and Sean laughed out loud. "Okay, that's it," Garrett called out when he came out of the water. "My shift is over."

"Not so fast, lover boy," Erica said as she approached the tank. "My watch says you got two minutes left."

"Step up to the plate, dearest sister-in-law." Jesse handed her three of his balls.

"If you love me, Rick," Garrett said, drying his face off with a towel, "You'll miss."

"Not a chance," Erica said, whipping out a fastball that would make any coach proud. She missed twice, but hit dead-on with her third ball.

"You guys are crazy," Austin said, shaking his head.

"Yeah." Sean loved this island. He loved the people—most of them, anyway. "But it's a good crazy." He glanced over at his son and took the opportunity to squeeze him quickly around the shoulders. Surprisingly, Austin didn't pull away.

WEARING ONE OF THE DRESSES—a dusty green in a soft modal fabric—Suzy had made from Grace's design, a light scarf, wide-brimmed hat and a large pair of sunglasses, Grace walked down Main, enjoying the warm summer sun on her cheeks, the sounds of laughter and conversation. Even the jostling crowds felt good today, and so far she'd remained entirely anonymous.

She bought herself a frosty tap beer and some fried cheese curds, two things that never would've passed through her lips during her modeling days, and wandered by the booths. Before long, she saw Austin standing in the midst of a group of teenagers. The moment he saw her, he waved.

"Hey, Austin."

"I'll catch up with you guys at the ninth hole in a little bit." He broke away from a group of both boys and girls and came toward her.

"The ninth hole? You guys golfing today?"

"No, we go there and play foosball sometimes." He looked away. "Don't tell Sean, but Hunter and Matt figured out where their dad keeps the keys to the vending machines in the small clubhouse at the far end of the course."

"Free soda and snacks."

"Exactly."

"You don't need to leave your friends," she protested, as she caught a young woman eyeing Austin.

"It's cool. Besides, you've got cheese curds."

With a smile, she held the basket toward him.

He grabbed a couple and they walked side by side down Main. "Someone should've told me sooner that summers on Mirabelle are one big party after another."

She laughed.

"So what do you think now?" he asked, munching on a curd. "Now that you've been back awhile. Did you make the right decision all those years ago in leaving Mirabelle?"

"Interesting question. On one hand, I can't imagine having stayed. But on the other hand, this place feels different to me today. I can appreciate the island so much more now than I could back when I was a kid."

"Do you think you might stay?"

"I just might." She glanced at him, studying his face. "What about you? Have you changed your mind?"

He snorted.

"I know you think Sean can't wait for you to leave, but I think you're wrong."

"He never wanted kids, remember? He doesn't want me here. He only agreed to take me because he thought I'd be able to help with the horses."

"You sure about that?"

"We might be getting along better, but that doesn't mean he wants me to stay."

"Do you want to go back to L.A.?"

"Not really, I guess. There's nothing there for me."

"For what's it's worth," Grace said thoughtfully, "whatever you do, don't run away from L.A. the way I ran away from Mirabelle. I never looked back. Never came home. Didn't do a very good job of keeping in touch with family. Don't make the same mistake. If you decide to leave L.A., do it for the right reasons. Do it because you *want* something else. Not because you can't—or won't—make something else work."

On reaching the city park, Austin pointed. "What's going on here?"

A crowd of locals had gathered, and Missy Abel was pushing her way to the front of the group.

"What's going on?" Grace asked.

"Come on." Missy grabbed her arm and tugged her along. "I promise it'll be good."

Grace couldn't see anything until she reached the front

of the crowd. She glanced around Missy to see Sean in a dunk tank.

Austin laughed. "This is just too good to be true."

He had that right. Water dripped from Sean's overly long dark hair. His cotton T-shirt clung to his chest, revealing every hard, flat plane and muscle. She had to admit the doctor looked damned good wet.

"That enough for you?" Garrett called as he tossed a baseball up and down in his hand.

"Bet you can't do that again," Sean challenged.

"Oh, man, you're asking for it."

Sean had no sooner resettled himself on the dunk tank seat, than Garrett whipped another ball, hitting the target dead center. Sean dropped into the water and came up laughing.

"Payback's a bitch, isn't it, Doc?"

Austin bought three balls. "My turn."

"Bring it," Sean taunted.

Austin dunked him two out of three tries.

"I'm next," Jonas Abel nudged Austin out of the way and dunked Sean twice. Missy even dunked him once.

Grace stepped to the front of the line and bought three balls. It'd been a long time since she'd thrown a ball, but it had to be like riding a bike.

"Oh, oh, Sean," Carl called out. "You're in for it now."

Sean's gaze caught with Grace's and his demeanor turned suddenly serious. "Come on, Grace. Hit me with everything you've got."

"Go, Grace!" Missy called.

She threw her first ball and missed.

"You can do better than that," Sean taunted.

"That was a practice shot." She hit the target dead-on with the next shot and the next.

"Okay, that's it," Sean called when he resurfaced. "My

shift's over." He came out of the tank area, rubbing a towel over his head. "Who's the next sucker?"

"That'd be me," Carl said, smiling as he headed toward the tank.

The line was already forming to take a shot at Carl, but Grace couldn't seem to take her eyes off Sean as he drew the wet shirt over his head and dried off his chest. He caught her gaze on him, but she refused to look away. Tossing the towel aside, he pulled on a dry shirt and made his way through the crowd toward her and Austin.

"Well, I'm off to go play bingo," Austin said.

"Okay, buddy. See you later."

The moment Austin stepped away, Grace said, "Everyone certainly loved getting you wet."

"Must be all that poking and prodding I do all year long in my exam rooms." He came close enough to whisper in her ear. "So do I get a shot at dunking you?"

"Not a chance."

They watched Carl get dunked a few times and then by unspoken agreement, she and Sean slowly drifted away from the crowd.

"Sean! Grace!" Missy waved at them. "Bonfire. Duffy's beach at dusk. Come."

"Will do."

They walked side by side down Main. He grabbed a beer and loaded a brat with every condiment known to man.

"Are you really going to eat that?" she asked as he piled sauerkraut onto the already bulging bun.

"You betcha." He grinned, took a big bite and swiped his mouth with a napkin.

"This really takes me back," she said, glancing out over the crowd. "When I was little this day even more than the other holidays was like a dream come true. My dad would give me twenty bucks first thing in the morning and I'd disappear until dark. The games, rides and treats. Even when I was a teenager, the Blueberry Festival still seemed a bit magical. Do you they still follow the tradition of giving all the locals the day off?"

"As far as I know." He took another bite of brat. "I did. Even hired a medical team from Bayfield to fill in for the day."

"My favorite part was the bonfires at night. It was one of the best days of the year to flirt with boys. I miss those days."

"Hey, what am I? Chopped liver?"

"That's not what I mean." She smiled. "I miss that carefree feeling. The feeling that everything was right in the world."

"Look around," Sean said. "Things look pretty right. At least on Mirabelle."

They spent what was left of the afternoon together, and before Grace knew it, the crowds had thinned and bonfires were being lit down along the shore. Unfortunately, she was all crowded out. "I'm not feeling like Duffy's."

"Ready to call it a night?"

"No." Heaven help her, but she wanted to be alone with Sean. She wanted to throw caution to the wind by turning this wonderful day into an amazing night. She laughed, surprising herself with her thoughts.

"Pretty happy with yourself, aren't you?"

"I just realized that you can come home again. And you can make it better than ever."

"This day has been…almost perfect," he said.

"I think I know what might tip the scale."

He looked into her eyes and, as if he read her every thought, pulled her into the nearest alley. "I hope you mean what I think you mean."

"Kiss me."

He did. Softly, at first. Then he groaned, tilted his head,

and opened his mouth. The first touch of his tongue made Grace arc toward him and wrap her arms around his neck, pulling him closer. He dragged his hand along her side and hesitated at the edge of her breast. "In a minute, I'm going to need a room," he murmured against her lips.

A phone rang.

"Dammit." He took out his cell.

"What is it?"

"Garrett. There's got to be a problem." He answered the call. "Don't tell me I'm needed at the clinic."

Grace couldn't make out Garrett's words, but Sean closed his eyes and shook his head. "Okay. I'll be right there." He disconnected the call. "Several kids were injured messing with fireworks, so the subs are outnumbered. I have to go in." He gave her a swift kiss. "Hold that thought for me, okay?"

"Okay."

Then he took off to his clinic.

The moment he left, though, her idyllic feelings all but dissipated. And when she caught sight of a certain someone she did not want to see, she knew there was no chance of those good feelings returning anytime soon.

The woman turned, caught sight of Grace and blinked. "Grace Andersen! Oh, my God, I can't believe it. I was so hoping I'd see you today."

"Hello, Gail." She'd managed to escape seeing the woman over July Fourth week, but there was no getting away from her now.

"Pam, Ann, Jan, Sybil! Come here quick." The women with Gail came toward them. "I told you she was here on Mirabelle. Now do you believe me? It's Grace Kahill!"

At that, several other heads turned nearby to stare at her. Then the whispering started. A couple of people even took pictures.

"Look," Grace said. "I need to go. It was nice seeing you, Gail."

"But wait!" She grabbed Grace's arm, far too forcefully as far as Grace was concerned. "You have to come with us. We're having a party at my mom's house."

"Some other time." She tried to pull away, but Gail wouldn't let go.

"Grace?" Missy came to Grace's side.

Thank God. And Sarah and Erica.

"Hi, Gail," Missy said. "I think I heard Grace say she needed to go."

"I *know* that's what I heard." Erica pulled Gail's hand off Grace.

"Go," Sarah whispered.

"Thank you." Grace glanced back to see Missy, Sarah and Erica all blocking Gail's path. Sean had been so right about these people. For the first time in a very long while, she felt safe. She felt like one of Mirabelle's own again.

CHAPTER EIGHTEEN

HOPING HE MIGHT FIND GRACE AT the bonfire behind Duffy's, Sean went to the beach the moment he finished at the clinic. Grace was nowhere to be found, and feeling oddly disconnected from his friends, he left not long after he'd joined the group. When a short walk through town didn't clear his head, he took off up the hill, decided to throw caution to the wind and stopped at Grace's house. She didn't answer the doorbell, so he knocked.

"Grace?" He knocked again. "Grace, it's Sean."

A dim light shone from the kitchen and another one from somewhere upstairs. Either she wasn't home and had left on a couple lights, or she didn't want to see him.

Frustrated, he took the short cut to his house. The moment he cleared the woods, he noticed a light on in the livery barn. She was there with Louie. He should've known.

Walking into the barn, he went straight to Louie's stall. Louie was out in the paddock area, standing in the moonlight sleeping. The horse ignored him when he opened the stall door and found Grace sound asleep in the clean hay. Curled on her side, her hand under her cheek, she looked as peaceful as he'd ever seen her. Her lips were parted and he could just make out the tip of her tongue. Her dress, a short, cottony type thing, had inched up on her thigh, revealing a narrow strip of her bottom curved toward him in almost sinful invitation.

What did she have on under that dress? Anything? Like a sucker punch to the gut, Sean was hit with a surge of desire unlike anything he'd ever known. He wanted her, and yet the need to protect and care for her ran strong.

Running a hand over his face, he took a deep breath. "Grace? Wake up." When she didn't open her eyes, let alone move, he knelt and lightly touched her arm. "Grace."

Still, no reaction.

Reaching out, he plucked some straw from her hair. Glutton for punishment that he was, he reached down and ran his fingertips along her side, the edge of her thigh, along skin as soft as Boss's muzzle. Then he leaned forward, brushed back her hair and kissed her neck.

Finally, she stirred. Rather than waking fully and pushing him away, she covered his hand and drew it from her side down, over the flat of her stomach. Then she made a small noise, half whimper, half groan, pressed his hand between her thighs and pulsed.

"Grace," he groaned, his erection pushing painfully against his jeans. "My God, wake up."

"Which one of us is dreaming?" she murmured.

"Neither. This is very real."

"Good." Slowly, lazily, she turned onto her back and opened her eyes. "I want you."

"You're still asleep."

"Oh, I'm awake all right."

"Grace—"

"Kiss me." Reaching up, she cupped his neck and pulled him down toward her.

For a moment, he resisted, but the lure of her lips and her sweet tongue was too much. Groaning, he pressed his mouth to hers. Their tongues clashed. Her nose smashed against his as she pulled him down on top of her. It felt so good to have her under him, but it wasn't enough. Running his hands down her torso, he felt her curves, but not her. He wanted bare skin, his against hers.

She bent a knee, baring her thigh and Sean, hungry for the feel of her, ran his hand along her leg. Her inner thigh was warm and as soft as a feather, but he wanted more. When he fisted the skirt of her dress and started to lift it off, she stilled his hands. "No."

"I want to feel you." He moaned in frustration. "See you."

She answered by kissing him, rolling him onto his back, and pinning down his arms with her knees. He was hers as she bent over him, licked and kissed his neck, his mouth. All the while her hands roved over his chest and along his arms. Then she sat back, rocking her hips against him.

He'd never seen her look more beautiful than in that moment. Her hair a wild, windblown mass of blond curls. Her lips parted. Her breasts moving up and down with each quick breath. He dipped his fingers under her dress, felt the warmth of her skin and moved upward to unsnap her bra. She closed her eyes as he cupped her breasts, rubbing her nipples with the pads of his thumbs.

"Let me see you." He started lifting off her dress. "All of you."

"I'm not ready for that," she said, half moaning as if in pain. "This will have to do." She stood, slipped off her thong, a lacy scrap of almost nothing, and straddled him.

Just the thought of her bare bottom rubbing against him made him groan. "You know this is what I want," he groaned. "But you? Grace, are you sure?"

"I've never wanted anything as much as I want you right now." Her eyes dark with need, she unzipped his fly. Then she dragged her hand down his boxers, freeing his erection. She poised herself over him.

"I'd like to savor this moment," he whispered, resting his forehead against hers. "But I just flat-out can't." The moment he came in contact with her sweet, wet center, he pressed her hips down as he thrust upward into her.

Moaning, she met him, taking him inside in one swift movement. He thrust into her and a pleasure so intense it was almost painful rushed through him. She was so tight, so wonderfully slick and tight. "Grace," he breathed, holding her hips still while he took a deep breath and struggled for control.

"Oh, no, you don't." She rocked against him. "I want this, and I want it now." She moved fast. Faster. When she cried out, the sounds of her pleasure all but swallowed by the night, her orgasm tightened around him like a slick, velvet glove and what little remained of his control snapped.

"Oh, Grace," he groaned as he pulsed out his own release. "Grace!" And, finally, he let himself go. Hard against her.

She cried out again and he drove into her, over and over, drawing out her orgasm. Finally, she collapsed on top of him and he held her tight, needing to feel every last ripple of her climax, wanting to make this last for as long as possible.

That was the most powerfully charged sex he'd ever had. He should've been at least content if not ecstatic. He was a guy. It didn't need to mean anything. But what he'd just shared with Grace meant more than something. It meant everything. To him, at least.

Without pulling away from her, he rolled them over, felt her slickness tightening around him and he was rock hard all over again. He moved against her softly, slowly, and felt her need building again. As he moved against her and watched her face, a sinking feeling in his gut grew more and more real.

Making love with Grace may very well have been the single biggest mistake of his life, but if this was going to hurt, he might as well seal the deal. He stopped and gripped her face with one hand and gently turned her face toward him.

Her eyes flew open. "What?" she said, breathless.

"You asked me not long ago what I want from you," he whispered. "Heading home from Duffy's. Do you remember?"

"Yes."

"At the time, I didn't entirely understand what I was feeling. Now I know. I want *you*, Grace. In every possible way. I want your body. I want your time. Your smiles. Your anger. Your tears. Every second of every day. I want everything from you. Every possible thing a woman can give a man."

For a moment, she said nothing. Her gaze skittered away from his face and he knew before she opened her mouth that she was going to, basically, chew him up and spit him out.

"I can't do that," she said, breathing hard. "I can't give you everything, but I can give you now. Right now." Then she rocked beneath him. She ran her hands along his sides, and then her fingers were in his hair, pulling him toward her.

His body was ready to comply all over again, but his heart said otherwise. He jerked away. "That's not enough. Not for me."

"This—this—is not enough?" She spread her legs wider, pulsed harder against him. "Then you're asking for too much."

"Or are you offering too little?"

She turned her head away. "I'm not ready, Sean. Not yet. I'm not sure if I ever will be ready for what you want from me. I…can't."

"Yes. You can." He kissed her again, but she pulled away from him. "I won't be another Jeremy in your life."

"That's what you think I want?"

"Maybe. Without realizing it. Someone who won't ask for too much. Someone you can keep at arm's length."

"What I just shared with you was more than I ever shared with Jeremy in all those years of my marriage to him." Without another word, she rolled away and snatched up her thong. A moment later she was running out of the barn.

"What are you afraid of, Grace?" he called after her. "It's my heart that'll be broken. Not yours."

HIS HEART, ALONE, BROKEN?

"I wouldn't be too sure about that," Grace said to herself as she ran off through the woods to her house. Her heart had most assuredly been involved in what had just happened between them. To what extent, she had no clue. These feelings she had for Sean were so different from anything she'd ever experienced. So frightening and wild. So wonderous and confusing. She couldn't begin to understand what it all meant.

One thing, though, was perfectly clear. Sean wanted a wife, a woman with whom to share the rest of his life. She, on the other hand, was just now rediscovering herself. She wasn't ready for happily ever after.

CARL KNEW SOMETHING WAS WRONG the moment he stepped through the back door and into the kitchen. Suddenly, he regretted leaving the festival early to get some work done at the lodge. Carol was sitting at the kitchen counter, her head in her hands, her skin as white as a sheet.

"What happened?" He set his laptop bag down on the counter. That's when he noticed a phone number scribbled across the piece of paper lying in front of her. "Did something happen with one of the kids?" he asked, trying to stay calm. "Are they okay?"

Her expression was oddly unreadable. "They're fine. They're at a bonfire downtown."

"You okay?"

"I couldn't believe it," she murmured. Her eyes misted

with tears, and she looked away. "Didn't want to believe it, I guess."

"Believe what? Carol? What's going on?" But he knew. He knew.

She glared at him. "Who is it?"

"Who is who?"

"The woman."

Like a kid caught with hands in the candy jar, all he could think to do was lie. "What woman? You're not making sense."

She thrust the paper in front of him. "Who's the woman who belongs to the voice on the other end of this cell phone number?"

"I don't know whose number that is."

"Don't lie to me, Carl. Don't make it any worse than it already is." She stood and paced. "You were acting so strange the other night in your office. Since when has a guest complaining bothered you enough to bring it home?"

He racked his brain trying to find an explanation, an excuse. Anything.

"Initially, I let it go," she went on. "After all the years we've been together, I know you. I trust you. I figured whatever was going on was something you needed to deal with alone." She turned away and put her face in her hands. "But then I started thinking. I didn't want to be a fool. I didn't want to be the last one to know."

Son of a bitch.

"So I did something I never thought I'd do," she said. "I pulled your phone records to see who you were talking to that night I came into your office. The number never showed the previous several months, but appears recently quite a few times. Every day. I know. I looked. I dialed it."

There was no explaining this away.

"Who is it?"

"I'm not having an affair, Carol. You have to trust me on this."

"Trust you. Trust you! Are you insane? Whether you call it an affair or not, you have...something going on with another woman."

He ran his fingers through his hair, feeling as if his life was unraveling at the seams, but then he realized he didn't deserve this. He'd been faithful for all these years. He'd never once cheated. This wouldn't have happened if she'd paid just a little more attention to him.

"All right. Fine," he said, turning on her. "You want to know the truth. Here it is. Yes, I've been with another woman. I was lonely. Lonely, Carol."

She swallowed.

"But then you wouldn't know what that feels like, would you?" Suddenly angry, he jabbed his fingers through his hair. "She turns me on. She pays attention to me."

"So this is my fault? You had sex with another woman and I'm to blame?"

He looked away. "That's not what I meant. I meant that I feel...wanted when I'm around her. Besides, it's only happened a couple times."

"Only a couple of times. As if that makes it all okay?"

"I've never cheated on you before, and it'll never happen again. I swear."

"So I'm supposed to let it go? Is that what you're saying?"

"No. It's just...the first night that it happened...it'd been a bad day at work. I'd had a martini. Another one with a burger. The third one...was a mistake. Started talking to her, and before I knew it I was in the bathroom. It all happened so fast."

"And the second time? The third time? The time after that?" Carol shook her head. "Who is it?"

"What's the point?"

"I want to know."

"Carol, it's not her fault. It's mine. I—"

"Oh, I know you're at fault. Don't think for one second that I'm blaming her. But I *will* know what woman on Mirabelle thought you were fair game. Tell me right now, Carl, or so help me God—"

"Sherri Phillips."

Carol shook her head as a sad, soft chuckle escaped her mouth. "I should've guessed. But I never thought you'd—"

"Carol, don't do this—"

"Leave," she said.

He glared at her. "This is my house. I work my ass off paying for the mortgage."

"Well, now it's my house, Carl. Leave."

"Carol, don't do this. I'm sorr—"

"Don't!" she yelled. "Don't you dare apologize. Leave this house right now and don't even think of coming back."

Indignation rose in his gut like a volcano. "You can't do this. You can't kick me out of my own house."

"I didn't break our vows," she threw at him. "And if you don't leave this minute, I swear to God, I will tell the kids what you've done. Then we'll see who goes and who doesn't."

He grabbed his laptop and stalked toward the door. "This isn't over."

"No," she said. "Not yet. But it will be soon."

CHAPTER NINETEEN

INTENSELY AWARE OF GRACE walking into the barn and stopping the moment she noticed he and Arlo working to replace a carriage wheel, Sean kept his gaze focused on the job at hand. She wanted space, and he'd give it to her. In fact, he'd avoided her as much as possible since they'd made love in Louie's stall just a few measly feet from where he now stood. And she'd been avoiding him.

God, he missed her. The realization settled with a sickening feeling in his gut. He missed everything about her, her face, her voice, her laugh, watching her riding Louie, working with Austin or simply walking across the yard in jeans and riding boots.

"Hello there, Grace," Arlo said. "Haven't seen you around much lately."

"I've been busy," she said. "Dad's thinking of downsizing, so he's clearing out the attic."

She looked good, as if she'd gotten some sun, and the neckline of her shirt was unbuttoned, exposing a sliver of her chest and even a little cleavage. He forced his gaze away.

"Is it okay if I let Louie out in the main pasture today with the rest of the horses?"

Arlo raised his eyebrows at Sean.

"Sure," Sean said without turning toward her again. "He could probably use the company."

"Thank you." She grabbed Louie's lead and went into his stall.

"What the heck is going on with you two?" Arlo muttered. "She walks into the barn, you leave. She leaves the moment you show up. You've both been polite and courteous to a fault. If I didn't know better—" the old man eyed him "—I'd say it was a lover's quarrel. And a doozy at that."

"Don't let your imagination—"

"Sean!" Austin ran into the livery barn, holding the house phone in his hand.

"What is it? What's the matter?" Quickly, Sean stood and wiped his hands on the rag sticking out of his jeans pocket.

"She said she's your sister." Austin handed over the phone as he caught his breath. "And it's urgent."

Sean grabbed the phone. "Vanessa, what's wrong?"

"It's Dad." Her sinuses sounded stuffy, as though she'd been crying.

"What happened? Is he okay?"

"He's alive, Sean, but he's not okay."

Sean turned away from Arlo and Austin and walked out of the barn and into the bright sunlight.

"He was in a car accident," she explained. "On the Santa Monica Freeway."

"Heading to the hospital?" As if it made a difference.

"Yeah. Traffic stalled and he had to break suddenly. A truck was behind him. A semi carrying a full load of new cars." She sucked in a breath. "There's practically nothing left of his Porsche."

"Where is he now?"

"In surgery. At Cedars-Sinai."

Good. Sean's old hospital was the best one in the entire L.A. area. "What was his status before he went in?"

The harsh sound of her breath whooshed over the phone line. "I can't... I don't..."

"Is Stephen with you?"

"Yes," she said.

"What about Rick?"

"He's on his way. So is Dana."

"Who was the E.R. doc?"

"Ellery."

"Good. He's good. What did he tell you after they took Dad into surgery?"

"I don't remember. I can't seem to think straight."

"Van, you're a doctor. Take a deep breath and tell me the extent of Dad's injuries."

There was a long silence over the line. When she spoke, the tone of her voice had changed. She went on to relay medical information in a clinical and unemotional manner. Until the end. "They gave him a ten percent chance of making it out of surgery alive. But…oh, God, Sean, they don't know…"

Tears burned Sean's throat. "It's okay," he said. "It'll be okay."

"No, it won't. You should come. You need to come. Now."

He ran his hands through his hair. What would be the point? Based on what Vanessa had told him, their father could be dead by nightfall.

"I have to go," she said. "Rick just got here."

"Okay," he said softly as the line went silent.

Grace was standing not twenty feet from him. A concerned expression on her face, she was holding Louie's reins. "How long have you been there?"

"Long enough."

He closed his eyes for a moment, ran a hand down his face and took in a deep breath. Then he gave her an abbreviated layman's explanation of his dad's condition. "He might not make it through the night."

"What are you going to do?"

"There's nothing I *can* do."

"You can go. If for no other reason than to be there for

your brother and sister. If you're very, very lucky, you'll have a few moments with your father."

"That's not likely." The physician in him put it in rational terms. "He'll be heavily sedated. He'd never know I was there." Surprisingly, his voice caught.

That's when Grace came forward and wrapped her arms around him. For a moment, he resisted. He didn't care if his dad died, he told himself. He'd cut off ties with the man long, long ago. "We weren't on good terms. You know that."

"Me neither with my mom. I can never get those years back with her. And now that she's gone, I can never make it right."

"I'm not sure I could ever make it right with my dad."

"If I had to do it over again with my mom," she said, "I'd have made peace with her. A long time ago. You still have a chance, Sean. Not to set everything right, but to be there. To do the right thing. If not for him, then for yourself."

The feel of Grace in his arms changed everything. He held her tight, breathed in the scent of her hair, felt her heat seep into his bones and he knew she was right. He had to go.

"Sean?"

Sean stepped away from Grace and turned. Both Arlo and Austin were standing in the barn doorway.

"Is everything all right?" Arlo asked.

"No." He explained the situation. "I'm going out to the hospital to see him." He glanced at Austin. "Did you want to come with me?"

"Why? What for?"

"To meet the rest of my—your—family."

Clearly unsure of the right course of action, Austin glanced from Arlo to Grace. When his gaze connected with Sean's, he asked, "Do you want me to go?"

"It's up to you," Sean said.

Apparently conflicted, Austin looked away. "Then, I don't—"

"On second thought," Sean interrupted. For some reason, he had a feeling this was an important event for him and Austin. An opportunity to turn something bad into something good. "I'd like you to come, Austin. You're *my* family, and I'd like you to be with me."

Austin's face immediately cleared. "Okay," he said. "When do we leave?"

"Right now. Go pack a carry-on bag as quickly as you can. You forget anything we'll buy it out there." As Austin headed for the house, Sean glanced at Arlo.

"Don't worry about this place," Arlo said. "Me and Grace." He winked at her. "We got things covered."

Sean turned to Grace. Suddenly, there was so much he wanted to say to her.

"Go," she whispered.

Not trusting himself to say another word, he turned and focused on getting to L.A. as quickly as possible.

SEAN WALKED THROUGH THE automatic doors to the Cedars-Sinai hospital feeling as if he'd never left. The smells, the sounds, the harried staff hustling about, the worried looks on all the strangers' faces. Nothing had changed.

"This is the hospital where I worked," Sean said.

"It's big," Austin said. "Do you miss it?"

"Not really."

Surprisingly, he and Austin had enjoyed several quality conversations about life and death and everything in between during the time they'd spent traveling from Wisconsin to California. They were finally completely comfortable around each other.

"So where are going?" Austin asked.

"One of the ICUs."

The moment he and Sean had stepped off the plane, Sean had called Vanessa for an update. Their father was alive and out of surgery, but his prognosis was, basically, horseshit. Avoiding the E.R. so as not to have to smile and chat with all his old coworkers, Sean took Austin directly to the ICU where his father, Austin's grandfather, was located.

The elevator door opened and Sean mentally prepared himself. *You've seen all this before. Including more death than anyone should ever have to witness. This is no different just because it's Dad. No different.*

With Austin by his side, Sean walked down the hall and immediately spotted his siblings along with their spouses sitting in chairs around a hospital bed. Vanessa glanced up, burst into tears and ran toward him. As he folded her into his arms, he held Rick's tear-filled gaze.

"I told him you were coming," Van said.

Never in a million years would Sean have believed he'd cry in this instance, but a few tears somehow managed to slip off his lashes before he gathered himself. Over his sister's shoulder, he glanced at the man in the hospital bed. That pale, weak-looking body couldn't possibly be his father. His father, a vital workaholic even at fifty-eight years old, ran five miles twice a week, dated thirty-year-old women, and managed the cardiology department at this very hospital.

Surreal, that's what this was. Maybe there was a difference when a member of your own family lay dying in the hospital bed.

"How's he doing?" Sean asked, as Vanessa stepped away.

"He's alive." She swiped at her cheeks. "Barely."

Rick gave him a hug, one of those brief man-type hugs including a couple pats on the back. "I'm glad you came."

Sean politely greeted his in-laws, Dana and Stephen, two

people he barely knew, and then turned to Austin, putting a hand on the boy's shoulder. "This is my son, Austin."

Based on the lack of surprise at that introduction, Sean figured Vanessa had told everyone about Austin after their phone conversation.

"I'm glad you came," Vanessa said, smiling at Austin. "It's good to meet you."

"You have cousins, you know," Rick added. "They're all about your age."

"Yeah, that's what Sean said."

While Vanessa, Rick and their respective spouses talked with Austin, Sean turned his attention to the readings on all the equipment hooked up to his father. He grabbed the chart at the end of the bed and read through all the notes. In the end, the conclusion was unavoidable. The doctors had done all they could for the man in this hospital bed and his life was out of modern medicine's hands. There was a short lull in the conversation and Sean glanced from his brother to his sister.

"He's going to fight this, you know." Vanessa squeezed his arm.

"I know."

"Talk to him, Sean," she said. "We've all had our chance. You, too, Austin." Then she walked away.

Before he knew it Rick, Dana and Stephen had all disappeared and Sean and Austin were alone with Sean's father—what was left of the man, in any case.

Sean sat in a chair close to the bed and looked into his father's pale, lifeless face. The respirator pumped oxygen into his father's lungs, the heart monitor beeped, and the ebb and flow of the ICU hummed around him. Still, he didn't know what to say, what to do.

"You should know, Austin, that your grandfather is a pioneer in the field of cardiac research. You'd find his name on any number of famous studies."

"But you two didn't get along."

"No. I think if my mother had lived, there may have been hope for me and my dad." He'd been eight when the buffer between him and his father had disappeared. Even at that young age, he'd known it had been a life-changing event. "It was all downhill from there between me and him." He glanced at Austin. "I'd like things to be different between us."

"Me, too," Austin said.

They held each other's gazes for a moment, but then things turned awkward. "If you want to go, you can. Go find Vanessa and Rick."

"You sure? I'll stay with you, if you want."

Sean smiled. "It's okay. I could use a few minutes alone with him."

As Austin walked away, Sean gently took his father's hand between both of his and warmed the skin. "Dad," he said, "I'm not going to lie. Your body took a beating, but you already know that, don't you? I can't do anything to save you," Sean whispered. "And Rick and Van have done all they can." He felt a slight squeezing pressure from his father's fingertips, but it was probably nothing. "You need to know. I have a son I never knew about. You have another grandson. His name's Austin. He looks like me. And a little like you."

Sean swallowed. The past couple of months had given him some perspective on fatherhood and, for the first time in his life, he had some small amount of appreciation for his own dad. Mistakes or not, maybe the man had done the best he could.

"Austin's pretty damned smart, too, so I...get it. Okay. The part where you want your kids to do the best they can. To be the best they can." He sighed, gripped his father's hand a bit tighter. "And I met someone. A woman..." Sean laughed. "I don't know where it's going, but it's a start."

He ran his fingertips along his father's face. "In spite of all our differences, Dad, I appreciate all you've done for me. I'm not sure I've ever said this before, and I'm sorry for that. I love you. I know you love me."

CHAPTER TWENTY

GRACE ROLLED OVER IN BED, marginally aware it was morning. The image of a silk jacquard dress, black like Louie, long like his tail and mane, with patterns in the fabric similar to the ornate tooling on the leather of one of Louie's saddles, lingered in her dreams. Her eyes popped open. That was it, the inspiration for her new collection. Something she'd been struggling to discover since Suzy had asked her for a spring and summer line.

She threw back the covers and reached for a sketch pad. Quickly, she outlined everything she could remember about the dress. The simple neckline, the asymmetrical hemline, the waist gathered with a buckle not unlike a girth strap.

Variations on this main theme raced through her mind and she couldn't get them down on paper fast enough. One after another, she sketched quickly, afraid she might lose the images. By the time she was finished, she had twenty new designs in various stages of completion to add to the dozen or so she'd already prepared these past few weeks, and she hadn't even left her bed.

She laid all of her designs out on the bedroom floor and soon realized that these were even better than the first set she'd sent to Suzy. Her confidence was building. She'd taken more risks. Although this meant she was opening herself up to the occasional flop, she was also experiencing much more satisfaction with the process. She could do this. She *liked* doing this.

She'd like it a whole lot more, though, if Sean were here. Sighing, she gathered the designs, set them on her bedside table and a gloomy mood swept over her. He'd been gone six days, and nearly every single moment of every single day had dragged on like an eternity for Grace. She'd gone through the motions of her new life on Mirabelle, taking care of her father, helping Arlo, working on her designs, eating and sleeping, but she was always intensely aware that something on Mirabelle had changed.

She missed Sean. The way he looked at her. The way he made her feel about herself, both strong and sexy at the same time. Even something as simple as the dark silhouette of his lean body coming through the livery barn door. She missed everything that was at once wonderful and irritating about him. And she was worried about him and how things were going with his family, had actually wished a time or two that she could've been with him. Although she had a feeling Austin returning to L.A. with Sean was the best thing that could've ever happened to their developing relationship.

Was this love? This aching rawness? This feeling of something lying unfinished in her life? She went to bed every night thinking she'd forgotten to do something that day. She woke every morning, the hours yawning in front of her like empty pages in a book. It had to be because Sean was gone. Were they just friends or was this something more?

The answer eluding her, she opted, instead, for keeping busy and starting her day. She turned on the shower, but even after the water warmed she couldn't seem to make herself step under the harsh spray. She needed pampering this morning. She needed a bubble bath.

The decision made, she filled the tub, dumping a liberal amount of her favorite scented salts. Then she dipped in her toes, testing the temperature and finally sank deep into the water. The bath felt wonderful. For the first time in a long while, she lingered, letting her fingers and toes wrinkle and her muscles relax. When she climbed out of the tub, she took time drying herself off. Then she slathered her favorite lightly scented lotion over her body.

Reaching for her shoulder with a dollop of cream, she stilled over the scar. It was odd the way she couldn't feel her own hand over the numb tissue, and without glancing in the mirror to see what she was doing she was never quite sure if she adequately covered the area.

Taking a towel, she wiped off the condensation on the mirror and studied her entire body. She analyzed herself as she imagined designers had done when deciding on what styles to drape over her frame. She needed a haircut. No doubt about that. She'd gained weight, and surprisingly liked the way it looked on her. Her breasts were a bit heavier, her face less gaunt and her skin looked healthier than ever. Only that ugly scar marred her appearance.

Get used to it, Grace. This is you.

She fingered the jagged edges, the twists and turns that looked not unlike the bays and peninsulas on a topographic map of a massive lake. It wasn't pretty by any means, but was it entirely repulsive? Something about it seemed...somehow... fascinating at the moment.

In the past, she'd dieted, she'd exercised and she suffered through too many pairs of too high-heeled shoes. She'd let makeup artists put things on her face, lips, eyes and eyelashes that seemed garish, if not downright hideous. She'd endured stylists tugging, pinning and ratting her hair in the most un-natural shapes. She'd done all that willingly for her career. All that in the name of what others defined as beauty.

Well, her career was over. She was done pleasing others. She smiled at herself and smoothed the lotion onto her scar. Her fantastic scar. It was time to be kind to herself, to be kind to the body that had been kind to her for so many years.

Slipping on a bra and panties, she pulled out an old favorite T-shirt made in the softest silk jersey. Heather-gray with a deep V-neck, she'd loved it because it was comfortable and draped nicely, the fabric as soft as down. She hadn't worn it since the accident. Pulling the shirt over her head, she glanced at her reflection. Her scars clearly showed on her arm and up on her chest and collarbone. It wasn't a bikini, by any means, but it *was* a start.

When her doorbell rang, she froze. This was it. Was she ready to show the world her scars? Yes. She could do this. She *had* to do. Marching purposefully down the stairs, she took a deep breath and opened the door.

A delivery man stood on her front porch, holding two packages. "Grace Kahill?" he asked, but the look in his eyes stated clearly he knew very well who was at the door.

"Yes."

That's when his gaze left her face and traveled over her skin. In a split-second, he took in the scars showing on her arm and chest. Then he blinked. That was all. Blinked. He smiled ever so slightly as his gaze returned to her face. "Can you sign for these?"

And that was that.

"Of course." She signed the log sheet and took the boxes from him. Champagne and something else, she thought, based on the size and shape of one box, but who? Why?

"Have a good day, Grace."

"Thank you. You, too." She smiled and went inside. One box did indeed hold a bottle of champagne, Dom Pérignon to be exact. In the other box she found a card from Jeremy.

If you're not indulging yourself these days, you should be. Heard from Suze that I can expect some competition. Welcome back to the fray, darling.

Inside were not one dozen, but two of the most extravagantly decorated chocolate-covered strawberries Grace had ever seen. He was wrong, though. She wasn't truly back, not yet. She called Amanda.

"Grace, hi. What can I do for you?"

"Can you call *Vogue* and my agent and tell them I'll talk about doing a story?"

"Seriously?"

"Yeah, but make sure they understand I won't do a back in the saddle thing." She had no interest whatsoever in returning to modeling. She was going to have her hands more than happily full designing clothes for Suzy. "This has to be something different." Something more real. More freeing. And, yes, a bit more frightening. She wanted to talk about the white elephant in the room. Her body, damaged but still lovely. "This is about an entirely new Grace. Scars and all."

"Good," Amanda said, her voice a little teary. "I can't wait to meet the new Grace."

They talked about details for a few minutes before Grace hung up. She popped one of the strawberries into her mouth and delighted in the combination of rich, dark chocolate and sweet, juicy berries. But she'd never be able to eat all these berries while they were still fresh.

She picked up the boxes and, following her instincts, walked down to the village. The moment she entered Whimsy, Missy waved her into the back room. "Grace! You're just in time for some lunch. Can you join us?"

She would face these women who could be friends. "Absolutely." Knowing she'd been too far away for Missy to see her scars, Grace followed Missy and greeted Erica and Sarah. Now that she was close to all three of them, there wasn't a chance they wouldn't see her scars.

Funny. She'd been prepared to talk about the proverbial white elephant in the room, but now that she was here, no words would come. She hesitated, almost turned to leave.

"Are they still painful?" Missy asked softly. "Your scars?"

Grace let go of the breath she'd been holding and smiled gratefully at Missy. "No," she said.

"So no more compression bandages?" Sarah said. "I mean, compression shirts or whatever you had to wear." She apparently knew something about bad burns, given what Jesse had gone through with his hands.

"Nope. No more compression garments."

"I have no clue what you're talking about," Erica said. "But it's nice to see a little more of you, Grace. Not that you need to go all *Vogue* on us, or anything."

Everyone chuckled.

"Okay, let's eat," Missy said.

"Salad," Sarah said, opening a large take-out container.

"Lasagna from Duffy's," Erica took a thermal container out of her bag. "Vegetarian, of course."

"And I've got dessert covered," Grace added.

"What is it?" Sarah asked.

Grace opened the box.

"Nummy!" Erica grinned.

"And this?" Missy tapped the box containing the champagne.

The presentation of the expensive bottle was met with appreciative sighs.

"Who sent these to you?"

"My ex-husband." Grace popped the cork. "Tell me you have glasses."

Missy produced four paper cups. "Will these do?"

"For Dom Pérignon?" Sarah raised her eyebrows.

"Why not?" Grace poured out four bubbly cups.

"What are we celebrating?" Sarah asked.

Grace smiled. "The car accident that gave me these scars!"

The other three women sobered.

"Really?" Missy asked.

"Really," Grace said. "Without it, I'd still be married to Jeremy, living in L.A. and hating it."

"Well, in that case," Erica said, "to change."

"Hear, hear." Sarah raised her glass.

"Something to which the three of us have been intimately acquainted."

"I had that feeling." Grace looked from one woman to the other as they all took a sip of champagne.

"So pull up a chair," Missy said. "I hope you've got a couple hours."

"That I do." Grace sat, grabbed a paper plate and scooped out some piping hot lasagna. "That I do." With Sean gone, the last thing she wanted to do was go home to an empty house.

"Have you heard from Sean?" Missy asked, as if she'd read Grace's thoughts.

"No." Grace glanced around the table. "Have any of you heard from him?"

"I have this feeling." Missy's smile was soft, sweet. "He'd call you before he'd call any of us."

Sean had made it clear before he'd left what he'd wanted from her. What, exactly, did she want from him?

AFTER A VALIANT STRUGGLE, Sean's father died in the middle of the night about a week after Sean and Austin had arrived in L.A. Sean and his siblings were all by their father's side when he took his last breath. Sean hadn't known what to expect with regard to his feelings. The numbness, though, took him by surprise.

The funeral was held a few days later, giving plenty of time for notices to be made in every possible news source. Dr. Richard Griffin had been a well-known member of the greater Los Angeles community, so Sean's sister and brother wanted an appropriate memorial. Hundreds, possibly even thousands, of people came to pay their respects. Friends, colleagues, even past patients and their families whose lives Sean's father had touched in one way or another.

While Austin was off connecting with his cousins, Sean stood in a reception line for an interminable amount of time, greeting people he, for the most part, didn't know and didn't care to know. It was worth it for Vanessa.

"He saved my son's life."

"He was a brilliant physician."

"The hospital will miss his expertise."

"My wife wouldn't be alive today if it wasn't for your father."

By the time it was all finished, Sean had heard every variation of accolade possible about his father's life as a doctor. What he hadn't heard was that his father had been a good friend, a kind and compassionate man, a lover. He was struck by the realization that while his father had been often respected, sometimes feared and always valued for his medical expertise, Richard Griffin hadn't been loved. At least he hadn't experienced, since Sean's mother's death, the love of one woman or the love of a close-knit family.

His father hadn't experienced the one thing that Sean now more than ever wanted in his life. Sean's life had been almost perfect. The only thing he'd been missing was someone with whom to share all that perfection. Two someones, as a matter of fact. Grace and Austin.

The funeral was over and the cemetery was all but deserted. Sean and Austin stood side by side over the grave, and what hit Sean more than anything was how much he missed Mirabelle. His horses. Arlo. More than anything, he missed Grace. Life was too short. When he got back to Mirabelle, he had a few things to say to Grace and she wasn't going to like one word of it.

He glanced at Austin, his son. "I'm ready to go home. You?"

"Yeah."

With one last look at his father's headstone, he turned and they headed to the car. "Do you want to see your mom again before we leave?" Sean asked.

Austin had spent a couple of hours with his mom and siblings at their house the previous day.

"No." Austin walked slowly beside Sean. "I actually kind of miss Mirabelle."

"I was thinking the same thing."

"Grace said she kinda liked growing up there."

Where that thought had come from, Sean had no clue.

"She's even thinking about staying for good."

Sean held his breath, didn't trust himself to speak. If Grace stayed, then what? "You mean she's thinking of living on Mirabelle?"

"Yeah."

"Did she say why?"

Austin chuckled. "No."

"Did she say anything about me?"

"What is this? Junior high?"

Sean laughed. "Stupid, I know. You'd think us adults would have it all figured out, huh?"

"She likes you. Isn't that all you need to know?"

"Yeah, I suppose."

A long moment of companionable silence filled the air.

"What if..." Austin hesitated.

Sean stopped beside the car they'd rented. Something inside him said this might be important. He needed to pay attention.

"What if..." Austin said. "I didn't want to come back to L.A.?"

Sean held his breath, waited.

"What if I wanted to stay on Mirabelle?"

"With me?" Sean asked. "You mean live with me?"

Austin nodded.

Sean racked his brain for the right things to say. All these weeks of them jockeying back and forth, arguing and then connecting, seemed to come down to this moment. Why was being a father—being a *good* father—so damned hard?

"Oh, forget it," Austin said, turning away. "Never mind."

"Wait a minute." Sean touched his son's shoulder. His son. God, would he ever get used to having a son?

Austin stopped, but kept his head down.

"You caught me off guard, Austin. I guess I never imagined, especially after the way things started between us, that you might want to live with me. Permanently. On Mirabelle." He swallowed, trying his best to gauge Austin's thoughts. "But if you want to stay…I mean really *want* to stay…I'll do my best to make it happen."

Austin spun around. "Yeah, but do *you* want me to stay, Dad?"

Sean felt his throat constrict with emotion. There was one thing he'd never felt from his father throughout his entire childhood. The man's vulnerability. Richard Griffin had no soft side. No give. Sean could do better. He had to do better.

"Austin, I want you to know that whatever you decide will be okay with me. It needs to be your decision. But I would like nothing better than to have you stay on Mirabelle."

"For real?"

Sean nodded. "I don't have a clue where we go from here. But we'll figure it out. Together."

"What if Mom won't let me stay?"

"You just think long and hard about what you want for yourself. Okay? Let me worry about your mom." That's when

Sean realized that Austin had inadvertently called him Dad. "If I can't convince her…"

"You'd fight for custody?"

"I don't want to have to go that far, Austin, but if that's what it takes I will fight for you." He squeezed his son's shoulder. "Let's go home."

CHAPTER TWENTY-ONE

"WE'RE GONNA NEED A MOVING truck to get all of this to a charity," Grace said, glancing through box after organized box of old clothes, books and household items stored in the basement. Now that they'd finished with the attic, it was time to tackle another project.

Her father stood. "Your mother always did have a hard time throwing things away."

"Why don't you let me hire some movers and arrange to have all this picked up?"

"Sounds good to me."

"Really? You're ready to just get rid of it all?"

He glanced around the storage room. "Life's too short, you know?"

She was beginning to understand that.

"You'll be happy to know that I set up a tee time with Doc Welinski." He smiled. "And I was the one who called him."

He'd turned the corner. She could see it in his eyes. "I'm glad, Dad." She hugged him.

"John? Grace? Hello?"

"Carol, what a surprise." Grace smiled as her sister-in-law appeared in the doorway to the basement storage room. "We're just assessing what needs to be done to clear out some old things."

"I'm sorry I haven't been over to help with things. A lot going on at home. I did bring a few casseroles over for you, though, John. Stuck a couple in the freezer and a couple in the fridge."

"Just in time!" John kissed her cheek. "I think I might head over to the putting green and practice a bit before my tee time with Doc Welinski."

"That sounds great, Dad. Have a good time." She and Carol followed him upstairs. The moment he left the house with his golf bag, Grace relaxed. "I think he's doing better."

"I'm sure it's helped having you here," Carol said.

"I hope so, but we've all played a role. Thanks for bringing him meals. He loves your cooking."

"Seems like I have a lot of time on my hands these days," she said, frowning. "The kids are so self-sufficient."

Grace couldn't remember Carol ever looking so down in the dumps. "Carol, is something wrong?"

"I'm all right," she said, but her expression belied her words. Something was weighing on her. "I'm thinking about looking for a job."

"I thought you loved being at home."

"I did. And I thought Carl liked me home, too. Now I'm not so sure."

"Carol?"

"Sometimes things aren't always what they seem, Grace. Did you know that? Take my life, for example. I thought I was happy. I thought everything was perfect." She laughed, the sound just a little off center. "I thought your brother was perfect."

That made two of them.

"He isn't. Not by a long shot."

What?

Carol turned and stalked down the hall.

"Carol, wait." Grace raced after her. "What's going on?"

"Why don't you ask your brother?"

That didn't sound good. For the first time since she'd met

Carol so long ago, Grace experienced some empathy for the woman. It was hard holding up the front of perfection. Grace knew.

"Carol." She stopped her sister-in-law. "I don't know what's going on, but I want you to know that if you need me...I'm here. I mean that."

Carol's eyes pooled with tears. "Thank you, Grace." Then she left the house.

Had Grace still lived in L.A. she wouldn't have had a clue any of this was going on. Even if she had somehow found out about Carl and Carol's having issues she would've never called to talk with him. She'd lived her life. Her family had lived theirs. Well, she wasn't in L.A. any longer, and her brother might actually need her for a change.

Grace left her father's house and walked toward Rock Pointe. She'd only been to the hotel once before, but if she remembered correctly Carl had an office in the main lodge. The moment she entered the lobby, people started staring. One person noticed her and whispered to another, "Grace Kahill." Then another said softly, "Accident." Within minutes, every tourist in the lobby was either outright studying her or surreptitiously following her every move, and for the first time since getting out of the hospital, she realized, she didn't give a damn.

Scars showing or not showing, stare away.

"Carl Andersen's office?" she asked, stopping by the concierge desk.

The young woman swallowed. "Down the hall on the left, Grace. I'll let him know you're here."

Grace was about to head into a glassed-in area clearly housing several administrative offices when a door opened farther down the hall and Carl appeared.

"Grace," he said, "come on down here."

She followed him into a large, rustically decorated corner

office where two walls of windows looked out over the lake and most of his resort. "So this is where you keep your thumb on things, eh?" she said, smiling.

"Yeah."

"It's nice, Carl."

"What are you doing here?"

"A sister can't visit her brother at work?"

"Not without something being wrong."

She took a deep breath and held his gaze. "Carol came to Dad's. She was pretty upset. What's going on between you two?"

"Nothing. At least, nothing that's any of your business."

"Carl—"

"She kicked me out of the house."

"Why?"

"Things haven't been good between us for a while. I suppose it was inevitable."

"Bullshit. Something happened—"

"I was seeing another woman," he blurted out. "Happy now?"

Grace stared at him. "You were having an affair?"

"It wasn't an affair. It was…sex. Just sex. And it only happened a couple of times." Carl turned away from her and went to the windows. He stood as stiff and straight as a board, like a king looking down upon his domain. "It's not like I've been cheating on her for years or anything. It's the first—and only—time all these years we've been married."

The guise of perfection from her brother, she realized, she could handle, but since when had he become so arrogant? So insufferable?

"Carl," she said, "listen to yourself. Not having an affair. It was just sex. Only happened a couple of times." She struggled for the right words, but could find none. "What would Sean say if he were here?"

At that, Carl turned and his eyes grew bright. "He'd kick my ass all the way to Bayfield."

"And Mom? What would she say?"

Tears pooled and suddenly slipped down his cheek.

Finally, some progress. "Do you want a divorce, Carl?"

For a long while, he didn't move, didn't utter a sound.

"Because a divorce is exactly what you're going to get if you don't do something to fix this."

He hung his head. "No. I don't want a divorce. But I don't want things to go on as they did before. I don't know how to start over."

"Do you still love Carol?"

"It's complicated, but I suppose when I get right down to it, yes, I do."

"Then you'll find a way. The very first thing you need to do is take responsibility for screwing up."

"But I didn't—"

"No, Carl! No buts. You are not Mr. Perfect."

No one was perfect. Not Grace. Or her body. She was just a small-town girl wanting to come home. And she wanted Sean.

"Carol's not perfect, either, Carl. I know, but she didn't break your marriage vows. You did. Guess what? You're human. You made a mistake. Now you need to make amends. Not excuses. No more justifications."

He stared at her, seemed to be absorbing, understanding what she was saying.

"She loves you, Carl. She still loves you. If she didn't, this wouldn't have broken her heart. And you did, you know. You broke her heart."

"You're right." He swallowed. "You're absolutely right."

Grace hugged him. For a long time, he held on to her as if he might never let her go. "I'm glad you're home, Grace," he said, stepping back.

"Would you be as glad if I was here to stay?"

"Yeah." He smiled softly. "Welcome home."

"I SCREWED UP," CARL SAID as he faced Nikki and Alex. "Big time."

They were sitting on the couch in the family room and he could do nothing but pace on the other side of the room. Carol sat by herself in the far chair, staring off into space, her face about as impassive as he'd ever seen it. He may have lost her for good. Who would blame her?

Everything Grace had said had been right on, and as he'd fallen down from his high horse, he'd realized that he'd been kidding himself. He had to make a last ditch effort to prove to Carol he was willing to do whatever it took to make things right with her.

"This isn't your mom's fault," he said. "It's mine."

"What did you do?" Alex asked.

"There's another woman, isn't there?" Nikki said. "You had an affair."

Clearly, she'd been looking for her own answers as to why he'd been sleeping down at the lodge and she was old enough to come to conclusions on her own. "It wasn't an affair."

A small scoffing sound came from Carol's direction.

"I saw another woman a couple of times. That's it."

"Did you have sex with her?" Nikki asked.

Carl didn't know what to say, how to stand here in front of his kids and admit the truth and still maintain any shred of integrity.

"Dad? Did you or didn't you?"

But that was it, wasn't it? He didn't have any integrity. Not any longer. And Carol hadn't taken it from him. He'd managed to throw it away all on his own.

"Yes," Carl said, trying his damnedest not to qualify or

excuse in any way shape or form what he'd done. "I had sex with another woman. I had an affair."

They both stared at him for a moment as if they couldn't believe what they'd just heard. How many times had he lectured them about trust? How many times had he set out his expectations as a father that they be honest with him? Didn't they deserve the same commitment from him? For the first time in all of this he realized it hadn't only been Carol whom he'd betrayed.

"That's just sick," Alex said, shaking his head.

"I can't believe it!" Nikki said. "That's not just sick. It's disgusting. How could you do that?" Then she started crying.

"No wonder Mom kicked you out of the house." Alex glared at him, then he focused on Carol. "Are you okay, Mom?"

"No," she said, her eyes turning bright with unshed tears. "But I will be."

Nikki went to Carol and hugged her. Then Alex did the same. They clung to one another for several long minutes. Carl stood there feeling like a scumbag, but then that was no more or less than what he deserved.

"So does this mean you two are getting divorced?" Nikki asked, her expression turning apprehensive. "Is that what this talk is about?"

Carl glanced at Carol. "I don't know." He wouldn't say it was up to Carol. That wouldn't be fair, and he'd been enough of an ass already.

"Well, I'd divorce you." Nikki stalked out of the room and up the stairs.

Alex clearly wanted to leave, but was feeling protective of his mother. Oddly enough, Carl was glad his son cared enough for Carol to be angry at him. In time and with a lot of luck maybe the kids would forgive him.

"Mom," Alex said softly, "did you want me to stay?"

"That's okay, honey. Your dad and I have a few more things to say to one another."

Alex followed his sister upstairs. From the sounds of their movements, both kids had gone into Nikki's bedroom, and then all was quiet. The dishwasher running in the kitchen was the only sound in the room. Suddenly, it struck Carl as one of the nicest, homiest sounds he could imagine.

"I love you, Carol." He swallowed the threatening tears. She didn't deserve to be manipulated by his emotions. He didn't deserve her empathy. "I know I don't do a good job of showing it, but I don't want to throw away what we have."

"You should've thought of that before you had sex with another woman."

"I know. I messed up. Badly. If I could turn back the clock…it wouldn't happen."

"You know…I tell myself that if this had been a one-night stand, that if you'd gotten drunk and this had just happened, I think I could almost, almost forgive once in all these years. But it wasn't once, Carl. You made the decision to break your vows several times."

"There's nothing I can say that will make it right. I'm just going to have to prove it to you. I love you, Carol. And I will spend every day for the rest of my life proving it. Just give me a chance."

"I don't know if I can." Tears streamed down her face. "I don't know if I will ever be able to forgive you."

"Maybe you can't. I wouldn't blame you. But if you don't try we'll never know."

"You broke my heart, Carl. Give me one reason why I should ever trust you with it again."

A reason that didn't seem self-serving? There wasn't one. "I'll live with whatever you decide. Now my heart's in your hands."

CHAPTER TWENTY-TWO

"BIG STORM'S COMING." ARLO glanced toward the southwestern sky.

"I heard," Grace said, following his gaze. The sky was an ominously strange greenish-gray color, the likes of which she hadn't seen since she was a kid.

She'd been at her father's house when a local news bulletin had interrupted his morning program. A massive line of severe thunderstorms was making its way northeast out of Minnesota, bringing with it the certainty of heavy rains and the possibility of damaging winds and tornadoes. Worried about the horses and Louie in particular, Grace had immediately left for the stables.

"Do you need any help getting ready for it?" she asked Arlo as they walked into the livery barn.

"Naw. Don't think so. The horses that won't be working this morning on carriage and trail rides are already out to pasture."

"Is that safest for them?"

"They'll fare better on their own than being stuck in a barn."

"What if there's a tornado?"

"That ain't gonna happen." He shook his head. "We've had bad winds come in off the lake, ripping up roofs, felling trees here and there, but Mirabelle's never been hit by a tornado. The lake protects us. All that cold water. Takes the heat right out of any storm."

"What do you think I should do with Louie?"

"Let him out to pasture with the rest of the horses."

Although there was no rain yet, let alone wind to speak of, already the clouds in the sky seemed to be churning with expectation. A damp chill was in the air and she buttoned her jean jacket. "You sure he'll be all right?"

"Horses can smell what's coming on the wind, Gracie. They're probably better predictors than our radar."

"All right. Anything else you need done around here?"

"Nope. Sean was up early and took care of everything before he went into the clinic."

Grace's heart leaped into her throat. "Sean and Austin are home?"

"Ayep. Got home after midnight is what he said."

"So you saw them?"

"Ayep."

"How is he?"

Arlo grinned. "Sean or Austin?"

She wasn't in the mood for teasing. A tempest was already brewing inside Grace that had nothing to do with the weather. "Sean."

"He looked tired, but okay. All things considered."

It was after lunch. He was likely finished at the clinic. "Where is he now?"

"Catching some shut-eye." Arlo glanced at his watch. "Probably about time for him to wake up, if you ask me."

She looked toward the ranch house.

"Austin's over at the community center with the Stall boys," Arlo said, a smile in his voice. "Probably be there till suppertime. In case you were wondering."

"I wasn't." There was only one male she wanted to see at the moment. Unfortunately, she didn't have a clue what to say.

She went to Louie's stall and walked him across the yard.

After bringing him through the main pasture gate, she kissed his forehead, patted his shoulder and set him free. "Stay safe, Lou."

He snuffled a few times, nodded his head, almost as if he were agreeing with her decision to release him, and then he trotted off to join the other horses. She watched for a moment, making sure he'd settle in. Then she headed to the main house and knocked.

Footsteps sounded from the kitchen a moment before the front door swung open. At once apparently glad to see her and unnerved by her appearance, Sean's face was a mass of conflicting emotions.

She understood. "When did you get home?"

"About two this morning."

"How was it?" she asked, unable to think of anything other than small talk to break the ice. "The funeral, I mean."

"All right, I guess. As funerals go."

"Your sister and brother? They doing okay?"

"Why don't you come in?" Abruptly, he turned away.

Closing the door behind her, she followed him into the kitchen. A plate holding a small corner of what was left of a sandwich sat on the kitchen table. Either finished or unable to eat any more, Sean picked up the plate and brushed the leftovers into the garbage.

"I didn't mean to interrupt your lunch."

"It's okay. I was done." He put the plate in the dishwasher. "Van and Rick are doing okay. Better than I am, anyway."

"When you live so far from your family, dealing with the death of a parent... is harder in many ways. If you're like me, you think, strangely, that time stands still back home. That your parents will always be the same. I forgot my mom was growing older. Then one day, poof, she was gone and reality sank in. Too late."

"That's it. Exactly. I always thought we'd have time. I hung up on him the last time we talked." He looked out through the window over the kitchen sink. "I wish he could've…gotten to know me…for who I am. Instead of wanting me to be someone I'm not."

"He might've lived to one hundred and twenty and never been able to do that," she whispered, going to stand behind him and wrapping her arms around his waist. He was hurting, and all she wanted to do was heal.

She'd thought he might stiffen at her touch. Instead, he put his hands on her arms and leaned into her. The sky darkened and rain, steady but gentle, sounded on the roof and spattered the windows. She spread one hand out over his abdomen and ran her other hand up his chest. He felt so good, warm skin and hard muscle. "I had a lot of time to think while you were gone."

Slowly, he turned within the circle of her arms and looked into her eyes. "And?"

"I missed you." She wrapped her arms around his waist and hugged him, rested her cheek on him.

Suddenly, she sensed a not-so-subtle change in his body. His muscles tensed. His chest rose and fell more rapidly. He tilted his face to her neck. In the blink of an eye, consolation turned to need, comfort to want. "Grace," he whispered against her skin, sending shivers down her spine. "What are you doing to me?"

"I don't know."

"Well, I know where this is going to lead if you don't stop touching me." He groaned and turned his head away. "We've been down this road before. If I remember correctly, you weren't too happy with the outcome."

"Maybe I'm ready for a different outcome." She stepped away, unbuttoned her jean jacket and tossed it over a chair.

When he saw the short-sleeved shirt she was wearing that didn't hide sections of the scars along her arm and neck, he smiled, a slight but sweet curve of his lips. "Austin could come through that front door any minute, or I'd whip that shirt right off you."

"Well, then, you're in luck. He's at the community center with the Stalls. Won't be home for hours."

His gaze darkened as her meaning sank in. Rain pounded harder on the roof. "And it sounds like you're stuck here."

She wanted to touch him, feel him so badly she was shaking. As she trailed her fingertips through the soft, curly hair on his abdomen and up to his chest, her legs nearly gave out. She felt his nipples pebble as she pressed her hands into his hard chest.

Impatiently, he yanked off his own shirt. Then he leaned against the counter and tugged her against him. There was nothing tentative or hesitant about the way their lips met, their tongues collided, their hands explored. Several long, delicious moments later, hungry for more, she reached for the belt buckle on his jeans.

"Oh, no. No, no, no." Sean pulled away and shook his head. "We've already done fast and furious." He brushed his fingers along her cheek, then across her lower lip. "This time, I want slow and luxurious. I want time. And I want you...in my bed." Taking her hand, he led her down the hall and into his bedroom. He closed the door, locked it and then went to the windows to close the blinds.

"Not in the dark." She stilled his hand. "Not this time." Instead, she drew the sheers closed, allowing the midday light to filter through without anyone in the yard being able to see into the house. "I want to see you when I make love to you. All of you. And I want you to see me."

He swallowed. "You sure about that?"

"Very." She wanted to do this for him. For herself.

Her heart racing, she reached down, gripped the hem of her shirt and dragged it upward. A quick tug over her head and she stood before Sean half-naked. As he stared at her, taking in every inch of her upper body, Grace felt a moment of panic. What if he realized that her scars were worse than he'd originally thought? What if he changed his mind? What if—

This was Sean. He wanted her just the way she was. He thought she was beautiful as she was.

"Damn." He reached out and fingered the lacy edges of her bra. "I never would've guessed a bra could be sexier than braless." It was a hot-pink thing that plunged low and barely covered her nipples. The small scraps of colorful fabric did nothing to hide her scars.

"The first time I saw you," he said, his voice husky. "I thought you were too skinny."

"I was." She loved her new softness, her curves. "And now?"

"Now—" he swallowed "—now...I can't think at all."

Emboldened by the intense look in his eyes, she unzipped her jeans and flung them aside. Her hands trembling, she drew off her thong and unsnapped her bra, letting it fall to the floor. Then she stood there. Free. Finally herself again. Grace. Just Grace.

The look on Sean's face made the risk more than worth it. No disappointment or pity. Only raw lust. Desire. A man wanting a woman more than anything else in the world.

"Okay, your turn," she said, laughing.

"In a minute. I just want to look at you." From her naturally highlighted hair to her beautiful blue eyes to those small, but perfectly shaped breasts, to the patch of light brown hair between her thighs, she was, in every way, perfect for Sean. Her scars were simply a part of who she was. He couldn't, didn't want to, imagine Grace any other way. "I don't know where to touch you first, but I know I want to touch you everywhere."

"Then you better get going. We've only got a couple hours."

When he didn't move, she came to him, took his hands and placed them on her breasts. Oh, sweet heaven. Her nipples felt cool against the warmth of his palms, but it was the contrast of her pale skin against his tanned hands, more erotic than he could've ever imagined, that set him to trembling.

He kissed her, wrapped his hand around her smooth back and pulled her against him. He loved that he could stand toe to toe with her, barely tilt his head, and their lips met. She fit with him. The perfect height. The perfect breadth. The perfect mouth.

Her tongue intertwined with his as her hands urgently pressed against him and she nipped at his lower lip. Her breath quickened. Her chest moved in and out as if she couldn't get any air. "I can't tell you how much I want you," she whispered. "How much I want this."

"You don't have to say a word. I can feel it." He dragged his hands down her cheeks, her shoulders, her chest, caressing every inch of her scars as well as her unblemished skin.

"I can't feel your touch on my scars."

"Then I'll describe how you feel. Soft. Beautiful. Real." He groaned and kissed his way down her neck, along her chest and, taking one sweet nipple into his mouth, tugged gently with his teeth.

On a soft whimper, she nearly collapsed. "Oh, Sean," she breathed. Then her fingers were at the waist of his jeans, quickly unzipping the fly and tugging the jeans down over his hips. She ran her hands along his erection.

Jerking away, he held her hands. "Slow and luxurious. Remember?" He shrugged off his jeans and boxers all at once and then backed up, pulling her with him onto his bed.

His bed. Grace in it. Was there a more wonderful feeling in the world? Maybe one.

When she impatiently reached for him again, he pressed her hands against the mattress. Then he kissed her, deeply. She spread her legs and lifted her knees, bringing him in direct contact with her sweet center. Instinctively, he moved back and forth. Already, she was slick. One thrust and he would be inside her, a place he wanted to be at this moment more than any other place in the world.

"Take me," she breathed, writhing against him.

"I will. Eventually," he said, his voice nearly unrecognizable to his own ears. The sky darkened and rain fell harder on the roof. "Besides, you're not going anywhere for a while." Slowly, he kissed his way down her neck and lathed his tongue over one peaked nipple. Softly, he bit down and tugged.

She exhaled harshly and bucked against him.

Then he did the same to her other breast, lingering longer, driving her wild and himself even wilder. By the time he made it to her thighs, he was so hard he almost came the moment he touched her swollen, slick folds. Rhythmically, he ran his fingers back and forth, then licked his tongue over her nub, as he pressed two fingers deep inside her.

"Sean," she cried. "I can't take any more."

"Then let go."

The words had no sooner left his mouth than she did, pulsing gently against his hand, his mouth. She clenched around his fingers. The moment her orgasm subsided, feeling drunk on the taste of her, he moved slowly up her body and entered her, slowly, deliberately. This was it. The one and only best feeling in the world.

She looked into his eyes, wrapped her legs around him and smiled. He'd never see blue again—the vibrant blue of her eyes—without thinking of Grace. As slowly as he could possibly move, he made love to her.

Grace raised her hips to meet his every torturously unhurried pulse. "Faster," she moaned.

"No."

"But I want—" Then she came again, violently this time.

He knew exactly what he was doing to her, breaking her apart, bit by tiny bit. Then his weight came fully down on her as he pressed his lips against her neck, her ear. "You're not going to want to hear this, I know," he said softly after his own release jolted through him. "I'm falling in love with you, Grace."

Love?

Had he just said *love?*

Not fair. Not fair at all.

She came again and again. She was panting as the ripples of one release after another throbbed through her. She'd never dreamed sex could be this way, but Sean's body, heavy over her, was the most wonderful thing she'd ever felt. He fit. Exactly as a man should. Exactly as *her* man should. But love?

Talk about ruining everything.

"Well, that's just…just perfect." She pushed him off her, grabbed her thong and slipped it on. She had no clue what the point was to putting on her scrap of a thong, but she had to *do* something. Where the hell was her shirt? Unable to find it quickly enough amid clothing strewn on the floor, she grabbed his and pulled it over her head.

He was quiet. Too quiet.

She didn't want to look at him, but the silence unnerved her. Slowly, she turned.

He was lying on the bed, naked, like his heart, his expression as calm as she'd ever seen it.

"How can you be so relaxed? We just… You just said…"

"I know exactly what I said." Then he smiled.

Smiled.

"I knew you'd do this," he said.

"Then why did you say it?" She threw his jeans at him.

"Why did you ruin everything?" she cried, stepping into her own jeans. "Damn you!"

"Because it's what I feel, damn you back. Do you think I want to fall in love with you?" He ran his hands through his hair and his calm disappeared as he sat up. "Putting my heart through a meat grinder. Yeah. That's what I want. That's what every man wants."

What she felt for Sean, she couldn't name. She'd never felt this way before. How could she possibly know what it was? All she knew for sure was that it hurt. Badly. "I'm sorry," she whispered and went for the door.

"Grace, wait! You can't leave in this weather."

Ignoring him, she yanked open the front door. "Oh, my God," she murmured. It had gotten ugly outside while they'd been...preoccupied. A massive storm front, black and boiling, was directly over Mirabelle.

Wind thrashed the trees around like toothpicks and the rain was quickly turning to hail the size of dimes. It hit the roof like nails being pounded into shingles and was accumulating on the ground like chunky bits of snow.

"Guess you won't be running away this time." Dressed only in his faded jeans, Sean came behind her and pushed the door shut. "You're stuck with me for a little while longer."

CHAPTER TWENTY-THREE

FEELING MORE THAN A LITTLE RAW and exposed, Sean turned toward his family room. He'd just spilled his guts to the woman he loved, had every word thrown in his face and there wasn't a damned thing he could do about it, at least not with this storm raining down on them.

First things first, unfortunately.

He flicked on the TV to get a weather update, acutely aware of Grace coming to stand behind him. Mirabelle was part of a severe thunderstorm warning area and tornado warnings had been issued in several counties. Two tornadoes had already touched down in the outskirts of the Spooner and Hayward areas. The likelihood of a tornado crossing the cold waters of Lake Superior and still holding any amount of steam by the time it hit the island was slim.

"A tornado has never touched down on Mirabelle," she said.

"There's a first time for everything." He called Austin on his cell phone. No answer. Immediately, he dialed Bud Stall's office number.

"Mirabelle community center."

"Bud, this is Sean Griffin. This storm's getting bad."

"Tell me about it."

While he was on the phone, Sean heard Grace calling her father. "Is my son there with your boys?" he asked Bud.

"Yeah, they've been here for a while. Playing basketball."

"Can you keep Austin there until this blows over?"

"No problem. I've already announced over the speaker system that everyone here should stay inside the center until this blows over. I'll make sure the boys heard me loud and clear."

"Thank you." Relieved, Sean hung up about the same time as Grace. "Is your dad okay?"

"Yeah. He's already in his basement."

The incessant staccato beat of hailstones hitting the roof and tapping the windows soon turned to outright pounding as the size of the stones grew larger by the second. In no time, golf-ball-size hail slammed down.

"The horses," Grace said. Without realizing it, she put her hand on his arm.

"They'll be all right." He put his arm around her. "The wooded areas will provide them enough cover."

Surprising him, she turned her face into his bare chest and closed her eyes. She wasn't doing it on purpose, she wasn't that kind of person, but she was ripping his heart out. "Grace, we have to talk—"

His cell phone rang. He glanced at the display and quickly answered. "Yeah, Bud, did you find them?"

"I hate to tell you this, Sean, but the receptionist said the boys left the community center a few minutes before you called. Have they come to your house?"

"No."

"Laurie says they're not at our house, either."

While he and Bud were on the phone, the island siren blared out a warning. Grace paced beside him.

"Hold on a second," Bud said.

In the background, Sean heard Bud get on his loudspeaker and direct all occupants to the center of the building away from all windows. He reiterated his directions and then got back on the phone. "The boys might be out in this," he said.

"And I can't leave the community center. There must be fifteen different families here and I'm responsible for them."

"I'll find the boys. Where do you think they'd go?"

"I don't know. Neither does Laurie."

"I'll call you when I find them." He turned to Grace. "Do you have a clue where he might've gone?"

"No, I—" She stopped.

"Think about it for a minute, Grace. He's probably shared more with you than me."

"The golf course," she said, hopeful. "There's a small clubhouse at the ninth hole."

"I know where it is."

"It has a foosball table and he told me they figured out how to open the vending machine for soda and snacks." She shrugged. "Sorry. I know he shouldn't have been doing that, but it seemed minor."

"I get it. Let's get you to the basement." He grabbed a clean shirt out of the laundry room off the kitchen, pulled it over his head and then led her down the old wooden steps off the kitchen. "It's dark and damp down here, but it's the safest place on this part of the island." He flipped on the light to reveal a small basement with a concrete floor, a few shelving units along one side and a furnace and water heater on the opposite side.

"There are candles here in case the electricity goes out." He pointed to the shelves. "Some food and water if this stays bad through the night. A battery operated radio and a couple of walkie-talkies. These should work anywhere on the island." He turned them both on and handed one to her. "Keep this on. I've got to go find Austin and the Stall boys."

"You can't go out in this."

"I have to. The boys will be sitting ducks in that small building if a tornado—"

"I want to go with you."

"No way. There's nothing you can do." He took a hard look into her eyes. "Promise me you'll stay here. I don't want to have to worry about you, too."

She clenched her jaw.

"I don't have time to argue, Grace, and there's absolutely no point in both of us being out there."

"All right, fine, but I'm staying under protest."

"Protest noted." He gave her a hard and fast kiss. "Whatever you hear going on upstairs do not leave this cellar."

Then he ran up the steps, grabbing a raincoat on his way out the door, and plunged into the hail and driving wind.

GRACE PACED THE LENGTH OF THE basement. She flipped on the radio and found it already tuned to a local weather station. The update declared another tornado sighting, this time two farmsteads had been destroyed outside of Washburn in Bayfield County. "That's too damned close."

A moment later, the lights went out. "Shit!" She fumbled around on the shelf and found a lighter and a couple of candles. Her hands shaking, it took a couple tries before she managed to light the wicks.

"Dad!" The sound of the voice came from upstairs. "Dad, where are you?"

"Austin!" She raced upstairs and pushed open the door to find Austin and the two older Stall boys standing in the kitchen, dripping wet. "Get downstairs!"

The moment they came down the steps, she shut the door behind them.

"Where's my dad?" Austin asked.

"He went looking for you." She found some towels on the shelf and handed one to each of them.

"So he's out in this?" Austin headed toward the steps. "I gotta go find him."

"No, wait. He's got a radio. I'll let him know you three are safe." She pressed the transmitting button and spoke into the radio. "Sean? Austin and the Stall boys are here. Can you hear me?" She released the button and waited a moment.

"I heard you!" Sean's voice came over the speaker.

The sound outside was deafening, a steady roar of wind like nothing Grace had ever heard.

"I'm at the golf course," he continued. "I'll be back in a few—"

A thunderous crack sounded over the line. It wasn't lightning. More like a branch or an entire tree—

"Sean?" she called into the radio. "Sean!"

Nothing but static came over the walkie-talkie.

Austin ripped the radio out of her hand. "Dad!" he yelled. "Dad!"

Oh, God. She couldn't think. She couldn't breathe. The room seemed to spin. If anything happened to him, she—

"I'm going to find him." Austin headed toward the door.

"No!" That snapped her out of panic mode. She grabbed his arm. "All three of you stay here. Your dads would kill me if something happened to any of you. I'll get Sean."

"It's bad out there, Grace. We got hit with hail and had to hide under some bushes in the woods."

"I'll be okay. You guys stay here. Promise me, Austin!" When he didn't answer, she grabbed his arms. "Promise me. Now! I have to get to your dad."

"All right, already! We'll stay. Just until it's over."

Grace hurried up the steps and slammed the door behind her. She grabbed a coat off the rack and ran full-out toward the golf course. Small hailstones hit her head and shoulders. The wind blew rain, leaves and even a branch or two straight at her, making it difficult to see. By the time she reached the ninth-hole clubhouse she was drenched. Sean wasn't inside the building, so she headed outside. That's when she noticed the tree, uprooted and lying on the ground at the edge of the woods and raced toward it. "Sean?"

"Grace! Get out of here!"

She rounded the downed tree and found him pinned beneath a large branch.

"Leave! Now! Get the hell out of here."

"No." She grabbed the branch and pulled, hoping to free him, but it wasn't moving. "I'm not leaving you."

"Grace, if that funnel cloud touches down—"

She glanced behind them and noticed a cloud swirling and dipping toward the ground less than a few hundred yards from them. Suddenly, tree branches and other debris blew into the air and spun.

"Grace, you have to get out of here. Please!"

"Listen to me." She stared into his eyes. "Either we both leave or we both stay. So let's figure out a way to get you out from under this damned tree!"

CARL PUNCHED DOWN THE ACCELERATOR on the golf cart, pushing the thing as fast as it would go. When the fallen tree branches across the road impeded his progress, he abandoned the cart and ran on foot toward Rock Pointe.

Finally, he reached the curve before the resort road. The moment he turned the corner, he was forced to stop and catch his breath. There was no denying the path the tornado had taken. It had hit Mirabelle at Rock Pointe and had continued inland straight toward his house.

"Oh, my God," he whispered, his blood turning cold. The roof and nearly an entire side of their house were gone. What remained seemed to be caving in on itself. "Carol!" he called, making his feet move up the hill. If anything had happened to her or the kids, he'd never forgive himself. "Carol, Nikki, Alex!"

He ran through the debris strewn across the yard, only

partially aware that trees had been snapped in half or entirely uprooted. Climbing over what was left of the front of his house, he picked his way from room to room. Upstairs. Downstairs. Into the basement. Either no one had been home, or the storm had taken them.

They had to be alive. Carol was smart enough to have taken the kids and gone someplace safe. Maybe she'd gone to the lodge.

Cell phones had no coverage. Phone and power lines were down. Somehow, he had to find them.

He raced down the hill to find the resort in complete chaos. Disheveled guests were racing this way and that, calling out for their loved ones. Within minutes, he was stuck in the thick of it, trying to calm everyone. He put his day manager and front desk staff in charge of locating missing persons. He organized his kitchen staff in the dining area to provide first aid for what were primarily cuts, scrapes and bruises. He promised full refunds to the guests too nervous or irate to calm down, knowing the sooner they packed and left the island, the sooner the rest of them could get on with more important tasks. And he asked every staff person he encountered whether or not they'd seen his wife and kids. No one had.

Slowly, but surely, a small degree of order replaced the initial mayhem the storm had left behind. In a daze, Carl glanced around him.

"Dad!"

That was Nikki! Carl spun around to find his son and daughter racing toward him. Carol followed slowly behind them.

"We didn't know where you were!" Alex said.

As he hugged his kids, he glanced over their head to hold Carol's gaze. She was crying. Was it too much to ask those tears might be for him? For the first time, he felt the tiniest spark of hope. Relief surged through him. She still cared.

They were going to be all right. One way or another, he had to make this right.

"Can you believe it?" Alex said. "That tornado was awesome."

"You idiot." Nikki glared at him. "It was totally scary."

As the kids bickered back and forth, Carl went to his wife. "Are you okay?" He so badly wanted to hold her.

"I'm fine. When I saw what was coming across the water, I was worried about being on the bluff. So the kids and I came down here and went to your office. I was hoping..."

"I was in town when it hit. I had to wait until it was over to come, and when I saw the house..." His voice broke. Something inside him broke. "I thought I'd lost you, Carol," he said. "Oh, God, I thought I'd lost you and the kids."

"I thought I'd lost you, too."

"I love you, Carol. I don't want to live without you."

She came into his arms and they held each other tight. He rested his lips against her hair and breathed in her scent. She was his life. "Just tell me what you want me to do, and I'll do it."

"Come home," she said. "I want you home, Carl."

WHILE THE ISLAND SIRENS continued blaring out a warning, Sean took in everything about Grace. Rain had plastered her hair to her forehead and cheeks. Wet leaves, dirt and grass stuck to her face, neck and jacket. She was a mess and she'd never looked more amazing. Or stubborn. There was nothing he was going to be able to say that would convince her to leave him stuck here under this tree.

Because she loved him. When this was all over, he was going to make her admit it, but first he had to get moving. There were bound to be injuries, possibly even deaths, resulting from this storm, and he needed to get to the clinic.

"Okay, Grace, let's do this!" He took a deep breath and

pushed himself to a sitting position. "Put everything you got into lifting the branch. I'll try to slide my leg out."

"Now you're talking." She squatted, getting as much of her body under the tree as she could. "Ready. Set. Go!"

He pulled with his arms, pushed with his good leg and as excruciating pain pulsed through his body, he managed to drag himself the few inches he needed to get free. "That's it! You did it."

Slowly, she lowered the tree. "Can you run?"

"No, but I might be able to walk," he said, clenching his jaw. "My lower leg hurts like hell." Most likely, his fibula had a hairline fracture, but that funnel cloud above the woods behind them had turned into a full-fledged tornado and was coming right at them. They had minutes, at best.

"Come on," she said, kneeling by his side. "I'll help you."

He swung his arm around her and hoisted himself up on his good leg. "The sand pit," he yelled above the roar. "Near the ninth hole. That's our best bet."

They moved as fast as they could and slid down to the lowest point of the pit. Before she could object, Sean rolled over Grace, covering and protecting her as the tornado touched down near them. The tumultuous wind drove rain and sand into them. Sean felt a tug on his body as if he were close to being lifted, and then it was over in a matter of seconds. Cautiously, he glanced around. The tornado had passed over them and was moving toward town. They could barely hear the sirens blaring above the roar of the storm.

Grace sat up. "Oh, my God." A path had been torn through the trees running right past where Sean had been stuck. "If we hadn't gotten you out…"

"Don't think about it," Sean said, trying to move his leg. "I have get to the clinic and put a splint on this leg. We're going to have injuries."

"Wait here." She ran to get an undamaged golf cart parked at the small clubhouse.

In no time they were on their way to his medical clinic. Sean got a hold of Austin on the walkie-talkie and made sure the boys were okay. "I'm going to need your help," he said. "You boys meet me and Grace at the medical clinic."

"What about the horses?" Austin asked.

"We'll worry about them later."

They hit the top of Island Drive and saw that the storm system had moved out over Lake Superior and dissipated. The silence that followed was almost as deafening as the storm itself.

Grace stopped the cart at the top of the hill overlooking Mirabelle's center. "Oh, my God!" she cried.

The tornado had not only touched down, it had ripped a path directly through town. Starting at the golf course, where Sean had been stuck, a line of trees had either been toppled over or been snapped off like tooth picks. The library had been obliterated as well as every little store and restaurant on that block. From there the tornado had apparently crossed to Main. Duffy's Pub. Whimsy. Sarah Taylor's flower shop. Every store on that block had been hit, some worse than others. Windows were smashed. Awnings had been ripped from their poles. Trees had crashed into the sides of the buildings and the brick had crumbled like the sand of a sand castle.

"Go, Grace," Sean said. "We'll take an inventory of the damage later. I've got to get to the clinic."

"Okay." As if in a daze, she drove the cart as far as she could before the debris inhibited their progress. "We have to walk from here."

Sean draped his arm around her shoulder and, within a few minutes, they were at the front door to the medical clinic. Austin and the Stall boys were waiting.

"Dad, you wouldn't believe the damage—"

"Later." The boys held open the doors for Sean. He limped to the supply cabinet and pulled out everything he needed to splint his lower leg, along with several ice packs. The phones weren't working. The power was out. "Grace, you know how to get the generator going?"

"No," she said. "But I'll figure it out or find someone who does. Where is it?"

"In the alley."

She took off and Austin helped him splint his leg. He slammed a couple over-the-counter anti-inflammatory meds just as Garrett yelled from the waiting area. "Sean? We need you, man!"

"In here!" Sean yelled.

Garrett raced into the exam room. "What happened to you?"

"A tree fell on him," Austin said.

"Can you—"

"I'm fine. Who's hurt?"

The lights came on. *Thank you, Grace.*

"Possible heart attack out at the Mirabelle Island Inn. He's stable, but Marty's bringing him in. A possible broken wrist out at Rock Pointe. Got a couple dumber-than-stump tourists who wanted to get pictures of the storm in your waiting room. I'd like to tell them to take a hike, but they got knocked out by some falling branches."

"Possible concussions."

Grace came back into the room. She was safe. Austin was safe. To Sean, that's what mattered most.

"Jesse and I have to clear the roads," Garrett said. "Can you—"

"Go! We'll manage."

Kelly and Donna showed up to triage. Even Doc Welinski came down to help. One patient after another streamed through the clinic over the next several hours. In the midst of it all, Sean glanced around and realized that his father may have forced him into the medical profession for all the wrong reasons, but this was what he loved and he did it well. He had the best of both worlds and he was making a difference on Mirabelle. He was exactly where he wanted to be.

CHAPTER TWENTY-FOUR

"THANK GOD YOU'RE ALL RIGHT!" Denise's voice sounded loudly enough over Austin's cell phone that even Sean could hear what she was saying.

"I'm fine, Mom." Austin held the phone away from his ear. "Don't worry."

"Is Sean okay?"

"Dad's got a broken leg, but he's all right."

"Dad?" There was an edge of surprise in her voice. "Bet that's freaking him out a bit."

Austin glanced at Sean. "Actually, he's pretty cool with it."

They'd finally attended to every last patient, so Grace had gone to Sean's property to help Arlo and the stable crew do some cleanup. Sean's leg hadn't swelled overly much, so Doc Welinski was able to cast it for him. The leg still ached, but that wasn't necessarily a bad thing. It never hurt for a doctor to have empathy borne of personal experience. It was late, but still light outside as Sean and Austin sat in the medical clinic waiting for Sean's leg cast to set, so Austin had called to check in with his mom.

"Austin, maybe I should come and get you a little early," Denise said. "School doesn't start for another few weeks, but if the news reports on the internet are anything to go by Mirabelle's a disaster."

"Umm...about that." Austin hesitated. "I think I want to stay on Mirabelle."

A long silence followed.

"You think?" Denise said more softly. "Or you do?"

"I do. I definitely want to stay here."

"What does Sean think about that?"

"He wants me to stay, too."

"Did he ask you, or was this your idea?"

"My idea." Austin frowned. "Mom, it's not that I don't want to be with you, Jeffrey and Erin, but I...want to be with Dad for a while. We just started developing a relationship. I don't want to lose that."

"What about school? Your friends? Your life here?"

"I don't have any friends in L.A., and I can go to school here."

"Let me talk to Sean—"

"Mom—"

"I want to talk to Sean."

Austin held his hand over the phone, blocking the sound. "I don't want to hurt her feelings."

"I understand." Sean took the phone. "Hello, Denise."

"Well, this is quite a turn of events," Denise said.

Austin paced the length of the exam room.

"Especially considering how rocky things started out."

"I need to know...have you coerced him into this in any—"

"No. Absolutely not."

Austin pointed toward the waiting area. "I'm going outside, so you two can talk."

His heart breaking just a little, Sean watched Austin head out of the room.

"Are you sure you're up for this?" Denise asked.

"I'm sure I'll do the best I can. Austin and I want to get to know one another better, and that'll be hard to do long distance."

"I'm not ready to lose him," she said, tears in her voice.

"You're not losing him, Denise. He'll always be your son."

"I was supposed to have two more years before he went away to college."

Sean didn't know what to say. The thought of losing Austin now, when they were just getting to know each other, made him ache inside. He couldn't imagine what Denise was feeling.

"I need to think about Austin," she said. "And what's best for him. I think he needs you now, Sean, more than me. If that changes, will you let me know?"

"I will."

They talked for a few more minutes and then Sean hung up. On crutches, he went looking for Austin and found him just outside standing on the sidewalk.

"She's accepting your decision," Sean said softly.

Austin appeared relieved. "So you're not going to have to fight for custody?"

Sean shook his head. "That doesn't mean she's not going to miss you. In fact, I think this is going to be really hard for her. They're all going to come out and see you before school starts. She said they'll stay a few days and visit."

"Cool."

"Although the island's going to still be in rough shape." He glanced up the hill and took in the damage. It was damned near a miracle that no one had been seriously injured. A small group of locals had gathered at the city park and were looking out over the damage. "Will you take me there on one of the golf carts?" he asked Austin.

"Sure." Austin ran to the medical clinic for a cart, picked up Sean and they made their way to the park.

GRACE STOOD ON THE FRONT PORCH of her father's house and glanced down the hillside. By the time the storm was all said and done, the Rock Pointe Lodge had lost a section of townhomes, and Carl and Carol's house had been leveled. Mirabelle Island Inn's iconic gazebo had been completely destroyed along with some of their historic rose gardens.

Sean didn't know it yet, as busy as he'd been taking care of patients, but he'd lost a barn and several fences. Minor damage, considering none of his horses had been seriously hurt and his livery barn containing all the carriages and supplies had been untouched. Although the island had lost a few of its centuries-old shade trees, most of the residential areas had been spared significant damages. Mirabelle's village center, on the other hand, had taken the brunt of the storm's wrath.

"It's hard to imagine this is part of some great plan, isn't it?" her dad said, coming to stand next to Grace.

"Yes, it is."

The town looked like a war zone. Wood siding, bricks and metal debris were scattered everywhere. Lampposts had been ripped off their footings. Trees had been uprooted, split down the middle or snapped in half.

The Taylor brothers and Jonas Abel had already made quite a bit of headway with the cleanup efforts. Chainsaws buzzed as crews cut fallen trees into manageable pieces, windows were being covered with heavy plastic, and debris from the buildings was being hauled away. The power was out across the entire island and the regional electric company was already here assessing damage and beginning repairs. All that was the easy part. Rebuilding was going to take time.

"I want to go down there," she said, surprising even herself. "I want to see if I can help."

"Let's go."

The walk down the hill took only a few minutes. She noticed a group of locals had gathered at the city park overlooking much of the mayhem, and she and her father headed straight for them. Missy, Sarah and Erica, Sophie and Noah, Arlo and Lynn, Marty and Brittany Rousseau, Jim and Josie Bennett. A few minutes later, Jesse, Garrett and Jonas put down their chainsaws and joined the group. It wasn't long before even Carl and Carol showed up. The people who would decide what to do for Mirabelle were all present and accounted for.

Grace caught Sean's gaze as she walked across the debris-strewn park lawn toward the group, and she went to stand next to him. "Doc got your cast on?"

He nodded.

"How does it feel?"

"Aches a bit, but I'll be all right."

She gave him an update on his property.

"Sounds like I got lucky."

It was all Grace could do not to take Sean by the hand and pull him away with her so they could settle things between them. Mirabelle be damned. She had a lot to say and most of it was going to surprise him.

"I've always hated storms," Sarah finally muttered. "And now I have a good reason."

Jesse put his arm around her and she leaned into him almost as if her legs wouldn't hold her weight. Missy's and Sarah's buildings had been hit hard. They'd likely salvage little from their businesses.

Next door, Duffy's Pub had been virtually flattened. The fact that the building had been brick hadn't made an ounce of difference to this storm. It had ripped the structure apart as if it'd been made of paper.

"We lost almost everything," Erica said, her eyes red-rimmed as if she'd been crying for hours. "Duffy's Pub is all but gone." Even now, her eyes glistened with unshed tears, and no one could blame her.

As Arlo and Lynn held one another, Garrett enfolded Erica

in his arms. Grace wrapped her arm around her father's waist. These businesses and buildings that had been destroyed didn't belong to her, but she felt their loss all the same.

"I'm almost glad Jean isn't alive to see this," Grace's dad said as he glanced out over the devastation.

"I have to admit," Carol said, glancing at Carl, "I'm feeling a little like the island right now."

"Me, too," Carl agreed, giving her a half smile before addressing the rest of the group. "The Rock Pointe phone has been ringing practically nonstop with cancellations."

The ferry had been operating since the storm had passed and visitors were already leaving in droves. The only people arriving on the island were the media.

"I guess the tourist season is over early this year," Sean mused.

"It's going to be a struggle just to survive for most of our businesses," Jim said. "A few won't even try."

Grace had already heard rumors that some of the newer residents, like Sherri Phillips and Tom and Carolyn Bent, people who'd never really gotten off to a solid start, were planning on packing their bags, taking their insurance money and starting over again someplace else.

"We have to make this right." Missy reached for Jonas's hand.

Garrett shook his head. "Missy, you've already done enough for Mirabelle."

"Losing the gazebo and a few gardens at the Inn was nothing compared to what some of you have lost," Marty said. "Whatever you need from me and Brittany, you can count on us to help."

"Us, too," Sophie said as Noah put his arms around her from behind.

"Add me to that list," Sean said. "All I lost was a barn, and the clinic's got minor damage. I'm not sure how much I'll be able to help until I get this cast off, but I'll do what I can."

"I hate to say this," Jim said, glancing from one face to the next, "but someone's got to be the voice of reason. Maybe it's time to let the island go."

Noah shook his head. "I can't believe you'd say that, Dad."

"He's got a point, Noah," Josie said, reaching for Jim's hand.

"This island either needs to stand on its own two feet," Jim added, "or sooner or later we all have to accept that maybe it just wasn't meant to be."

"Don't say that." Missy shook her head. "Mirabelle's my home."

"Well, the way I see it," Arlo said, glancing from Lynn to Jim and Josie, "it ain't actually up to us retirees to decide."

"No, it's not," Lynn agreed. "Us older folks have had our time on Mirabelle. Each and every one of these kids has sunk heart and soul into this place. They're just getting started. They're the ones who need to decide what to do with Mirabelle."

"Arlo and Lynn are right," Grace's dad said.

With a worried look on his face, Jim sighed, but seemed to accept the consensus.

Grace glanced at Sean. To her surprise, he was watching her. "I'm staying," she said.

Every head turned in her direction.

"I know most of you probably don't care what I plan on doing," she added. "The fact that I turned my back on Mirabelle for a lot of years probably takes away my right to an opinion. Technically. But now that I'm home again, Mirabelle means more to me than ever."

She glanced around at all their faces, faces she'd come to know and care about in such a short amount of time. "All of you have fought for years to make this your home. Don't give up. Don't forget that we have something special here on Mirabelle." She glanced at Sean, held his gaze. "Once in a lifetime is kind of special."

"She's right," Carl said, placing his arm around Carol's shoulder. "We're staying, too."

Carol nodded. "Sometimes you need to fight and fight hard for the things you love."

Grace smiled inside. Apparently, her brother and his wife had decided to work things out.

"What about you guys?" Missy asked Garrett and Erica.

Erica dried her eyes and shifted slightly, staying within the circle of Garrett's arms. "A damned tornado isn't going to run me off this island."

"We're staying," Garrett said.

"Same goes for us," Jesse said. "Sarah, Brian and I can't think of a better place to raise our new baby."

"Did you say *baby?*" Garrett said.

"I'm pregnant." Sarah grinned at the group and then glanced at Sean. "I'll be heading to Sean's office for confirmation, but I'm not sure it's necessary. All five quick tests couldn't be wrong."

"Five tests." Sean laughed. "I'd say you're pregnant."

Missy screamed in delight and lunged toward Sarah for a hug. "Auntie Missy has such a nice ring to it, doesn't it?"

"If there's one thing I've learned from personal experience," Sophie said, "it's that Mirabelle wasn't meant to stay the same. Change is good."

"So that's that," Garret said decisively. "We're all staying."

Everyone nodded.

"What's the first step?" Jim asked.

"Well, this is too big a job for me and Jesse," Garrett said. "The town will have to bring in a commercial contractor,"

Jesse added. "There's got to be someone out there who specializes in rebuilding after this kind of disaster."

"Well, as mayor," Carl said, "I've already made some calls to see if Mirabelle will qualify for federal or state disaster aid, so the ball's rolling."

"It's gonna take some time," Arlo said softly. "But you're all going to see Mirabelle through this."

"We need to get to my shop to see if anything's salvageable," Missy said, grabbing Jonas's hand and they slowly walked away.

"Me, too," Sarah added. She and Jesse followed the Abels.

One by one, the group disbanded, leaving only Grace and Sean standing beside each other. He glanced at her. "You sure about staying?"

"Yes," she said, smiling sadly.

"You don't sound too happy about that."

"It took me most of the summer to figure this out, but Mirabelle is my home. It's where I belong. In some strange way, this place centers me. I know myself when I'm here."

"So where does that leave us?"

"Sean, I—"

"Don't. Okay? I don't want to hear any more excuses, Grace. No more pussyfooting around this." He shifted both crutches to one side and reached out with his free hand to caress her cheek. "To be honest, I'm feeling a little like those buildings down there, too. Torn up and broken. Didn't this storm prove anything to you about your feelings for me?"

She leaned into this hand. "It proved a lot."

"Yeah. Like what?"

"You said you love me." Her heartbeat thundered in her ears as she held his gaze. "I think I'm in love with you, too."

"You think?" He smiled gently.

"I've never been in love before," she whispered. "I've

never…but when you were out in the storm…when I thought…" She closed her eyes for a moment and then opened them again. "No. I know," she said. "I love you, Sean. I do love you."

He dropped his crutches on the ground and reached for her hands. "Do you love me enough to marry me, Grace?"

As she looked at him, tears welled in her eyes, but she couldn't speak.

"Grace?"

It'd been only months since they'd first met. She should've felt wary, as if they were moving too fast. Instead, she'd found that she couldn't move fast enough with Sean. It was as if she'd been waiting her whole life for him and hadn't even known it, as if her life had started the moment she'd come home to Mirabelle. The moment she'd met Sean.

"Yes," she said. "I'll marry you."

"Now." He kissed her, softly, slowly. "My life is perfect."

"I hope not," she said, smiling. "Perfect isn't all it's cracked up to be. I'll settle for happily ever after."

* * * * *

Be sure to look for Helen Brenna's next book,
REDEMPTION AT MIRABELLE,
the last book in her
ISLAND TO REMEMBER miniseries!
Available in September 2011
wherever Harlequin books are sold.

COMING NEXT MONTH

Available September 13, 2011

#1728 THE SHERIFF'S DAUGHTER
North Star, Montana
Kay Stockham

#1729 THE BABY CONNECTION
Going Back
Dawn Atkins

#1730 WINNING OVER THE RANCHER
Hometown U.S.A.
Mary Brady

#1731 REDEMPTION AT MIRABELLE
An Island to Remember
Helen Brenna

#1732 THE ONE SHE LEFT BEHIND
Delta Secrets
Kristi Gold

#1733 A FATHER'S NAME
Suddenly a Parent
Holly Jacobs

You can find more information on upcoming
Harlequin® titles, free excerpts and more at
www.HarlequinInsideRomance.com.

REQUEST YOUR FREE BOOKS!
2 FREE NOVELS PLUS 2 FREE GIFTS!

Harlequin®

Super Romance®

Exciting, emotional, unexpected!

YES! Please send me 2 FREE Harlequin® Superromance® novels and my 2 FREE gifts (gifts are worth about $10). After receiving them, if I don't wish to receive any more books, I can return the shipping statement marked "cancel." If I don't cancel, I will receive 6 brand-new novels every month and be billed just $4.69 per book in the U.S. or $5.24 per book in Canada. That's a saving of at least 15% off the cover price! It's quite a bargain! Shipping and handling is just 50¢ per book in the U.S. and 75¢ per book in Canada.* I understand that accepting the 2 free books and gifts places me under no obligation to buy anything. I can always return a shipment and cancel at any time. Even if I never buy another book, the two free books and gifts are mine to keep forever.

135/336 HDN FC6T

Name	(PLEASE PRINT)	
Address		Apt. #
City	State/Prov.	Zip/Postal Code

Signature (if under 18, a parent or guardian must sign)

Mail to the **Reader Service:**
IN U.S.A.: P.O. Box 1867, Buffalo, NY 14240-1867
IN CANADA: P.O. Box 609, Fort Erie, Ontario L2A 5X3

Not valid for current subscribers to Harlequin Superromance books.
**Are you a current subscriber to Harlequin Superromance books
and want to receive the larger-print edition?
Call 1-800-873-8635 or visit www.ReaderService.com.**

* Terms and prices subject to change without notice. Prices do not include applicable taxes. Sales tax applicable in N.Y. Canadian residents will be charged applicable taxes. Offer not valid in Quebec. This offer is limited to one order per household. All orders subject to credit approval. Credit or debit balances in a customer's account(s) may be offset by any other outstanding balance owed by or to the customer. Please allow 4 to 6 weeks for delivery. Offer available while quantities last.

Your Privacy—The Reader Service is committed to protecting your privacy. Our Privacy Policy is available online at www.ReaderService.com or upon request from the Reader Service.

We make a portion of our mailing list available to reputable third parties that offer products we believe may interest you. If you prefer that we not exchange your name with third parties, or if you wish to clarify or modify your communication preferences, please visit us at www.ReaderService.com/consumerchoice or write to us at Reader Service Preference Service, P.O. Box 9062, Buffalo, NY 14269. Include your complete name and address.

HSR11

New York Times *and* USA TODAY *bestselling author*
Maya Banks presents a brand-new miniseries

PREGNANCY & PASSION

When four irresistible tycoons face
the consequences of temptation.

Book 1—ENTICED BY HIS FORGOTTEN LOVER

Available September 2011 from Harlequin® Desire®!

Rafael de Luca had been in bad situations before. A crowded ballroom could never make him sweat.

These people would never know that he had no memory of any of them.

He surveyed the party with grim tolerance, searching for the source of his unease.

At first his gaze flickered past her, but he yanked his attention back to a woman across the room. Her stare bored holes through him. Unflinching and steady, even when his eyes locked with hers.

Petite, even in heels, she had a creamy olive complexion. A wealth of inky-black curls cascaded over her shoulders and her eyes were equally dark.

She looked at him as if she'd already judged him and found him lacking. He'd never seen her before in his life. Or had he?

He cursed the gaping hole in his memory. He'd been diagnosed with selective amnesia after his accident four months ago. Which seemed like complete and utter bull. No one got amnesia except hysterical women in bad soap operas.

With a smile, he disengaged himself from the group

around him and made his way to the mystery woman.

She wasn't coy. She stared straight at him as he approached, her chin thrust upward in defiance.

"Excuse me, but have we met?" he asked in his smoothest voice.

His gaze moved over the generous swell of her breasts pushed up by the empire waist of her black cocktail dress.

When he glanced back up at her face, he saw fury in her eyes.

"Have we *met?*" Her voice was barely a whisper, but he felt each word like the crack of a whip.

Before he could process her response, she nailed him with a right hook. He stumbled back, holding his nose.

One of his guards stepped between Rafe and the woman, accidentally sending her to one knee. Her hand flew to the folds of her dress.

It was then, as she cupped her belly, that the realization hit him. She was pregnant.

Her eyes flashing, she turned and ran down the marble hallway.

Rafael ran after her. He burst from the hotel lobby, and saw two shoes sparkling in the moonlight, twinkling at him.

He blew out his breath in frustration and then shoved the pair of sparkly, ultrafeminine heels at his head of security.

"Find the woman who wore these shoes."

Will Rafael find his mystery woman?
Find out in Maya Banks's passionate new novel
ENTICED BY HIS FORGOTTEN LOVER
Available September 2011 from Harlequin® Desire®!

ROMANTIC
SUSPENSE

NEW YORK TIMES BESTSELLING AUTHOR

RACHEL LEE

The Rescue Pilot

Time is running out…

Desperate to help her ailing sister, Rory is determined
to get Cait the necessary treatment to help her fight
a devastating disease. A cross-country trip turns into
a fight for survival in more ways than one when their plane
encounters trouble. Can Rory trust pilot Chase Dakota
with their lives, and possibly her heart?

**Look for this heart-stopping romance in September
from *New York Times* bestselling author Rachel Lee
and Harlequin Romantic Suspense!**

Available in September wherever books are sold!

www.Harlequin.com.

RSRL27741